Christmas at Hope Ranch

by

Loretta C. Rogers

This is a work of fiction. Names, characters, places, and incidents are either the product of the author's imagination or are used fictitiously, and any resemblance to actual persons living or dead, business establishments, events, or locales, is entirely coincidental.

Christmas at Hope Ranch

COPYRIGHT © 2020 by Loretta C. Rogers

All rights reserved. No part of this book may be used or reproduced in any manner whatsoever without written permission of the author or The Wild Rose Press, Inc. except in the case of brief quotations embodied in critical articles or reviews.
Contact Information: info@thewildrosepress.com

Cover Art by *The Wild Rose Press, Inc.*

The Wild Rose Press, Inc.
PO Box 708
Adams Basin, NY 14410-0708
Visit us at www.thewildrosepress.com

Publishing History
First Champagne Rose Edition, 2020
Trade Paperback ISBN 978-1-5092-3187-4
Digital ISBN 978-1-5092-3188-1

Published in the United States of America

Her head was spinning. This was not a sensation she enjoyed. "My heart was ripped to shreds by Rowan... He mangled my soul and then had the audacity to laugh. So you'll forgive me if I've closed the door on my *trust* department. I won't be your latest fling."

He snarled. "My latest... What the hell are you talking about?"

"Oh, don't play coy, Wade. The other night, when you kissed me, you called me *Gracie*. She must be some deep, dark secret. Even Nell wouldn't talk about her when I asked."

When he didn't answer, Addison arched a brow. "Whoever she is, I won't compete with her, and I won't let you use me to hurt her." Her heart was knocking against her ribs.

Casually he lifted her hand and turned it to kiss the palm. "It's not what you think, Addison."

She harrumphed. "No, it never is."

The radio in his cruiser crackled. A voice said, "Sheriff, everything a 10-17?"

"Shit." Wade hissed between his teeth as he opened the car door and leaned in to grab the radio's mic. "Freddie it's a 10-4. I'll be in shortly."

Overhead, the sky was brooding and turgid with snow clouds pushed by the wind. Addison hugged the cloak closer as chills raced up and down her spine. Her teeth threatened to chatter.

He stepped forward, and she stepped back. The lines that bracketed his mouth might have been carved with a knife. "Things are a bit hectic, especially with Friday being Freddie's last day. I'll be in touch."

Praise for Loretta C. Rogers and…

MURDER IN THE MIST: "Lots of suspense, great characters, and some romance tossed in for good measure."

~*Coffee Time Romance*

BANNON'S BRIDES: "I was so taken with the story and characters I read this book in one day."

~*Reading for the Love of Books*

THE WITCHING MOON: "Part paranormal, part western, and part suspense romance. 100 percent enjoyable."

~*A Reader*

SHADOWED REUNION: "Action packed with a riveting blend of romance and suspense."

~*Book Lover*

WHEN COMES FOREVER: "A visual and engaging Historical with romance and suspense."

~*Netgalley*

MURDER IN THE MIST: "Fast paced suspense is a nail biter!!"

~*Audible Audio*

LADY ADEL'S CAPTAIN: "Fast paced and filled with passion, a bit of mystery, a soldier's sacrifice, and lots of love."

~*My Book Addiction and More*

FORBIDDEN SON: "This book is a keeper."

~*Night Owl Reviews*

**Other books by Loretta C. Rogers
also available from The Wild Rose Press**

ISABELLE AND THE OUTLAW
MCKENNA'S WOMAN
BANNON'S BRIDES
FORBIDDEN SON
LADY ADEL'S CAPTAIN
CLOUD WOMAN'S SPIRIT
MURDER IN THE MIST
SHADOWED REUNION
TAMING THE LYON
FATE COMES SOFTLY
WHEN COMES FOREVER
BITTER AUTUMN

"It's not what's under the Christmas tree that matters.
It's who is gathered around it."
~Anonymous

Chapter One

Sheriff Wade Grey scanned the baggage carousel area and spotted her. Addison James's gold bracelets glinted in the light as she raised her hand to brush a wayward strand of platinum blonde hair. The color of her hair accentuated the large bandage above her left eye. She wore a leather-trimmed cape that covered a navy blue pants suit, and high heels definitely not suitable for snow.

She stood watching the carousel making its revolutions. He groped the corners of his mind trying to remember if he'd known her when they were kids. A woman of her beauty wouldn't be someone he'd easily forget. Except for the pictures in the scrapbook Nellie Hopewell had recently shown him, and the few times he'd seen Addison on talk shows, he didn't remember ever knowing her.

The way she tapped her foot clued him that she probably wasn't a patient person. Her internet profile had stated she was thirty-two. She looked younger. She also looked frazzled and like someone who never slowed down.

What he did know was that she'd been one of Nell's kids, and that's all he knew. Aunt Nell wasn't much on divulging information about the children she had fostered. He'd read about all the toes Ms. James had stepped on to become a successful model. His lawman curiosity made him question why a woman of her caliber would return to an out-of-the-way ranch in an out-of-the-way small Idaho town. Maybe she was hiding. If so, from whom or from what?

The whirring vibration of his cell phone interrupted his mental meandering. Frowning, he read the text from his deputy: *twins arrived safe at Nell's*. The frown changed to an inward smile as he replied with a thumbs-up emoji. Uncertain of how Ms. James might react, he decided to keep the information about Nell's two unexpected guests to himself, for now.

****

If disaster happens in threes, then surely my life can't get any worse. This thought rattled around inside Addison James's head as she struggled to retrieve her large suitcase from the airport's luggage carousel.

"Here, let me help you." A hand reached out to grasp the oversized piece of luggage.

"Thank you…ah," Addison's gaze went straight to the gold badge pinned to the brown canvas jacket. "Sheriff…"

"Wade Grey. I was told to look for a beautiful woman with a broken arm. I'm hoping you're Addison James?"

She felt him studying her face and hoped he wouldn't notice the smudges that looked like dark bruises under her eyes and the pallor beneath the carefully applied blush on her cheeks.

Addison's shoulders squared and her chin lifted. She cradled the sling that held her throbbing arm. "I thought Nell was going to meet me."

"Too much snow on the roads and too far to drive."

He shifted his eyes toward the revolving conveyor. "This your only suitcase?"

Addison pointed to three other large pieces of maroon-colored leather.

Wade rolled his eyes when she declared she was traveling light. He collected the bags and set them on the rolling cart. "Would you like a cup of coffee, food, or to use the facilities before we leave? Meadow Creek is about an hour's drive."

"No, I'm good." She followed him through the airport and out the double electronic doors. A blast of frigid air tugged at her navy blue cashmere cape. Fingers of cold air nipped at her flesh. She shivered and pulled the wrap closer.

"I hope you brought a warmer jacket. It gets pretty cold around Christmas time." Wade lifted the luggage to the bed of his sleek black vintage Ford pickup truck.

Her voice sharper than she'd intended, Addison said with a gasp, "That's real Italian leather. It's not meant to be in the weather." She lifted the sling. "And in case you haven't noticed, fitting a cast through a sleeve is next to impossible." She grabbed the door handle and yanked.

Addison stepped on the truck's running board. With her right arm incapacitated and nothing to grab hold on to with her left, she found herself in the awkward position of not being able to get inside the cab. She stepped back to the ground. "Well, don't just stand there. *Do* something."

She wasn't sure why the blush creeping up the handsome sheriff's neck gave her a morbid sense of satisfaction. Her list of disgruntlements was increasing.

Before she realized what he was doing, Wade put

his hands around her waist and lifted. "Sorry, I didn't realize...well, I don't generally use the department's cruiser for personal business."

His warm palms jolted her. She swore to herself. He was looking at her too closely. His gray eyes were as gray as his name. She should have felt complimented, but the circumstances of her recent breakup had left her feeling cynical. Nonetheless, she settled in the seat and offered a conciliatory smile. "My bad. I shouldn't have snapped."

He reached across Addison and secured the seatbelt in place. "Don't worry about your luggage. I'll cover it with a tarp." He shut the door, then leaned over the side of the truck to grab a silver tarpaulin lying in the bed of the truck. He unfolded the canvas and spread it over the expensive luggage like a neat package, careful to tuck the edges underneath each piece before he secured the heap with bungee cords.

Once inside the truck, Wade turned on the heater. "You'll be warm as toast in a few minutes." He also turned on the radio. "Jingle Bells" filled the interior.

"Do you mind?" She spoke through clenched teeth. "I'm not in the mood for Christmas gushiness."

Wade stopped at the Exit Airport sign and checked both ways before pulling onto the highway. He looked into her eyes again. "Are you always so testy, Ms. James?"

She expelled a loud sigh. "Perhaps I should have taken you up on the coffee offer. I haven't had my usual dose of caffeine today." She hugged her arm close. "It's just that Christmas carols don't exactly evoke the usual warm and fuzzy feelings for me that they do for others."

His eyes crinkled at the edges when he offered a baffled smile. "Really? What about Christmas parades, trimming the tree, gifts wrapped in pretty paper, and—let's not forget—Santa Claus?"

Addison shrugged. "Overly commercialized, all overrated, and as for presents..." She drew a deep breath and reminded herself that she was here to get away from all the recent upsets in her life and to forget about her fiancé. Ex-fiancé! But here she was, after fifteen years, returning to the place she had loathed as a teenager. Small town USA. The only secure place she had known and the only person who had taken care of her without asking for anything in return.

"Perhaps I've made a mistake in returning to Meadow Creek. If you'll drop me at the local hotel, tomorrow I'll—"

Wade interrupted her. He flashed a frown. "No, ma'am. I won't disappoint Nell by leaving you in town. You're all she's talked about for days. When we get to the ranch, if you don't want to stay, *you* tell her."

Surprised by the harshness of his response, Addison blinked, noting the lines of irritation etched across his forehead. "Okay, I'll stay the night."

Warmth from the heater settled around her, and Addison relaxed. Her thoughts turned to Ruby Raye. She had invited her best friend to join her at the ranch, more for moral support than company, and was disappointed when Ruby had gracefully declined, stating she planned to spend Christmas in South Carolina getting to know her fiancé's family. Addison felt no warmth for the spirit of the season. Instead she was cold inside, as cold as the snow banked on both sides of the highway and as empty as the plains ahead of her.

Her phone vibrated. She lifted it from the outer pocket of her purse, then smiled at the simple text from Ruby: *Give Aunt Nell a hug. Relax and enjoy life.* And she'd added, *Merry Christmas! Don't be a Grinch!!*

Wade's voice startled her. "Better get all your business taken care of before we get to the ranch. There's limited cell phone reception and no internet."

Addison lifted her eyebrows. "No internet! You mean Nell is still living in the dark ages?"

He laughed. "Not in Nell's mind. She doesn't own a computer, says they are the ruination of the world. Although she won't admit it, she enjoys the television Emmett gave her on her birthday. Oh, and just so you know, there's no cable, so she's limited to one, maybe two channels at the most."

"Emmett Oxbow? He must be ancient by now."

Wade harrumphed. "Well, you know, seventy is the new fifty, or so they tell me. At any rate, Emmett's a good man. Solid as they come and can work circles around most of us."

Addison groaned at her own remembrance. "How long have you known Nell?"

He looked as if he were doing a quick calculation inside his head, but he responded, "Long enough."

Addison touched the bandage. She didn't know which ached the most—her arm, the laceration above her eye, or the emptiness in her heart.

Wade offered a sympathetic smile. "The accident was on a few news channels. I'm sorry you were hurt. From the size of the dressing, that must be some gash."

"A scarred face is a career buster in my business." Her voice came out more harsh than she'd intended.

"Fifty-six stitches, in case you're wondering."

She'd let sensitivity and pride rule her emotions, again.

He nodded and concentrated on the road ahead.

She shivered.

"Are you cold?" Wade reached toward the heater.

"No. Just anticipation, I guess."

He glanced at her. "Want to talk about it?"

She bristled. "Is this a subtle way of interrogating me?"

His jaw tightened. He noted the misery in her eyes. His cop intuition told him she was hurting—emotionally. "Sorry. I wasn't trying to pry." His voice softened. "Is your arm hurting?"

Addison shrugged, looking out the window. "Some. It's bearable."

Wade kept his eyes on the road. Minutes later he huffed out a lungful of air. "My sister is a doctor. Her office is in Meadow Creek. I'll point it out when we get to town."

"A country doctor. How quaint." Addison let out a ragged breath. Her voice was apologetic. "I'm sorry. That didn't come out right. I'm sure your sister is a fine doctor."

He stared at her for a long moment. "Forget it."

There was nothing in the blandness of his face to indicate he was angry, but the expression in his eyes spoke otherwise.

The conversation played out. Wade once again increased the volume of the radio. Addison turned her head and gazed out at the lovely countryside. As twilight descended, the rest of the drive took place in silence except for the Christmas music.

Addison sat quiet and stern, still cradling the sling, trying to ignore the throbbing in her arm. After her recent disasters, she needed a place to escape, a place to rethink her life, and her future.

Wade's voice interrupted her pensiveness. "Another twenty minutes and we'll be at Nell's."

When he spoke, Addison realized she had lapsed into a mental abyss, allowing time and scenery to wing past. She looked up just as they drove under the quaint town's archway that welcomed visitors. Tears welled in her eyes and her throat tightened, just for a moment, though for the life of her she couldn't explain either phenomenon. There was no room in her life for tears. She stared out at the festive decorations lining both sides of the street and at shoppers bundled in scarves and jackets, some laden with packages, bustling down the sidewalk to the next store.

At the town's center, Wade slowed to maneuver the roundabout that circled the courthouse. Several people called out a greeting and waved. He rolled down the window, allowing a blast of frigid air to collide with the heat inside the truck, and acknowledged each person by name.

Addison shivered under her light wrap; while pretty and expensive, it didn't exactly warm her. The town reminded her of a postcard, leaving her feeling as if she'd stepped into a time warp. The traditional twenty-foot ornately decorated Christmas tree graced the front courtyard. Seasonal banners hung from the street lamps, and pots of bright red poinsettias lined the sidewalk. Cora's Beauty Shop, Flowers by Flo, BB's Café—all looked the same as they had the day she boarded the Boise State Transit bus and left Meadow

Creek, never to look back.

At the end of the block Wade pointed to a red brick building. A decorative holiday wreath adorned the door. A large white sign announced Dr. Ava Grey Montgomery, MD.

Addison raised a brow. "Let me guess—your sister?"

"Ava is my twin sister. She's also a first-rate general surgeon."

Addison wasn't quite sure why his air of casualness annoyed her. "The town is just as I remember—still stuck in the nineteenth century."

Wade tossed her a rascally glance. "Oh, I assure you, we've moved beyond the horse and buggy days. As a matter of fact, we even have indoor plumbing."

"Touché." She glowered at the fine-looking man next to her. Deep clefts accentuated each jaw, and between them a strong chin, not like the weak ones that some men hide behind a beard. She thumbed her finger minus the emerald-and-diamond engagement ring that had weighed heavily on her finger. Sheriff Wade Grey was not at all like Rowen Sarkozy, her millionaire ex-fiancé.

Exhaustion continued to settle in. Shifting in her seat, she flashed an annoyed glance at Wade. "How much farther?"

White flakes feathered down from the sky to land on the windshield. Wade turned on the wipers. The sound of the rubber blades scraping away the snow echoed in Addison's already throbbing head.

"About ten more minutes."

"Peachy."

When the headlights swung off the main highway

and onto a long drive, Wade braked to a stop. He turned to face Addison. His look was contemplative, and not altogether friendly. She cocked an eyebrow. "Something wrong?"

She could see the anger in him no matter how tightly he reined it in. His voice was matter of fact. "Don't make coming back to Hope Ranch all about you."

A surge of righteous anger filtered through Addison. She opened her mouth to argue. "What's that supposed to mean?"

His eyes held hers. He didn't smile. "Meadow Creek is far removed from the glitz and glamour of the big cities, including Boise, and most certainly New York City, Paris, and Istanbul. I'm sure you get my meaning."

Her mind raced forward. Was she so transparent that he could see right through her? Her chest rose with a heavy sigh. "I hope you're not accusing me of something I haven't done."

The smile that had earlier danced in his eyes had definitely disappeared. "I do have internet, cable TV, and the international news channels. You've made quite a reputation for yourself as the most beautiful woman in the world, and the world's top model, and…" His voice drifted off. "I can't imagine what it's like to live under the microscope of the paparazzi's constant snooping. One thing I can tell you is that Nell's not as young as she used to be, and though she'd never admit it, she isn't as spry as she was even a year ago. Don't expect to be waited on hand and foot, Ms. James. Just remember that you were once one of Nell's kids. I don't care who you are now, how much money you've made, or that you own *real* Italian leather luggage, Nell is not your maid. Broken arm or not, you will pull your weight for as long as you plan to stay at the ranch."

"Or what…you'll *arrest* me?"

He was looking at her too closely. "If you find Meadow Creek so distasteful, then why did you return?"

Addison squirmed under his scrutiny. She opened her mouth to say something, then changed her mind. Instead she managed a brittle smile as she thought, *Disaster number four—meeting Sheriff Wade Grey.*

She gave a curt nod. "Just to set the record straight, I'm here for my own reasons—none of which include taking advantage of Nell."

Chapter Two

Addison forced herself not to fidget under Wade's lingering gaze, and was relieved when he finally shifted the truck into gear and proceeded down the long drive. There were a few slick spots on the icy road that threatened to send the truck into a ditch. Addison was thankful for the way Wade handled the old Ford. She was even more thankful when he rounded the bend and the headlights shone on a porch that spanned the length of the house.

Small white flakes continued to sift from the sky as Wade switched off the engine. Her thoughts were interrupted when he opened the door. The moment she slid unassisted from the truck, the wind tugged at her cape and whipped her hair around her face. The cold increased the nagging ache in her arm. She expelled a mild curse when her high heels sank in the snow as she struggled to walk to the front of the truck.

"My instincts tell me you're here for more than rest and relaxation, Ms. James. Whatever your reason, make sure it brings no harm to Nell."

Even though she knew there was no need to deliberate the answer, Addison replied in a firm voice, "Not that it's any of your business, but I'm here to find something I lost a long time ago."

He cocked an eyebrow. "Let me know if I can

help."

Her voice rasped, "If only it were that easy."

Wade frowned. He looked at Addison with concern. "I can't imagine your life being so complicated."

She deliberately looked away from him, and then she inclined her head. "Are you familiar with the children's rhyme 'Humpty-Dumpty,' Sheriff?"

Before he could respond, a dog barked and the porch light flicked on. The front door opened, and a large black Labrador bounded down the steps. A voice called, "Boomer, mind your manners. It's only Wade, and—oh, my lands!" Nellie Hopewell put her hands to her cheeks, "Addy, my sweet Addy, you're home."

Addison gritted her teeth. She really hated the childhood nickname. Her mind reeling, skeptical, wary, Addison walked up the steps into outstretched open arms. "It's good to see you, Nell."

The elderly woman hugged Addison, patting her on the back before she pulled away. "Don't just stand there gawping, Wade Grey. Grab Addy's bags, and the two of you come inside. There's a toasty fire in the fireplace, and I've got coffee and fresh baked gingerbread with homemade clotted cream."

A shiver that had nothing to do with the temperature traveled down Addison's spine.

"C'mon before you catch your death." Nell held the door wide.

Addison inhaled the gingery aroma, quickly brushing aside unwanted memories as she stepped into her childhood home's hallway.

His arms loaded, Wade trudged up the steps. He set the bags inside the foyer. "I'll take a rain check, Nell.

Gotta get back to the office."

Nell whistled the big black dog inside and closed the door. "There's nothing so pressing that Freddie can't handle. Besides, I'd like you to take a peek at my new arrivals."

Addison shot a skeptical glance toward Wade. She needed rest and relaxation—not visitors filled with questions about her life. "I didn't realize you had guests. Perhaps I should have Sheriff Grey drive me back to town."

"I'll hear no such nonsense." Nell's blue eyes lit with adamant affection. "They're all tuckered out from the long drive from Seattle." She placed a finger to her lips to signal silence as she opened a door down the hall.

Two blonde heads peeked out from under the heavy quilt. Addison turned a questioning glance toward the older woman. "Children…I thought you were retired?"

Nellie Hopewell stood tall, rawboned, and still feisty. As long as Addison had known her, Nell had never worn a dress. Plaid shirts, jeans, and cowboy boots, her hair worn in a single long braid. Addison remembered how Nell had always bustled through the house and around the ranch making sure every child did their assigned chores. She was the only family Addison had ever known. There were never any elaborate meals, and clothing was mostly hand-me-downs, but no child went hungry, and there were always gifts for each birthday and at Christmas. Though vibrancy still shone in her blue eyes, the long braid was laced with more silver than red, and Nell, nearing the downside of seventy-five, was barely the woman Addison remembered.

"There's retirement, and then there's retirement." Nell nodded emphatically. "Until permanent arrangements can be made for these two six-year-old tadpoles, I'm *un*-retired." She eased the door shut and motioned Addison and Wade to the kitchen, where she poured two cups of coffee, set out a plate of gingerbread, and hovered the coffeepot over a third cup. "Wade?"

He acquiesced, then reached for a square of gingerbread. "Better wrap a couple of pieces for Millie and Freddie. Millie'll skin me alive if she smells gingerbread on me but without any in my hand."

Addison inhaled the spicy aroma that still lingered in the kitchen. She remembered that Nell's gingerbread was dark and gingery and made with what Nell referred to as her *secret* ingredient. She also recalled that Nell made two different types of this lusciousness—one for the children and a grown-up version for the adults. She never knew what the secret was because when any of the children would ask, her foster mother would only smile and say, "Nosey is as nosey does. Now go mind your business."

Nell settled in a chair at the long kitchen table. Addison glanced around the room. The house was still as shabby as she remembered except for the kitchen, which had always been Nell's pride, a place that was both welcoming and efficient. The old Formica countertops had been replaced with white quartz. That plus a new five-burner gas stovetop, wall oven, and double-door refrigerator with a bottom freezer seemed to be where Nell had spent money for upgrades.

Addison had dined in the most expensive

restaurants in the world, and yet no one made coffee like Nell. Preferring it without cream and sugar, she savored the beverage. "If the children are orphans, then why didn't they go to the orphanage?"

Nell plopped a generous dollop of the rum-flavored clotted cream on a slice of gingerbread and forked it into her mouth. She munched for a moment. "The children were willed to me."

"Willed... How does that happen?" Addison sputtered.

The gray-haired woman offered Wade a wink as she explained, "Easy as putting pen to paper, I reckon. Even though she lived in Washington State, Claire Reed was my best friend for near seventy years. Joey and Julie are...were...her great-grandchildren. I won't go into circumstances, but Jenny, that's Claire's granddaughter, found herself in a financial predicament, with no husband, and with no education to get a good-paying job, and no other family to help out. She left the children with Claire and joined the Army. Jenny's parents died when she was a little girl. Well, Claire took sick. When she knew she wouldn't be around much longer, she gave me a call, asking if I'd take the children until their mother could make a life for them." Nell drank deep from her own cup. "Naturally, I wasn't about to say no to a dying friend. I have temporary custody until their mother returns."

"What about the children's father?" Addison glanced toward the closed bedroom door.

Nell harrumphed. "From my understanding he—whoever *he* is—has never been in the picture. According to Claire, his name isn't even on the children's birth certificates. In fact, the twins bear their mother's maiden name—Wallace."

Addison was startled by the depth of emotion in Wade's voice. "The twins are lucky to have you, Nell." He cut a glance toward Addison. "None of us would be where we are today if you hadn't taken us in."

So he was one of Nell's kids, too. Addison's curiosity was piqued. She didn't remember Wade Grey, and she had lived at the ranch for eleven years. "Is there any chance of contacting the mother?"

Wade furrowed his forehead into a frown. "Her unit is deployed to a remote region in Afghanistan. We've contacted the Red Cross to help bring her home, hopefully by Christmas." He gulped the last of his coffee before he slid from the stool and bent to kiss Nell on the cheek. "Hate to leave good company, but duty calls." He grabbed the paper sack Nell had prepared for his dispatcher and deputy.

An awkward interval of silence fell. Addison also slid off her stool. "Thank you for picking me up at the airport and for driving me out here."

The two women followed him to the foyer. "I'm putting Addy in her old room. The one she shared with Ruby Raye. Would you mind, Wade?" The older woman shifted her gaze to the luggage, and then toward Addison. "My old knees aren't what they used to be. A downstairs bedroom is much easier for me these days."

"Sure thing." He didn't crack a smile as he tucked one piece of luggage under his arm and grabbed the others, one in each hand, and labored up the steep stairs.

Addison didn't know why, but she was mesmerized by him. He was different from the men she'd met in the fashion industry, different from the jetsetters with enough money to buy small countries. He was introspective, with intensity in his dark eyes that revealed a soul weary with pain.

Once Wade returned to the foyer, he kissed Nell on the cheek and thanked her for the goodies, and with the assurance that he was only a phone call away if she needed him. He situated the hat on his head. "Let's keep bringing the twins' mother home for Christmas to ourselves. I'd rather give them a happy surprise instead of disappointing them."

Addison quirked a smile as he tipped the brim of his hat to signal his departure. Western boots, a tan felt cowboy hat, denims, starched white shirt beneath a tan jacket. So different from Rowan, she thought. No expensive designer slacks, silk shirt and tie, and hand-stitched leather loafers. Yes, very different. She was still smarting from the painful disillusionment that her fiancé was a frog and no amount of kissing would turn him into a prince charming.

Nell escorted Wade to the door and locked it behind him. She wandered back to where Addison still stood.

"Earth to Addy." Nell's voice jolted Addison back to the present. "You look all done in. Why don't you go on up? We can talk tomorrow." She made a shooing motion with her hands.

Addison opened her mouth to object when her subconscious reminded her of Wade's warning that Nell was not her personal maid. She forced herself to soften her voice. "I am tired."

Nell gave a quick nod. "How long has your arm been in the cast?"

"Fifteen days." She sighed. "Although it seems like

forever."

"Uh-huh. I remember when Ruby Raye thought she was superwoman and jumped off the barn roof and broke her arm. She was in a cast for six weeks."

Addison walked to the photo-laden mantel over the fireplace. Nostalgia filled her voice. "I'm very proud of Ruby. She's become quite successful with her real estate business."

Both women were quiet for a moment. Nell looked at Addison with a concerned expression. "How did you break your arm?"

"Nothing very glamorous." Addison blinked away the vision of herself falling eight feet and landing in a crumpled heap on a cement floor. "We were doing a show in Budapest. Inferior workmanship caused the runway pedestals to collapse. I wasn't the only model to suffer a nasty fall. Actually, I'm lucky only my arm was broken."

"Did you suffer a concussion?" Nell indicated the bandage over Addison's eye.

"Yes, but the doctors said there was no brain damage." She tried to stifle the yawn. "I'm more tired than I thought. Do you mind if I retire early?"

"Off to bed with you. We have plenty of time to visit tomorrow or for as long as you plan to stay." Nell patted Addison's shoulder.

Chapter Three

Mindful of the sleeping children downstairs, Addison eased her bedroom door shut. She stood in front of the three-door wardrobe, with its two bottom drawers and a tall mirror. The dark cherry wood was scarred with age...and memories from how many more children after she had left Hope Ranch? She faced her image, which seemed to hold all the forgotten years, including the Addy who used to be reflected back at her. A deep, long-forgotten gladness stirred in her heart. It almost felt as if the room was putting its arms around her...welcoming her home.

The reflection of her old bed showed a new pink chenille spread had replaced the tattered patchwork quilt she and Ruby had slept under. She peered again at her image. The mirror revealed the face of a six-year-old orphan who had silently cried herself to sleep there that first night so many years ago. Ah, but this mirror couldn't be tricked. Addison touched the large white bandage above her left eye. "I'm not as young as I used to be," she spoke only to the image staring back at her.

Doubts and fears nagged at her. Beauty in the world of modeling was truly only skin deep. There was no room for wrinkles, facial flaws, and certainly not a large scar that would take a skillful plastic surgeon hours to mend the disfigurement. At thirty-two, she was nearing retirement age as a runway model. The mirror was no longer her friend. She looked pale and tired…and unwanted.

She wandered to the window. It had been fifteen years since she'd left Hope Ranch, and what did she have to show for all those years? Fame, fortune…the creeps who came crawling out of the woodwork with their long-range camera lenses to sneak candid shots of her…and a broken heart. Her warm breath fogged the window as she peered out at the yard. The moon hung like a giant silver ball casting a sort of moonlight rapture over the trees and the snow-laden ground. The tree limbs barren of leaves reminded her of children holding their skinny arms up to the visitors who used to visit the orphanage, children desperate for a loving home.

A light tap at the door drew her away from the window. She swallowed hard and brushed away unwanted tears.

"Addy, may I come in?"

Addison opened the door to find Nell standing there wearing an apologetic smile. "I never thought to ask if you needed help undressing." She nodded toward the blue sling that cradled Addison's arm. "I suppose it's the mother hen in me. Of course, I don't want to intrude."

Addison held the door wide as an invitation. "It is a bit awkward with one arm."

Unbuttoning the silken blouse and slipping it from Addison's shoulders, Nell sucked in a deep gasp at the sight of the purplish-yellow bruises that lingered from the fall. The younger woman's spine resembled a railroad track, and her ribs were almost visible through the bruised flesh.

Nell's gaze shot up, horrified. "Addy, I don't mean to pry but, my goodness, child, you're skin and bones. No wonder you look so pale and washed out."

Addison tried to make light of her foster mother's alarm. "Flab is not acceptable in the world of fashion."

"You…you aren't anorexic, are you?"

Addison looked into her foster mother's worried eyes. "In the beginning, yes, I did purge. Not anymore. Not for years. I've simply learned how to subsist on very little."

The answer didn't seem to satisfy the woman who had raised her. Addison smiled at Nell. "I would never turn down your blueberry pancakes, or homemade chili. I won't promise to eat a lot. I must maintain a size four or I won't fit into any of my clothes."

Addison felt a foolish, almost overwhelming urge to fling herself into the older woman's arms and sob, but she was no longer a child. Besides, years on the runway had taught her there was no room for displaying private emotions.

Childhood remembrances continued to sweep over Addison as Nell's deft fingers wove the silken strands into a long braid. "I've missed being home, Nell. My life…" With a hitch, her voice trailed off.

Nell patted the young woman on the shoulder. "I suspect there's more than a broken arm that's brought you home, Addy. No pressure. When you're ready to talk, you know I'll listen, and without judgment." She bent and kissed Addison on top of the head. "Now, off to bed with you, and don't get up until you're ready."

At the opened door, an upturned smile on her lips, Nell said, "Blueberry pancakes, scrambled eggs, and bacon for breakfast. You'll need your strength. There're chores to do, you know."

"Yes, I remember." Addison held up her arm. "I'm not sure how much I can do with a bum wing."

Nell winked. "It only takes one hand to load a dishwasher, or feed the chickens, or collect eggs." She eased the door shut.

In the moonlit room, Addison snuggled under the covers and relaxed against the downy pillow. She swallowed hard to avoid giving full rein to her emotions. She fell asleep and dreamed of Humpty Dumpty, except the face on the large white egg was hers.

****

On the drive back to his office, Addison intruded on Wade's thoughts. He wondered what she was running from, and why after fifteen years she had suddenly returned to Meadow Creek. There was no doubting Addison James was beautiful. He wondered what really lay beneath the layers of makeup and false eyelashes—not just her physical features, but her integrity, her heart and soul.

He silently recited the nursery rhyme "Humpty Dumpty." Why had she asked him if he knew the poem? He suspected it had a lot to do with the sadness in her eyes that she'd tried to hide behind an artificial smile.

She did appear slightly jaded. Her sarcasm hadn't affected him in the way he thought it would, and her laugh had left an ache that mystified him. Her female scent permeated the truck, and he inhaled deeply. The memory of how their brief contact felt when he'd lifted her into the truck and the momentary heat that had flickered in her eyes caused a soft moan to slide from his lips. *What the hell?*

He played good-cop-bad-cop with himself. The good cop wanted to believe that Addison had returned for rest and relaxation, to recuperate from the fall. From what he'd read on the internet, it was fortunate she had survived virtually unscathed, well, except for a broken arm and a gash over her eye. Unfortunately, one young model had been crushed to death under the weight of the scaffolding.

His bad-cop persona argued Addison was running from…what? He figured she hadn't returned to Meadow Creek to catch up on old times with her foster mother. He justified this thought because Nell had mentioned on occasion that unlike the other children she had fostered, Addison never sent Christmas cards or greeting cards of any kind, and on Nell's sixty-fifth birthday bash, out of the fifty kids that Nell had opened her home and her heart to, Addison hadn't responded to the invitation.

Wade wheeled his truck into the parking space in front of his office. He sat in the warmth and listened to Dean Martin crooning "Walking in a Winter Wonderland," while mulling a rampage of concerns about Addison. Whatever her reason for returning, as long as Nell's heart didn't get hurt he was willing to give Addison the benefit of the doubt. When the song finished, he switched off the radio and stepped into the cold night air. He battened his hat against the wind as he sprinted up the steps.

Inside, the night dispatcher glanced up from the mystery novel she was reading. Millie Mann pointed over her shoulder. "Coffee's fresh and hot."

He set the bag on the desk. "Gift from Nell—fresh gingerbread."

Millie opened the bag and removed a wrapped dark brown wedge. She sniffed and purred her pleasure before removing the protective paper wrapping and uncapping the plastic container of clotted cream. "Perfection."

Wade shucked out of his coat and hung his hat on the hall tree. He poured two cups and set one in front of the dispatcher, who was old enough to be his grandmother. She always claimed the only way she'd retire was if she was carried out with her boots on and toes turned to the sky. "Anything exciting happen while I was out?"

Millie chuckled. "The widow Turley called in, frantic, saying someone was trying to break into her house."

Wade propped his long legs on his desk and leaned back in the chair. "Did you remind Freddie not to turn on the siren?"

"I did." She was thoughtful for a moment. "I swear I don't know how that poor boy made it through the police academy."

Wade waggled his eyebrows. "That's why he isn't allowed to keep his revolver loaded." It was common knowledge that Freddie Sumner was easygoing, good-natured, and about as bumbling as they come. "And…"

"Yeah, yeah, I know. His daddy's money…" Millie's voice trailed off when the young deputy entered the office, cat hair clinging to his coat.

The deputy expelled a series of sneezes. "False alarm."

"Freddie Sumner, what in Hades happened to your

jacket and your face?" Millie set her book and the gingerbread aside. She rushed to get the first-aid kit from the filing cabinet.

The deputy touched the long red scratch on his cheek. "Like I said…false alarm. Busby—that's the widow Turley's tomcat—was outside, and was scratching on the bedroom window and yowling up a storm. I guess he was cold and wantin' to get inside."

Freddie obeyed when Millie ordered him to sit down. "Anyhow, fool cat started hissin' and spittin' when I grabbed hold of him. Scratched my face and then dug his claws into my jacket when I tried to set him down." Freddie guffawed. "For a minute I wasn't sure who was gonna win…me or Busby." He peeled the gloves off his hands. "Good thing I was wearin' these."

A smile played in Wade's voice. "How is Busby, and Mrs. Turley?"

"Oh, they're both okay. Mrs. Turley apologized for Busby, and said she was sorry for bringing me out on a wild goose chase."

Millie swabbed antibiotic ointment along the scratch. "Looks like you got the worst end of it." She patted the young deputy on the shoulder. "You'll live."

Freddie sneezed again. "Guess I'll write out my report and file it."

Concern laced Millie's voice. "I hope you're not coming down with the flu. It's going around, you know."

In the middle of another sneeze, Freddie managed, "Ca-ca-cat hair."

Millie returned to her desk and picked up the novel. "Better cat hair than a bullet."

Although only three years separated them, in some

ways, his deputy seemed much younger, and definitely less mature, than the sheriff. The crestfallen look on the Freddie's face tugged at Wade. "Take the rest of the night off, Freddie."

Freddie accepted a tissue and honked out a hefty blow. "Anything on my transfer to Baltimore, Sheriff?"

"You'll be the first to know, Freddie."

The deputy sighed. "Nothin' excitin' ever happens in Meadow Creek." He hefted on his coat, and thumbed a finger at his chest. "I'm tired of chasin' cats and helpin' round up stray cows. Wastin' my talent as a lawman is what I'm doin'." Situating the hat on his head, he bemoaned, "Wade, don't you ever itch for some excitement, like an armored car heist or a shootout with gang members?"

Wade reared back in the chair; he placed his hands behind his head. "Nope. The only itch for excitement I have is taking home the grand prize in next year's big-mouth bass tournament." He nodded toward the dispatcher. "Millie will fill out a requisition to get you a new jacket."

The zipper snagged as the deputy pulled it up. He made a frustrated gesture with his hands. "*Freddie* is a kid's name. I'd appreciate it if everyone would call me Fred. I'm thirty-three years old, for gosh sakes."

Millie glanced at Wade. She winked. "Tommy Jenks is sixty-five. I've never heard him complain about folks not calling him Thomas."

The material tore as the deputy gave a forceful yank on the zipper. "Don't make fun, Millie. I'm serious."

The chair squeaked as Wade set his feet to the floor and stood. He walked over and clapped Freddie on the back. "A name doesn't make a man; it's how he wears it that earns the respect he wants." He glanced at the wall clock. "Go on home, Fred. Relieve me at six."

"*Fred!* Dang it! Don't say it like you're pokin' fun at me."

Millie handed him the paper sack. "Here. Maybe this will take the sting out of your harrowing experience. Nell sent gingerbread and clotted cream."

"Well…well. Dang it…just…well. That's all." He grabbed the sack and without another word, Deputy Freddie Sumner turned on his heel and pushed through the double glass doors. Wade watched him trudge down the steps, one hand jammed inside a pocket of the tattered jacket and the other gripping the paper bag.

"You know, with the political pull and money to back it, ol' Ed Sumner could easily get Freddie the transfer he so badly wants." Millie plopped a large piece of rum-cream-soaked gingerbread in her mouth, then picked up the mystery novel and opened it to the bookmarked page.

Wade sauntered to his desk and sat in his office chair. "Uh-huh. For Freddie's sake, let's hope his father doesn't do that."

Waking the computer from its hibernation mode, he typed Addison's name in the search engine. He clicked on a link that opened to an article titled "Supermodel Set to Wed Billionaire Rowan Sarkozy."

The punch to the gut reaction surprised Wade when he looked at the picture of Addison wrapped in the arms of a man who looked as if he were in his late forties and wearing a killer smile, clearly a playboy, with a touch of gray at the temples and a manicured five o'clock shadow. Holding long-stemmed fluted glasses, the couple stood on the bow of a yacht. Addison was nothing to him, so why should he care who she married? And he'd never heard of Rowan Sarkozy. Wade emitted a low whistle when he read the price of the engagement ring.

Quickly scanning through several articles and not finding what he was looking for left Wade frustrated and dissatisfied. He shut down the computer. "Millie, what do you remember about Addison James…when she lived with Nell?"

The night clerk-dispatcher set her book aside. Swiveling her chair around to face her boss, she furrowed her forehead as if trying to recall long-lost information. "Best as I can recall, I think she was about six when Child Protective Services showed up on Nell's doorstep with Addison and another little girl." She pondered for another second. "I believe that was Ruby…uh-huh, Ruby Raye. I remember because I was at the ranch. It was late September. I and several other ladies from the church were helping Nell plan the annual bazaar for the Christmas festival."

She was thoughtful for a moment as she plopped the last bite of gingerbread in her mouth and washed it down with a generous sip of coffee. Wade thought perhaps her thoughts had meandered elsewhere and was about to prod her back to the present when she spoke.

"I don't know that it's my place to be talking about Nell's business. You know everything with foster kids is s'posed to be confidential."

"Millie, I'm the sheriff. I can spend hours researching CPS's files, or you can tell me what you remember." He made a zipping motion across his lips. "My lips are sealed. Whatever you say is between the two of us."

The dispatcher harrumphed. "Sometimes I forget you're the sheriff, because you're so...so..."

Wade smiled. "So dadgum young. Yeah, I know. You keep reminding me."

"Smarty pants!" Millie smirked. "So where was I? Oh, yes, wide-eyed with fear those two little girls were. They gripped each other's hands like they'd never let go. Like I said, I think they were about six years old. Anyhow, Addison's story is about as pitiful as it gets. Ruby Raye's is fairly typical."

"How so—for Ms. James, that is?"

"As I recall, it seems someone found her at the bus station in Boise. She was just sitting on a bench crying. Apparently no one saw who left her. Barely a toddler, she was too young to talk. There was no note or anything to identify her. Nell asked if the police had looked at the bus station's security camera to see if it showed who left the little girl." Millie stopped to make a sound of disgust. "Apparently, from what the caseworker said, the station manager reported that the camera had been out of commission for a couple of weeks. Humph. How convenient. From that point on, it seems the little girl was shuffled from one foster home to another until she came to live with Nell."

Wade felt the scowl on his face deepen as he leaned forward. "Then how did the authorities know her age, and how did she get her name?"

"Nell asked the same questions. A doctor determined her age by the number of teeth she had cut. As for her name, apparently CPS named her."

Silence filled the office, broken only by the ticking of the large wall clock. Millie picked up her book and opened it to the marked page. "I can tell you one thing. From the very beginning it was obvious the girl was a natural beauty—and sassy-mouthed and defiant. Nell gave her heart and soul to all her kids. She made excuses for the girl and always said that Addison was—spirited."

Millie looked Wade square in the eye. "Remember when we celebrated Nell's sixty-fifth birthday—all of Nell's kids that could come came, and the ones who couldn't either called to wish her well or sent cards and gifts? But there was nothing, absolutely nothing from *Ms. Addison James*." She made a motion that reminded Wade of a hen ruffling her feathers.

"I guess she had her reasons." This last bit of information piqued his cop curiosity even more. "I was one of Nell's kids. I can't seem to remember knowing her."

"Well, it's no wonder. First, you're a few years older, so you would've been several grades ahead of her in school. Plus you and Ava had already been adopted." It appeared Millie was doing a mental calculation. "By the time you graduated high school and joined the Marines, Addison would've only been fourteen or thereabouts."

He smiled. "Yep, in those days the only thing on my mind was football and…Gracie." His eyes blurred. After all these years, the memory of the fiasco with his one and only love still stung.

He stifled a yawn. "I'm grabbing a nap. Unless there's an emergency, wake me before you clock out."

"Humph, it'd be nice to have a little excitement around here. Dull as a cemetery."

He chuckled. "Now you're beginning to sound like

Freddie."

Millie gave him one of her *Don't be a smarty-pants* glares.

Wade made himself comfortable in the jail cell reserved especially for him and his deputy. He lay on the cot, his hands folded behind his head as he stared at the ceiling. He didn't like the direction of his thoughts. He had a sudden wild desire to run his fingers through Addison's silvery strands of silken hair, and to frame her face with his hands, and to…he hadn't realized he had fallen asleep until Millie's voice jerked him back to reality. His eyes clouded with sleep, he blinked until they cleared and he was able to focus.

"It's midnight, Wade."

He grunted a reply.

"You were babbling a lot of nonsense." Millie voiced her concern. "You okay…one of your bad dreams?"

Wade swung his feet to the floor and sat up. He stretched and yawned, and made light of the dispatcher's concern. "Nothing that a week-long fishing trip wouldn't cure."

"Yep, I reckon. Anyhow, all's quiet, coffee's hot, and I'm taking my weary bones home."

He yawned again and riffled his hands through his hair. "It's freezing out. I'll drive you home."

"Not on your life. I can walk two blocks faster than you can get the heater going in the squad car." Millie hefted into her jacket, tied a scarf over her head, and pulled on a pair of gloves. She collected her purse and pushed through the office door. "Call if you need me."

Wade merely nodded. After splashing water on his face, combing his hair, and straightening his tie, he poured a cup of coffee into his favorite mug, the one with a bass-shaped handle, and walked to the double-paned glass doors to stare out into the night. Meadow Creek was a beautiful old town with hiking trails, not far from Sun Valley and Jackson Hole, and with a population of less than a thousand. Nothing much out of the ordinary happened. Even the tourists seemed to respect the quiet ambiance of Meadow Creek.

He realized he wasn't studying the town or his current surroundings. Instead he was recalling another time, another place. Both hostile. Closing his eyes, he pressed his head against the cool glass. He understood his deputy's urge for excitement. Once upon a time, he'd been a gung-ho eighteen-year-old eager to conquer the world. With a fifteen-year stint in the Marine Corps, including deployments in Africa, Iraq, and Afghanistan, he'd seen enough injustices to last him a lifetime. He'd put up plenty of safety nets these past four years to make sure he never slipped back into the darkness he'd so painstakingly left behind, and he continued to shove back the unpleasant images that threatened to escape from his mental closet. He surmised that Freddie might never appreciate the peacefulness of home until he'd experienced the ugliness of elsewhere.

He opened the drawer where Millie kept her novel. The cover, picturing a cop with a badge attached to his belt and a woman on the run, had piqued his curiosity. He opened to the bookmarked page. A chill raced through him as he read about Texas Rangers finding headless corpses. He closed the book and read the title: *Shadowed Reunion.* Some imagination, he thought. This was exactly the kind of exhilaration Freddie Sumner craved, and it was this kind of danger that could very well get him killed.

If the transfer to Baltimore, Maryland came through, Wade faced the dilemma of deciding whether to approve it and send Freddie to a dangerous and uncertain future, or deny the transfer and watch his deputy wither in a job he was slowly growing to hate.

Chapter Four

Wade ambled down the sidewalk toward BB's Café. He greeted visitors as well as folks he'd known most of his life. A tooting horn drew his attention toward a beat-up red pickup that wheeled into a parking space. A lanky man in his seventies stepped out of the truck. "Mornin', Wade. Glad I spotted you."

"Same to you, Emmett, what's on your mind?"

"I'm runnin' a few errands for Nell. She's in need of chicken feed, a few bales of hay, sack of oats, and such."

"Join me for breakfast?"

"Already ate, but I could go for another cup of coffee. Besides, I was comin' to see you."

Wade grabbed the door handle and held the door wide, then followed Emmett Oxbow inside the bustling café. The aroma of bacon tantalized his taste buds.

"Morning, Wade…Emmett." Brenda Brown greeted the men with a wide smile. She pointed them in the direction of an empty table. "Seat yourselves. I'll bring the coffee."

"Same to you, Brenda." Wade removed his hat and seated himself. "I'll have my usual."

The stout woman cocked an eyebrow toward Emmett. He said, "Two spudnuts."

"Plain or glazed?" She held the pencil over the

order pad.

Emmett groused, "You already know the answer, Brenda. Why do you always ask?"

She grinned as she tweaked his leathery cheek. "Somebody's got to keep you mentally alert."

The old rancher expelled an aggravated snort. "Maybe I'll surprise you and order a chocolate-covered one."

"You feisty ol' goat, you don't like chocolate, and you know it." Brenda grinned as she filled their cups and then bustled toward the kitchen to place Wade's order of two pancakes with scrambled eggs and a double order of crispy bacon, and two glazed spudnuts for Emmett.

Wade wrapped his cold hands around the cup to garner the heat. "Why were you coming to see me?"

Emmett glanced around the crowded room. He leaned forward, his voice lowered. "I haven't mentioned this to Nell, no need to worry her. I've been seein' flashes of light up on the northern ridge of her property. At first I didn't pay no never-mind, thinkin' it was just the sun glintin' off the snow. Thing is, it's happenin' regular-like. Thought maybe you'd go with me to check it out. We'll have to horse it in. Too much snow for a truck."

"How about if I bring the snowmobile?"

"Nope. Makes too much noise—spoil the element of surprise."

Brenda bustled over and placed the food on the table. "How's Nell, Emmett? Haven't seen her out and about in a while."

The rancher cut a large piece of spudnut with his fork and held it in midair. "She's feisty as ever. Got a couple new young'uns, girl and a boy—six-year-old twins. Besides, you know she doesn't like to drive on snowy roads."

Brenda harrumphed. "Yeah, I hear you. Makes me glad I live upstairs." The café owner was thoughtful for a moment. "Those babies can consider themselves lucky. In fact, half the people in this town can count their blessings that Nellie Hopewell opened her heart and her home to them." She shook her head. "Still, she's no spring chicken."

Emmett guffawed. "I know it and you know it. Thing is, Nell hasn't figured it out yet."

Brenda refilled the half-empty cups. "You fellas have a good day."

Wade waylaid her. "Brenda, have you seen any strangers in town lately?"

Brenda answered with a good-natured grin. "Look around you, Sheriff. Seventy-five percent of the people in here are strangers. What kinda question is that?"

Wade offered a sheepish grin toward the plump woman with rosy cheeks, who wore her customary Mrs. Santa hat to celebrate the season. "I stand corrected. What I meant to say, have you noticed anyone who doesn't resemble the usual touristy type?"

She bent low to the table, her voice hushed, as she asked, "You mean nefarious types…suits?"

Emmett snorted. "You and Nell read too many dang mystery novels. What Wade's tryin' to say is—"

"Oh, don't go gettin' your suspenders in a tangle, Emmett. I'm just joshing. Anyhow, I'll keep an eye out and let you know, Wade."

Someone yelled, "Brenda, telephone."

Emmett finished off the remaining bite of the donut

made from mashed potatoes, then cut into the second one. He was thoughtful for a moment. "Well?"

Wade frowned. "Could be campers thinking the land is part of the park."

"Yeah, sure, and it could be poachers, or Christmas tree thieves. That's why I don't want to go up there alone. I'm not a young pup anymore. Can't run very fast with these ol' arthritic knees."

Wade rolled his eyes. Crime in Meadow Creek was limited to jaywalkers and occasional squabbles over a parking space, but the last thing he wanted to do was rile the older man. "All right, we'll check it out."

Emmett downed the last of his coffee. "Good. I got things to do. When can you come out?"

Wade checked his watch. "It's seven. If you can wait until I check in with Freddie and Millie, and then go by the barn to hitch up the snowmobiles, I'll follow you out to Nell's and help you unload the hay bales."

"Nope. Like I said…horses! You can hear a snowmobile a mile away. Don't want to scare off whoever it is that's trespassin'."

Wade lifted his eyebrows and offered a sardonic smile. "What about your ol' bones?"

Emmett answered with an aggravated snort. He pulled money from his wallet and laid it on the table. "Well, don't just sit there. Time's a-wastin'."

****

The morning sun crept into the room. Comforted from a restful night's sleep, Addison lazed with her eyes shut. The bedroom door's squeak alerted her that someone had entered. Soft shuffles toward the bed, followed by whispers, prompted an inner smile as she listened to the cherubic voices of two youngsters. She remembered that Nell had called them Joey and Julie.

"She sure is pretty." Addison surmised the little boy had made this comment.

"As pretty as our mommy?"

Without opening her eyes, Addison almost felt the little boy's shrug as he answered his sister. "Dunno."

The little girl whispered, "She looks like a princess."

"Who, our mama?"

The little girl countered with a hushed pitch in her voice. "No, dork, her."

Addison envisioned the little girl's annoyance and almost laughed out loud. Instead she decided to keep up the pretense of sleeping to see what she could learn about the children.

"Maybe she'll 'dopt us and be our mommy."

"Don't be silly, Julie. Gram promised Mama would come get us."

"But Gram's in heaven. What if she don't? Who's gonna take care of us?"

A wave of compassion washed over Addison at the worry in the little girl's voice. She remembered, all too well, what it was like to be a six-year-old in a strange place and afraid that no one would come get her.

Joey's voice lowered, and Addison strained to hear what he said. "Let's write a letter to Santa. If we're extra good, betcha he'll bring Mama home for Christmas." And then, "Shh, don't tell anybody, Julie. It's our secreeee…"

The word "secret" came out as a surprised screech when the half-closed bedroom door burst open and seventy pounds of Labrador retriever bounded into the room and in one leap landed on top of Addison.

****

Addison's scream, accompanied by the twins' frantic shrieks and Boomer's barking, sent Wade bounding up the front steps with Emmett close behind.

Nell labored up the stairs. "Oh, thank goodness, Wade. I can't get up the stairs fast enough to see what's causing all the ruckus."

Wade took the steps by twos until he reached the landing. He sprinted toward the woeful sobs and the children's pleading voices. "No…get down…Boomer!"

He burst through the open doorway to find a chaotic scene with the twins struggling to drag the big black dog off the bed, and Addison shielding her face with her good arm to ward off slobbery kisses from the rambunctious two-year-old dog.

He grabbed Boomer by the collar and hauled him off the bed while Nell scolded everyone. "Wade, get the dog out of here and outside where he belongs." She pointed to Emmett. "Make yourself useful. Take the twins downstairs and fix 'em a bowl of cereal." She scowled at the youngsters. "What're you doing up here anyhow?"

Joey and Julie clasped hands and stood close together, tears puddling in their eyes.

Addison's breaths came in deep gasps. After the initial shock of being pounced on by the dog, followed by the hullabaloo, her already stretched thin emotions erupted into a combination of sobs and laughter. "It's okay, really. Don't be mad, Nell. They were just curious."

Emmett guided the children through the door. "C'mon, young'uns, and don't mind Nell. Her bark is worse than her bite."

Wade spoke gently. "You look a little shell-shocked. The dog didn't hurt you, did he?"

Addison's heart stilled in her throat when she looked up at him; a shiver wracked over her. Too soon, she silently chastised herself. Her emotions were still raw from the break-up with her fiancé, and she certainly didn't want to get involved in a relationship on the rebound.

Her voice wavered. "I'm more startled than hurt, I think." She reached up to touch the bandage on her forehead.

"I'll telephone my sister and ask her to come out to take a look at you."

"That's okay. I don't want to be a bother."

The dog whined and tugged against Wade's grip. "No bother. Just call it my civic duty to keep the citizens of Meadow Creek safe from attack puppies."

Addison knew the sheriff was making a joke. Her voice was sharper than she intended. "Then someone should teach *the puppy* some manners. Please, if you'll excuse me, I'd like to get dressed."

A lazy grin spread across his tanned face. "C'mon, Boomer, let's give the lady her privacy."

Her heart was still in her throat when Wade left the room, the Labrador walking obediently beside him.

As soon as the room emptied, Nell eased the door shut. She sat on the edge of the bed, her voice calm. "I know hysteria when I see it. I won't push you into telling me what's brought you back after all these years and why you call me Nell instead of Aunt Nell." She reached forward and smoothed a wisp of hair from the corner of Addison's mouth. "I don't keep up with the news, but I hear things about most of the kids who called Hope Ranch their home." Nell stood and smoothed her hands down toward the knees of her jeans. "I'll listen—and without judgment—when you're ready to talk about whatever's eating at you."

Addison's brows were drawn into a single tense line. Nell had a right to know everything, and she didn't want the information coming from gossips, or news rags spouting fake reports just to sell magazines. She forced a smile. "You're right. I did come back for a reason." The smile crumpled. She sank back against the pillow and tried to shove the bitterness aside. "I—I just can't talk about it right now."

Nell leaned forward and lifted Addison's hand into her own. "It's okay. Like I said, when you're ready, I'll listen."

Addison removed her hand from Nell's and swung her feet over the side of the bed. "Do you mind helping me into my robe? I'll dress later."

Nell grabbed the cream-colored silk robe from the door hook. "Why don't you stay in bed? I'll bring up a tray."

"Absolutely not!" Addison hugged her foster mother.

Although she'd been catered to by beauticians, makeup artists, and housekeepers, feeling helpless wasn't Addison's style. She tamped down her annoyance at having to depend on Nell to do simple things like pulling her hair into a ponytail. *Note to self: go shopping for practical ranch clothing.*

She lifted her nose, sniffed, and found the perfect opportunity to change her thoughts. "No one makes coffee like you, Nell. Besides, I'm hungry." And she really was—for the first time in years.

Addison followed the older woman down the stairs and into the kitchen. The twins sat at the counter munching on slices of gingerbread. Each wore a milk ring around a full mouth. Her heart melted when they lowered their eyes to keep from looking at her.

Nell set out two mugs. She hovered the coffeepot over the cups as she addressed the two men. "You and Wade had your breakfast yet?"

Wade answered, "Yes, ma'am, at BB's. I came out to help Emmett unload the hay bales and sacks of feed."

"Yep, and speakin' of that, times a'wastin'. Let's get to it." Emmett doffed his cowboy hat. "Nell, holler if you need any chores done. I'll send over one of my hands." He winked. "Don't let her boss you around too much, Miss Addy."

Addison didn't miss the slight blush that pinked Nell's cheeks. Who could blame her? Tall and whipcord lean from years of ranch work, Emmett Oxbow was still a handsome man. She thought he was easily Sam Elliot's doppelganger. Even when she was a kid Emmett had always been around, doing things like trimming the horses' hooves, patching the barn roof, or taking the boys fishing…and sitting in the kitchen sipping coffee. She brushed aside the thought of why he and Nell had never married.

A lazy grin swept across Wade's face as he thanked Nell for the coffee, yet his gray eyes were sincere when he said, "Let me know if you need anything."

Addison knew he'd directed the comment toward Nell; still, it seemed the statement was open-ended. She didn't know why she was mesmerized by him. He was different. Under all that handsomeness his dark eyes hinted at personal secrets. *Note to self: find out more about Wade Grey.*

"Sheriff, perhaps I spoke a bit too hasty, before…upstairs." She touched the bandage over her eye. "Rather than flying back to New York for a doctor's appointment, it would be much more convenient to see your sister. May I have her number?"

He removed a business card and a pen from his shirt pocket and jotted his sister's office number on the back. A tiny smile quirked the corners of her lips when he extended the card toward her. "Ava makes house calls if it's an emergency. Otherwise, I can send my deputy out to drive you in if Nell doesn't feel comfortable driving in the snow."

Nell guffawed. "Don't you worry, Wade Grey. I can still hitch up the sleigh. It won't be the first time Bud and Chipper have driven me to town. Besides, the exercise will do 'em good."

He leaned over and kissed her on the cheek. "You are one in a million. I can't think of any good reason why some man hasn't claimed you. Can you, Emmett?" He winked at the crusty old rancher.

Addison nearly choked to keep from laughing out loud at the indignant expression on Nell's face and the crimson creeping up Emmett's neck.

The awkward moment was broken when the twins chimed in unison, "Where's the bathroom? We forgot."

Wade stood behind Emmett trying to hide his own amusement. His wink brought a spurt of laughter from Addison. She was suddenly conscious of her bed-mussed hair and that she wore no makeup.

Nell cleared her throat. "Don't you two have hay to unload?"

Chapter Five

Joey tugged on Addison's sleeve. "Lady, we really have to go."

Still chuckling, she held her good hand toward the brother and sister. "C'mon, I'll show you."

Joey scrunched his face into a concerned frown. "What's so funny?"

She had no idea why the moment had struck her as humorous. "You know, I really don't know." She led the twins down the hall and pointed to the bathroom. "One at a time. Little boys need to respect a girl's privacy even if they are brother and sister."

"You go first, Joey. I want to ask the lady somethin'." Julie waited until her brother had closed the door, then looked up at Addison. "Lady, are you mad at us?"

Blue eyes brimming with tears and deep concern on the freckled face tugged at Addison's heart. "First of all, my name is Addison, and second, why would you think I'm mad at you?"

Julie's face puckered, and Addison wasn't sure what she should do to comfort the child. "Please don't cry. It's okay, you can tell me." She knelt to be on eye level with the little girl.

"W-we didn't mean for the dog to jump on you. P-please don't let the grouchy lady send us away. Our

Gram is in Heaven, and…and…and…" The emotional dam broke, and tears streaked down both cheeks.

Addison mustered a smile. Images of her six-year-old self flashed through her brain as she gathered the little girl into her arms and cooed, "I'm not mad, and neither is Aunt Nell. Things happen."

Julie pulled back a little and snuffled. "But…she yelled…and really loud."

"Yeah, and she looked real mad." Joey added as he came to stand next to his sister.

"Aunt Nell isn't mean, really and truly. She loves children, and you know how I know?" Addison was careful to keep her smile bright but sincere. The fact was that it hurt more than she expected that she had put pride and fame first in her life.

The twins watched as if not fully convinced they should believe whatever Addison was about to tell them. Joey blurted, "I bet she's a *witch*."

This time Addison frowned. "You mustn't ever think such horrible thoughts about Aunt Nell. You see, when I was six years old, I and my best friend, Ruby Raye, came to live with Aunt Nell. She's my foster mom, and the kindest and most loving person I know. Oh, she yells, and sometimes she huffs and puffs, but that's only when little kids do something they shouldn't."

Two sets of blue eyes widened in dismay. "You didn't have a home and nobody to love you either?"

"Hmm, just like you." She pointed toward the bathroom. "Julie, go do what you have to do. Joey, get your jackets and caps. When I've changed into my clothes, we'll go to the barn and collect the eggs. When I was a little girl, Aunt Nell always had barn cats to keep the mice away. Maybe we'll see them, plus the horses and a milk cow."

Nell yelled, "Sold ol' Buttercup. With just me, didn't have any use for a cow."

The twins had already squealed with delight and scampered off in different directions.

"That was nice, Addy. Real nice." Nell walked forward and placed her hand on Addison's cheek.

"I'm sorry, Nell, for—"

"There's no need for explanations, Addy. You had your reasons for staying away. The thing is you're home for however long you choose. And when you decide to leave, there'll be no questions asked."

Addison leaned forward and kissed Nell's wrinkled cheek. "You are the best! Now, do you have a pair of boots I can borrow? Italian-made high heels aren't for trudging through snow."

With a chuckle, Nell said, "I believe I have an extra pair in the closet. I'll come up and help you get them on." Nell turned toward her own room. "Like I said before—welcome home!"

The twins skipped around the corner and stopped short when they saw Nell. Julie hid behind her brother. Joey swallowed hard. "Um, are you going to send us away?"

Nell smiled at the youngster. "'Course not. Whatever gave you that idea?"

The little boy shifted from one foot to the other. Although her knees ached, Nell squatted to his level, much as Addison had. She reached out and stroked his cheek. "I'm not a mind reader, Joey. I can't fix whatever's on your mind if you keep it to yourself."

Joey looked at his sister as if summoning up

courage. There was a slight quiver in his voice when he asked, "Um, can Boomer sleep in our room..."

Julie finished out the sentence: "So we won't be scared?"

"You betcha." Nell winked as she struggled to stand. "You know, I hadn't planned on putting up a tree this Christmas, but come Saturday we'll hitch up the horses, pack sandwiches and hot chocolate, and go find us a jim-dandy tree."

Two pairs of blue eyes widened. The twins spoke in unison. "You mean we're gonna cut it down all by ourselves?"

"You betcha. Now, I heard you were going to collect eggs. Dixie and Trixie are my barn cats. They're friendly and so are the horses. Don't let their size scare you."

"Wow, c'mon, Julie. Let's get our coats. We've never seen a real live horse before."

Nell offered Addison a wink over the children's heads. "Soon as I help you get the boots on, I'm off to bake a couple of quiches. The ladies auxiliary is coming over to work on plans for the Christmas bazaar. You remember the annual bazaar?"

"I certainly do." Addison smiled at the twins. "It's a fun time. You'll love it." With that, Addison made her way up the stairs and into the bedroom. She removed her arm from the sling and, though awkward, managed to dress herself. She sat on the edge of the bed and in an instant wondered about her life and how she'd gotten there. If she had made different choices, would she be happier than yesterday or even today?

Hearing Nell's footsteps on the stairs, Addison shook away the doldrums. Now was not the time to indulge in a pity party.

"Knock…knock. Okay if I come in?"

"Door's open." Addison wrestled with the buttons on her shirt. She looked up as Nell entered the room. "You mentioned the horses' names were Bud and Chipper. What happened to Cinnamon and Nutmeg?"

Nell drew in a deep sigh as she brushed Addison's silken strands into a ponytail. "Oh, my, you have been away a long time. When you were here, both horses were nearing twenty years old." She sighed again. "They crossed the rainbow bridge, one pretty close after the other, a long time ago. Emmett helped me bury them up on the ridge. We planted alder trees to commemorate them. Replaced 'em with two young Percheron geldings. Brothers and good boys, too."

Addison replied in a congenial tone, "I'm sorry. Nutmeg and Cinnamon were gentle giants, even though I always was a little bit afraid of them. Probably because of their size."

An awkward silence rolled between them.

Two exuberant voices chimed, "We're ready."

Nell secured the elastic band around Addison's ponytail. "Good. The egg basket is on the kitchen counter. Addy, I'll leave it up to you to teach these two how to get the eggs out from under the hens."

Addison rolled her eyes in an *Oh, brother* expression. "Yes, ma'am."

Nell fastened the arm sling over Addison's shoulder. She lifted the coat from the bed and guided Addison's good arm through the armhole. She pulled the front together and buttoned it. "It's a might large, but it'll keep you warm until we can go shopping, and here's a sweater cap to keep your noggin warm." She pulled the red cap over Addison's ears.

The twins hopped down the stairs. Nell called after them, "Joey, go in the kitchen and get the egg basket."

"Yes, ma'am."

He raced to the kitchen and returned in a flash with the wire basket clutched in his hand. "Ready!"

Outside, the twins squealed with delight as Boomer raced around and frolicked in the snow. Addison beckoned the twins to the barn. They entered through a side door that led to a small office and then to the barn's wide aisle. Nickers greeted them, followed by clucking.

"Come, let's meet Chipper and Bud." Addison led the way down the barn's wide aisle to the stalls where two dapple-gray Percheron geldings stood.

Julie screamed and clung to her brother, who took several steps backward. "I'm afraid, Joey."

The little girl's fright brought back memories for Addison. Just like Nell had done when Addison had refused to go near the horses, she kept her voice quiet, calm, and even. She clasped Julie's hand. The size of the horses caused Addison's own heart to thump. She couldn't remember the last time she'd been near a horse, much less ones that were the size of a two-story building.

"Joey, hold your sister's other hand." For the children's sake, she put on an armor of bravado. "These are Percherons, otherwise known as gentle giants. You mustn't be afraid. It will hurt their feelings, and we wouldn't want that, would we?"

Addison walked to the feed barrel and with her free hand lifted the lid and set it aside. She reached in and scooped oats into a small pail. She held out her hand, palm up. "Joey, place about a cup full of oats in my hand. I'll show you how to feed the horses."

His eyes widened with skepticism. "His mouth is gi-normous. Won't he bite your hand off?"

She hoped her smile didn't wobble. "Not if you hold your hand out flat. Like this." She approached the stall labeled "Bud" and held her hand forward. "Hello, Bud. I'm Addison, and this is Joey and Julie. Aunt Nell says you and your brother are good boys."

She didn't know who she was trying to convince, herself or the twins. The massive neck stretched forward, and almost as if he knew to be careful, Bud lipped the oats from Addison's hand. Once he'd finished with the oats, she inched closer and reached to scratch his forehead and crooned, "You are a good boy."

When she'd coddled the horse for several minutes, she brushed a few loose strands of hair from her own face and said, "I see that Sheriff Grey and Mr. Oxbow have already put hay and oats and water in the bins. It will be our jobs to help Aunt Nell feed the animals for as long as we're here."

Chipper stretched his neck and nickered. Addison laughed. "Joey, more oats, please."

The youngster hastened to obey.

This time Addison didn't hesitate. For the first time in a long time she felt awakened and confident as she stretched her hand forward, allowing the big horse to lip the oats. She patted the animal's silken neck. "See how careful they both were?" She faced the twins. "Either of you want to try?"

At their hesitancy, she said, "It's okay. There's plenty of time." She offered a reassuring smile. "The chickens are over here."

Joey puffed out his chest. He took a hesitant step. "Um, wait. Can I try?"

His sister pleaded, "Don't, Joey. Your hand is little, and they have big teeth. Please, Joey, don't."

"Stop being a 'fraidy cat, Julie. He didn't bite Addison."

"Her hand is bigger than yours." Julie scrubbed the toe of her shoe against the barn floor. Her head lowered so that her chin almost touched her chest.

Addison patted the top of Julie's head. "There's plenty of time, Joey. Once Julie gets used to the horses, I'm certain she'll be eager to feed them."

Julie scrunched her face and stuck her tongue out at her brother.

Addison scooped oats into the little boy's hand. When he stepped forward with his palm flat, she realized then just how small his hand was compared to the massive horse's mouth. She held her breath, ready to pounce if necessary.

Joey giggled as the horse lipped the feed. "Look, Julie, I did it...I did it!" He stood on tiptoes and patted the black silken nose that stretched forward to sniff his hair, leaving Joey to squeal with delight.

The trio moved to the next stall. Chipper met them with a stretched neck and soft blowing snuffles. Addison placed a scoop of oats in Joey's hand.

"Me...too." Julie made a hesitant step toward the stall.

Addison offered a reassuring smile as she filled the girl's tiny hand with feed.

Julie cast a doubtful look toward her brother, hesitated for a moment, took a step backward. Joey encouraged, "You can do it, Julie."

Wearing a tenuous smile, she offered her tiny palm. Gentle, like his brother, Chipper lipped the meager offering with care. When he finished, he stretched his neck for more.

"See, Joey, I'm not a 'fraidy cat." She pooched her lips into a pout. "Well, maybe a little bit."

Addison laughed in spite of herself. "Before long you'll both be experts at feeding the animals. If I remember correctly, the chickens are down here."

The twins followed her to the nesting boxes. "We're not tall enough," Julie lamented.

Addison glanced around until she spotted a wooden box. "Joey, bring that crate over here so the two of you can stand on it."

Four nests each held one egg. Addison cautioned the children to lift the eggs carefully and place them inside the basket. A hen with black-and-white feathers sat in the fifth box.

"Wow," both twins exclaimed. "What kind of chicken is that?"

Addison prided herself on remembering the breed. She looked at the name plate above the nest. "Penny is a Dominique. She lays brown eggs."

Addison spoke to the hen. "Be nice, Penny. All we want is to collect your eggs." She scooted her hand beneath the hen to lift her. "Julie, reach under her and get the eggs."

The little girl stepped up on the box. She gave Addison a skeptical look. Addison's voice was firm when she said, "Quickly!"

Julie did as instructed and carefully withdrew two brown eggs. She giggled as she placed them in the basket. "I did it, Joey. Did you see?"

"Um-huh." He shot Addison a curious look. "Gosh, Addison, how do the eggs get out of the chicken?"

The question stopped Addison. While she weighed the answer, Julie spouted, "I thought there were kittens. I want to see the kitties."

A bit relieved that the little girl had saved her from having to answer Joey's question, Addison turned in a circle. "It's very cold. Don't you think they might be nestled up some place warm? I'm sure we'll see them another day."

Julie snuggled close to Addison. "I'm cold."

As the trio retraced their steps to leave the barn, an orange striped cat leapt from nowhere, followed by a calico cat, and hot on their heels Boomer gave chase. A large dark rat raced between Julie's legs. To get away from the frenzy, Julie tripped over her own feet and fell.

The commotion was over as quickly as it had begun. The cats and the rat disappeared. Boomer gave up the chase and flopped at Addison's feet.

Joey helped his sister from the floor. Addison didn't know whether to laugh or cry. In retrospect, the surprised expressions on the children's faces had been funny. Her voice was crisp when she said, "Well!"

Julie scrunched her face into a frown. "I don't like living here. I don't want to collect eggs, and I don't want to have horse slobber on my hands either. Why can't we buy our eggs from the grocery store the way Gram did…and…what if the rat gets in the house and in our bed?"

Addison understood the alarm in the little girl's voice—saw the flash of panic in her eyes—like herself when she was six—and knew Julie's feelings of displacement were genuine.

Addison searched for the right words. "Fresh eggs are healthier and make the best pancakes and puddings—ever!" She held up two fingers. "Scout's promise. And no one will make you hand feed the horses. But…as Aunt Nell used to tell us kids when I lived here, if you want to eat, you have to earn your keep, and that means feeding the animals, helping in the kitchen, and making your bed. Besides, Aunt Nell can't always get to the grocery store."

"Aw, don't be a baby, Julie. 'Sides, Boomer's gonna sleep with us. Aunt Nell said so."

Julie pooched her lower lip into another pout. "Okay, but if that old hen pecks me, I hope Aunt Nell turns her into fried chicken."

Addison didn't laugh out loud, but she didn't bother to hide her grin either. *Out of the mouths of babes.*

Chapter Six

The morning sun moved across the sky and glistened off the snow. Vapors of air formed when Wade breathed. He trailed behind on a sturdy appaloosa gelding, allowing Emmett, riding his favorite buckskin, to lead the way to where Emmett thought someone might be trespassing on Nell's land. The horses loped easily up the woodland's gentle slope. A herd of grazing elk lifted their heads and stared as if annoyed that the two humans had disturbed their morning meal.

Wade had to admit that taking this little adventure on horseback was a lot more relaxing than on a snowmobile. He breathed deep, the cold crisp air hurting his chest. It felt good to be away from the office, paperwork, and the same daily dull routine. Adjusting his sunglasses against the glare bouncing off the snow, he truly understood his deputy's need for excitement.

His thoughts strayed to Addison. He wasn't sure why he was drawn to her. She was something special—beautiful, sophisticated, definitely out of his league—and he'd wanted to kiss her ever since he'd seen her impatiently tapping her foot at the airport's luggage carousel. Something deep in his belly reacted strongly to the sensual rocking motion of his body in the saddle that jackhammered his heart. Tamping down his frustration over his body's betrayal, he shifted in the saddle to ease the hardening discomfort in his crotch.

No other woman had affected him this way. Not since Gracie. Gracie Howard. High school sweetheart, prom queen, wife, mother of—if he knew what was good for him, he'd throttle his thoughts and never let them get away from him again, and that included wayward fantasies about Miss Addison James.

He gigged the appaloosa forward to ride alongside Emmett. He kept his voice low as he leaned toward the old rancher. "How much farther?"

Emmett lifted his arm and pointed. "Best as I can recollect, up in that grove of blue spruce."

"When did you last spot the lights?"

"Yesterday around two in the afternoon. Brought back memories of when I was in Nam and the Viet Cong would use signal lanterns to send messages to their comrades."

Wade understood about such flashbacks. Even now a smell or a sound would trigger an unwanted memory of his own battle scars. "What made you take notice?"

Emmett's eyes were unreadable behind his sunglasses. "Can't rightly say. I had walked out of the barn and suddenly the hairs on the back of my neck prickled." He stopped to clear the hitch in his voice. "You know what I mean…like when you know the enemy is there but you can't see him."

Wade nodded his understanding; he knew more times than he cared to remember his own bowel-wrenching forewarnings.

"Anyhow, I turned around, and a flash bounced off the barn's metal roof and near 'bout blinded me. That's when I figured the other times weren't just the sun tap-dancin' across the snow."

A few hundred yards later, the men dismounted and tied their horses to a nearby tree. Wade stretched to relax the kinks in the backs of his legs. Emmett pulled the wool-lined collar of his coat higher around his neck. Clouds of mist evaporated in the air when he spoke. He reached for the rifle in the saddle boot. "I don't exactly know who or what we're lookin' for, but we'll know it when we see it."

"You expecting trouble, Emmett?"

"Pays to be cautious. You're a Marine. You orta know that."

Wade didn't miss the hint of sarcasm in the older man's voice. *Once a Marine, always a Marine.* Emmett had served three tours in Vietnam and had earned a purple heart. "All right, Emmett. I stand corrected."

Wade checked the cylinder of his .38 police special Smith and Wesson. "Whatever or *whoever* we happen upon, you just remember that I'm the sheriff."

Emmett tsked and offered a slight nod. "Want to fan out or stick together?"

Wade motioned with his hand for Emmett to lead the way. "Fan out, maybe keep thirty feet between us."

The shallow but solidly packed snow made climbing easier. Not sure what he was looking for, Wade kept his eyes alert. About the time he'd spotted the orange ribbon, Emmett whistled one of his bird chirps. Wade answered by pointing to his eyes, then down to the ground, signaling that he, too, had spotted something.

Wade pulled a plastic evidence bag from his pocket. He knelt and carefully scooped snow from around the ribbon lest he spring an animal trap. What he found was a wooden surveyor's spike. He removed the phone from his pocket and snapped several pictures before pulling the spike out of the dirt and slipping it into the bag. He labeled the picture as number one. He searched around for a small branch to mark the spot before trudging toward Emmett.

Emmett knelt. Like Wade, he had used caution to remove snow from around a ribbon that was a twin to the one Wade had discovered. The old man had seen animals that had literally gnawed off a paw to escape the steel jaws of a spring trap. No traps here, though. He added his discovery to the plastic bag that Wade held forward.

Emmett brushed the snow from the knees of his pants. As he situated the hat on his head, he turned. "Well, I'll be gawldanged, Wade. Look yonder."

Wade's gaze followed where the old man pointed. He swallowed the profanity threatening to spew in response to what he saw. "We're high up enough that this would make a perfect ski slope right straight to Nell's back door. In fact"—he cast a view along the vista to where the Kootenay River bordered Nell's six hundred acres of prime land—"I'm thinking someone is doing a little secret surveying to scope out Nell's land as a spot for some sort of resort."

"Sonafabitch. Ain't that trespassin'?"

"It is, especially if it's done without the owner's permission." Wade held up the plastic bag. "I might even toss in a littering charge, just for the hell of it."

"How are we gonna find out who's doin' this?"

"*We* aren't." Wade gave the old man a *stay out of my business* look. "I'll let you know if I need your help."

"Not a word to Nell about this, least not until you find out who the culprits are that're tryin' to steal her land. Probably one of them super real estate corporations that has more money than brains and doesn't give two hoots in hell about preservin' nature."

Although he agreed with the old man, Wade knew he needed to keep his thoughts to himself. Fueling Emmett's fire wouldn't serve any good purposes. "Don't go making assumptions, Emmett. We don't know that anyone's up to no good. I'll check it out."

"Yeah, well, Brenda said she hadn't seen any strangers in town."

"Wade laughed. "Uh-huh, and as she also pointed out, almost everyone in town was a stranger."

Emmet said emphatically, "I'm here to tell you, if I find out it's one of our locals, I'll nail his sorry hide to the wall."

Wade clapped the older man on the back. "I've got to get back to the office."

Reaching where they'd left the horses, the men rode down the mountain toward Emmett's ranch. To break the silence, Wade said, "You're very protective of Nell. It's none of my business, but why haven't you asked her to marry you?"

Emmett scowled. "You're right. It's none of your business." In the next breath, he added, "Besides, who says I haven't?"

"Tell me about it."

"Nope. 'Nuff said."

Wade had known Emmett Oxbow his entire life. Until he took up ranching full-time, he'd been a deputy when Ward Grey was sheriff. Meadow Creek was a small town, and if anyone would have the inside scoop on old flames and forgotten romances, it would be his mother.

Losing himself in thought had made the ride down the mountain and into the ranch yard seem shorter than when he and Emmett had first set out. Dismounting, Wade led the gelding to the barn where he unsaddled the horse and led it into a stall to be brushed down and a warming blanket tossed over its back.

"You know, Emmett, as much as I hate to admit it, going in on horseback was enjoyable." He rubbed his backside. "Tomorrow morning my muscles might disagree."

Emmett stepped out of the stall where he'd put his gelding. "Better soak in a hot tub before goin' to bed tonight. If that doesn't work"—the old man guffawed—"I have a bottle of horse liniment that'll do the trick."

Chapter Seven

Addison smiled as she eased the bedroom door shut. The twins had had a full morning collecting eggs and having other barn adventures that included finding and cuddling Dixie and Trixie, the barn mousers. After a midday snack, Joey and Julie didn't argue about taking a nap. Addison planned to use this time to catch up on a few phone calls.

She peeked into the kitchen where Nell had just hung up the phone. The crestfallen expression tugged at Addison's heart. "What is it?"

Nell heaved a sigh. "I guess the meeting's off. Edith says the roads are too slippery, Dorothy has the sniffles, Maxine... Well, everyone has an excuse." She picked at the crust of one of the quiches. "Can't say as I blame them. We're all a bunch of old women. Our numbers have thinned out due to deaths, or living in nursing homes, or just too old and tired to plan the annual Christmas bazaar." She wiped a tear before it fell. "We've tried to recruit younger people." She shrugged. "These days, it seems the younger generation just isn't interested in keeping tradition alive." She sauntered slowly to the kitchen door. "I think I'll go watch my programs and maybe take a nap. Help yourself to the quiche."

Addison longed to give her foster mother comfort

and didn't know what kept her from going to her and giving a hug to someone who desperately needed one. Instead she offered a sympathetic smile. "I'm sorry, truly."

She automatically glanced at the phone. As if reading her mind, Nell said, "There's a phone in my office if you'd like some privacy."

"Oh, I didn't mean to imply my business was more important than talking to you."

Her voice dejected, Nell said, "It's okay." With that, she left the kitchen and headed to her combination bedroom-sitting room equipped with a television.

Addison trailed down the hall to the small closet-like room that Nell called her office. She sat in the large black leather office chair. The antique rolltop desk was littered with unopened envelopes, old calendars, and newspaper clippings. Addison picked up the stack and filtered through article after article that followed her career. Included were articles and pictures that announced her engagement to billionaire Rowan Sarkozy, and the most recent photo of the collapsed runway. A shiver chilled Addison at the sight of her lying on the ground like a crumpled doll.

She opened her cell phone and groaned at the *no service* message. She scrolled to her contacts list and, using Nell's old-style rotary phone, dialed her agent.

"Glamour Plus, Carl speaking."

"Carl, its Addison."

"My god, Addison, it's good to hear from you. How in the hell are you? I haven't seen you since you were released from the hospital, and better yet, where in the hell are you? I can't begin to count how many times I've called you."

Addison laughed. "Take a breath, Carl. First off, I'm at my aunt's ranch in Meadow Creek, Idaho, where there is no cell phone reception. You won't believe it, but I'm calling you from an antique rotary phone."

"Rotary phone...you mean as in the Christopher Columbus days? My god, girl, you need to get back to civilization."

"I will..." Addison sighed. "Just as soon as I can get an appointment with a doctor to remove the stitches."

"Yeah, about that, if you have a pen, jot this down. It's the name and number of a top-notch plastic surgeon. He's in Vegas. Comes highly recommended because he makes ugly beautiful again." Carl's namby-pamby voice rose an octave. "As you know, scars of any kind are not a model's friend—especially if the scars are on the face."

Addison blinked hard, trying to funnel her agitation. "I understand, Carl. Tell me, what are my rankings?"

The exaggerated sigh told her more than she wanted to hear. "Dropping, my darling. You know the old saying, *Out of sight...out of mind.* Taylor Tagget's rankings are moving up fast. Oh, hold on, my darling, I need to get this."

While she waited on hold, Addison absentmindedly rifled through a stack of envelopes. She noticed that the majority of them were from First Federal Holdings of Seattle. She wondered why Nell hadn't opened the envelopes and why a mortgage company had sent her over ten letters.

Her agent's voice cooed, "Addison, forgive me, darling, some sort of emergency with the Egyptian shoot. Too bad you're not available. You'd be perfect. Call me as soon as your face is fixed. Love you, ta." She heard the smack to indicate a kiss and then the line went dead.

"Carl...Carl...I... Shit!" Addison wanted to throw the receiver against the wall. Instead, she dialed the number of her doctor in New York only to learn that it would be four months before he had an available appointment date. Four months—to April—wouldn't do. The stitches needed to come out. The receptionist suggested a local physician could remove the stitches.

"Oh, great...just great!" She reached into her sling and withdrew Wade's business card, flipped it over, and dialed the number for Dr. Ava Grey-Montgomery.

Addison breathed a sigh of relief. "Yes, I'm sure Friday at one o'clock will work. However, Nell doesn't drive. She may insist on bringing us to town in the sleigh."

The good-natured voice on the other end said, "It won't be the first time Nell has come to town driving her sleigh. She's one of Meadow Creek's more colorful characters, but she's also one of the most loved. I don't think there's a citizen in this town that she hasn't helped in one way or another. So, if you're a little late, don't worry. Your appointment is set, and we look forward to meeting you, Miss James."

Addison added the appointment to her phone's calendar. She leaned back in the chair and closed her eyes. The news that her archrival, Taylor Tagget, stood to replace her as top model stung. Part of her dreaded getting the stitches removed and seeing how badly her face was scarred, and part of her...what? No, she couldn't believe she was actually thinking that a scarred face would give her an excuse to retire from days of subsisting on cucumber water and plain yogurt to maintain her size four figure, from doing bikini shoots in freezing waters during the winter months, or posing in ski outfits during July's summer heat, and always expected to look fresh after eighty-hour work weeks and twelve-hour flights from one country to the next.

This brought another thought—what would she do with her life if her career came to an end? She wasn't sure what she felt...relief, skepticism...worry?

Maybe she should swallow her pride and call Rowan. No! That was begging, and begging was beneath her. She would never be that desperate.

Tears stung her eyes. She blinked them away, telling herself to get over it. She eyed the stack of unopened envelopes. Glancing at the open door, Addison listened closely until she was satisfied that Nell's television was still on. Part of her felt like a sneak thief as she reached for one of the envelopes, but the curious part of her slid the letter opener under the flap and carefully wiggled it downward and then upward until she was able to open the envelope without tearing it. Once she peeked at the contents, she would glue the flap shut. No one would be the wiser. Except her, of course.

To reassure that Nell was still occupied, Addison glanced again at the door. She turned her attention to the letter. The gasp sounded overly loud in the small room.

The hell with it. She grabbed another letter and looked at the date, then decided to stack the envelopes in chronological order by date mailed. One by one, she opened them, each one a notice of arrears on the mortgage, the more recent ones threatening foreclosure if payment wasn't received, and the last on the pile stated that foreclosure was imminent if the arrears were not brought current by... Addison opened her phone calendar. "Oh, no, that's in three days!"

She lifted the old-fashioned desk phone's yellow receiver and dialed.

"Sheriff's office. Millie Mann speaking."

"May I speak to Sheriff Grey?"

"Sorry, he's on a call. If this is an emergency, I can send Deputy Sumner."

"No, the deputy won't do. I need to speak to the sheriff immediately. It's...a personal matter, but important. Well, maybe it's an emergency...sort of."

"I can send Deputy Sumner, ma'am. He can be at your location in less than an hour."

Addison let her head fall back against the chair. "When do you expect the sheriff?"

"Can't say, ma'am. He's in the field doing some investigating. If you'd like to leave your name and number, I'll have him call you as soon as he returns."

"Yes...no, wait. Maybe I should talk to him in person. This is Addison James. I'm a guest at—"

"Oh, Addison, this is Millie Mann. Remember me? Well, it's been eons since you left Meadow Creek."

"Hi, Millie. Of course, you and Nell were best friends. Really, I do need to speak with Sheriff Grey as soon as possible."

The tone of Millie's voice changed from affable to serious. "Is Nell okay...the twins hurt?"

"No, nothing like that. It's...just tell him it's personal but needs immediate attention. Really, it can't wait."

She heard Millie suck in a breath. "He's with Emmett Oxbow. I'll give Emmett a call and relay your message. That's the best I can do."

The thought of seeing Wade caused her heart to pound. "Thank you, Millie. It's good speaking to you."

She felt even more like a thief when she gathered the letters, tucked them inside her sling, and slipped toward the door.

The phone's obnoxious ring caused Addison to jump. She was nearly out of the office and raced back to grab the phone before Nell came charging out of her room to answer it.

"Hello?"

"Addison, this is Wade. Millie said you had an emergency."

She kept her voice to a low whisper. "Can you hear me?"

"Yes. What's all the mystery?"

"Can you come over right away? I don't want to risk Nell hearing our conversation. Wade, it's terrible. I mean it's really *awful*."

"You're scaring me, Addison. Do I need to have Millie get an ambulance out there?"

"No, it's not that kind of emergency. It's of a personal nature. But when you get here, act normal. Nell doesn't know about this, and I'd prefer to keep it private until after I've talked with you."

"Okay, get dressed. I'm taking you to lunch."

"Perfect. Oh, what should I wear? I don't have flannel shirts and jeans."

She thought he snorted...a sound of disgust, probably. "Nothing fancy. You remember Smitty's?"

She thought her jaw dropped. "Smitty's Pub?

That's not a restaurant. It's a bar."

"I never said I was taking you to a restaurant. Besides it's the only place in town loud enough to drown out private conversations. And the hamburgers are dynamite. I'll be there in ten minutes."

Ten minutes. It took at least an hour just to put on makeup. Not to speak of trying to do something with her hair. She raced up the stairs and hid the letters inside her large designer purse. Then she walked to the stair rail and yelled, "Nell, I need your help." She laughed delightedly. "No need to come up here. I'll bring everything down to your room."

She felt like a giddy teenager getting ready for her first date. It dawned on her that Rowan had never had this effect on her.

Addison adjusted the sling as Nell tidied the long blonde braid. "Nell, why are some couples happy together and others not?"

Nell glanced at their reflections in the mirror. "I suppose some people just aren't right for each other."

Addison watched Nell watching her. "I saw the newspaper clippings on your desk. I wasn't snooping. They were just there."

"That fiancé of yours sure was a handsome man. I guess you'd be referring to him and you, about being right for each other?"

The tears surprised Addison. She thought she was over Rowan. "It still hurts more than I realized." She dabbed the moisture with the tips of her fingers. "If I don't stop this foolishness, I'll ruin my makeup."

"Addy?"

"Someday, Nell, I'll tell you. All of it. Just not today."

Boomer rose from the round braided rug and trotted to the window. He loudly announced they had a visitor. Nell scolded, "Shush, Boomer. You'll wake the twins."

"Hello," Wade called from the foyer.

There he stood. All six foot two inches. He wore jeans, cowboy boots, and a long-sleeved tan shirt, and he smelled slightly of horse, an aroma that mingled sensually with his musk aftershave. He reminded her of a young Tom Selleck—rugged—manly—sexy as hell.

She didn't miss his survey of her. Long and male, but his smile made it polite and not suggestive.

Chapter Eight

Smitty's was busy, especially for a weekday, and mostly filled with tourists. Leo Smith stood behind the bar. He looked up when Wade entered, nodded, and cut his eyes toward a booth in a darkened corner. Wade answered the discreet nod and led Addison to his usual place. Leo followed.

"You on duty, Wade?"

"Yep. My usual."

Addison looked at him. "What is your usual?"

"Coffee—black. Hamburger, ketchup and mustard, extra pickles, hold the onions, fries crisp."

She glanced at the bald man whose nose looked as if he'd lost one too many fights. "I'll have the same, except no bread and no fries, no ketchup, and a glass of water with lemon."

Leo rolled his eyes and walked away.

There was an awkward silence before Wade asked, "So what's the big emergency?"

"These." Addison opened her purse and lifted out the stack of envelopes. "Nell is on the verge of losing the ranch. All of it." She shoved the letters toward Wade. "She would have my hide if she knew I'd snooped through her personal stuff. I didn't mean to, but they were right there in the open. So I looked."

She handed him another envelope. "This is her

most recent bank statement. Wade, Nell is barely surviving. She has no income other than her Social Security, and that's precious little. She doesn't have enough in savings to bring the mortgage account current and barely enough in her checking account to pay next month's electric bill. We have to do something."

A waitress approached the table with a smile. "Fresh coffee and water with lemon. Your food will be ready soon."

Wade lifted the cup to his lips and blew. He ventured a couple of sips. "Nell is too proud to ask for help. She inherited the ranch when her father died. I can't imagine her allowing the bank to repossess it." He set the cup down.

Addison took a napkin and ran it around the rim of her glass. "What are you thinking?"

Wade leaned forward so she could hear above the noise without him having to yell. He related his outing with Emmett and how they had discovered the survey stakes. "Someone apparently knows about Nell's financial situation and is looking to snap up the property." He seemed to drift off.

Addison looked into his eyes. His lips seemed to beckon her. She really wanted to kiss him, felt herself leaning forward, her lips tingling with anticipation. Wade's voice intruded into her yearning when he said, "There has to be a way to find out who's behind this."

The world went blurry when she drew in a deep lemony sip that went down her windpipe. She covered her mouth with a napkin to keep from spewing the cold liquid. Her eyes teared, and she was attacked by a spasm of coughing. Wade slid out of his seat to pummel her on the back. She managed to squeak out, "Stop! I'm okay. It went down the wrong pipe, that's all."

"Good. I've never had a woman die on me on the first date."

Addison's eyes widened with humor. "We're on a date?"

"Whoa. That didn't come out quite right."

By the time the food arrived their laughter had subsided, and they were ready for drink refills. Addison ordered a cup of hot tea. Wade chowed down on his burger while Addison took her time chewing each bite of the large quarter-pound patty. She set her fork down and leaned forward so he could hear her.

"I've got it! Ruby Raye. Of course! She owns her own real estate brokerage firm in New York. She's in South Carolina at the moment. If only I could use a phone other than Nell's, I'd give her a call to see what she can find out."

Sheriff and model stared at each other for several seconds without speaking. Wade reached out and used a napkin to wipe a speck of mustard from the corner of Addison's mouth. It was a simple gesture that aroused her in an oddly sensual way.

The moment stretched on as she continued to stare at him. She felt pathetic, wanting him. He wanted to kiss her. It was there—in his eyes, the way he leaned forward. Minutes ticked by with her looking at him and feeling like she was a total failure in the love department. Her heart skipped an apprehensive beat as she leaned forward.

His voice was husky. "I remember Ruby. She came to Nell's sixty-fifth birthday party."

The mention of the party felt like cold water tossed

on a blazing fire. Addison drew back. "I was in Qatar for a shoot. I didn't know about the party until weeks later." She laced and re-laced her fingers. "It was thoughtless of me to not send a card or a gift."

"Nell didn't care about gifts or cards. She will never tell you how hurt she was that you didn't call. *Thoughtless* isn't a strong enough word. She never forgot about you. How could you forget about her? A five-minute phone call, Addison, would have meant the world to Nell."

Suddenly angry, she blasted, "Don't scold. You know nothing about my life, my hectic schedule, the demands on my time, and the heart-wrenching pain of walking in on my fiancé humping my matron of honor just an hour before we were to walk down the aisle…" Her voice trailed off until she added, "And then the accident."

Squeezing her eyes shut, this was the first time she'd spoken of the break-up. Her throat constricted with pain as she tried to suppress the sobs that threatened to rip through her chest. "An-and all he said was, 'It's just sex. Don't take it personally.' "

Her appetite had diminished. She pushed the plate away and shook her head in a mixture of disgust and humiliation. "Oh, God," she whispered.

Wade helped Addison from the booth. He led the way through the crowd of dancing tourists and prayed none of the locals would spot him and want to chat. He called out to tell Leo to put the meal on his bill.

The cold hit Addison like an arctic blast. "I-I'm sorry. I didn't mean to break down like that and just…just blurt it out." A fresh wave of sobs had her trembling before Wade could get her into the police cruiser. "I still can't understand why Rowan would betray my love in such a terrible way."

Wade opened the car door and held it wide until she scooted inside. He reached inside the glove box and pulled out a wad of napkins. "He's an asshole."

"Who?" Addison wiped her eyes and blew her nose.

Wade jogged to his side of the vehicle. He shivered as he slammed the door shut and turned the key in the ignition. "Rowan what's-his-name."

"Sarkozy. He's a Hungarian prince with an unlimited supply of money."

"Did you love him?"

Addison blew her nose and wiped the tears as she mulled the question. "After all these weeks, honestly, I don't know. Maybe I was in love with the idea of *being* in love with such a wealthy and powerful man." She loosed a shuddering sight. "It still stings to think I wasn't good enough to be his one and only."

Wade lifted her hand and brought it to his lips. "Like I said, he's an asshole."

Addison's restraint snapped. She couldn't figure out what was going on inside her head as she leaned forward to press her lips against Wade's. She simply knew she was eager to taste him and was surprised when he placed his hands on her shoulders and gently pushed her back.

His voice was equally as gentle. "There's nothing I would like more than to take you to my house and make love to you. But your emotions are all tangled up with what your fiancé did to you. I don't want him in your head when I take you to my bed. When I do, it'll be just you and me."

He guided her hand to his chest where she could feel his heart was rapidly thumping. "Believe me, my testosterone is working overtime, which is not a good thing because I'm still officially on duty. I'd hate to go on a call with an obvious boner." He winked.

She laughed. He'd let her down without insult and with a bit of humor. "Lend me your phone so I can call Ruby Raye." She put the phone on speaker. While she waited for the call to connect, she said, "Thank you."

"Hello?"

"Ruby…Addison, hi."

"Merry Christmas. How is Aunt Nell? You're not being a scrooge, are you?"

"Absolutely not! Aunt Nell is as feisty as ever, but Ruby, there is a problem." She explained about the letters from the bank, Nell's lack of income, and the survey stakes that Wade and Emmett had found.

Addison sucked in her breath and said as casually as she could, "Is there any way you can discreetly find out who might be interested in Nell's property?"

"I don't know what to say. I'm flabbergasted. Yes, of course, I'll do my best. You know I will, Addison."

"We only have three days. That might not be enough time. Another thing, Ruby—is it legal for me to bring the account current? I mean, will the bank accept my check to pay Nell's mortgage?"

"If you can get a coupon payment book or access to the account number, it doesn't matter who writes the check. However, with the large amount due, the mortgage company will probably require a certified check, a bank draft, or a credit card."

Addison looked at Wade. He said, "I'll pick you up in the morning and drive you to the bank." He spoke a little louder for Ruby's benefit. "J.T. Elsworth is vice president of Southern Idaho National. I'm sure he'll help us."

Ruby laughed. "You mean Jonas Theodore Elsworth, the skinny, four-eyed kid who cried all the time?"

Wade countered back. "I don't know about the crying, but he's not skinny anymore. Besides, he's quite influential in the banking world."

"That's good to know. I'll take care of things on my end and will definitely get back with you asap! Hugs, Addison. Good talking to you, Wade."

Before disconnecting the call, Addison suggested Ruby touch base with Wade since there was no cell service at the ranch.

Addison returned the phone to Wade. "You're a good man, Wade Grey."

He rewarded her with a wink and a smile.

On the drive to the ranch, Addison said, "I have an appointment to see your sister on Friday. The stitches are itching something fierce. I'm hoping she'll take them out."

"I'll drive you in?"

"No need. Nell wants to give the twins a sleigh ride, and I've promised her we'll go shopping and then have lunch at BB's Café. I'd hate to disappoint Joey and Julie."

He adjusted the heat and shifted the cruiser into gear. "We have a couple of hours before the bank closes. Let's pay J.T. a visit."

Chapter Nine

The interior of Southern Idaho National was quaint by New York standards. Artificial garlands adorned the span of teller windows. A Christmas tree decorated a corner of the reception area. A receptionist greeted them. "Merry Christmas, Sheriff Grey. What can I do for you?"

Wade removed his hat. "Is J.T. in?"

The young woman punched in a number and lifted the phone's receiver. "One moment. I'll let him know that you and a guest are here." And then she smiled and said, "You know where his office is."

Addison also smiled, a little piqued, perhaps, that the receptionist hadn't recognized her. But then, Addison reminded herself, Meadow Creek didn't always get international news. She followed Wade inside a glassed cubicle.

If she had passed him on the street or if he had sat down beside her in a restaurant, she would not have recognized the skinny kid who had worn round, black-rimmed glasses that made him look like an owl, and who'd cried at the drop of a hat. With his chiseled face and athletic body, Jonas Theodore Elsworth had developed into an attractive man with a gentle smile. His slight squint cued her that he probably wore contacts, which accentuated his blue eyes.

He came around his desk to give her a friendly hug. "Addison, I would have known you anywhere. My wife and daughters would love to meet you." His eyes drifted to the blue sling and the sizable bandage next to her eye. "Even as a kid, you always were a survivor." He extended his hand to indicate the chairs. "Would either of you like a cup of coffee?"

Without waiting for an answer he buzzed the receptionist. "Ella…"

She answered as if she'd read his mind. "I've already got a fresh pot brewing, Mr. Elsworth."

After a few minutes of general chit-chat, the receptionist arrived with a tray of cups and a carafe of coffee. "Shall I shut the door, Mr. Elsworth?"

He nodded. As he poured, Addison filled him in on Nell's situation and Wade explained about finding the survey markers.

She sat very still, as if her emotional gears had been disconnected. "I'd like to bring the account current—without Nell's knowledge, of course."

"I'll be happy to make that transaction happen, Addison." J.T.'s fingers flew across the computer's keyboard. He made a notation on a slip of paper. "Paying with a credit card will expedite the payment."

Addison fumbled around in her purse. She handed over the piece of plastic. "Add two additional payments to that." Both she and Wade sat sipping coffee while they waited for J.T. to key in the information.

He returned the credit card. "Here's the thing, Addison. While this brings Nell's mortgage out of arrears, it really doesn't solve the problem." He lifted a cup to his lips.

"I don't understand. What do you mean?"

He shifted in his chair. "If you recall, when we were kids, we always had food but nothing fancy. We always had clothes, but never anything new, except socks and underwear at Christmas. It didn't matter because most of us were happy to have a safe place to live and regular meals. There's no question that Nell loved us unconditionally, and now that I know what I know, she always put us kids ahead of her own needs."

Addison met his eyes directly. "Don't keep us in suspense, J.T. What is it that you know?"

The banker's gaze flicked from Addison's to Wade's. "Years ago, when I was a loan officer, Aunt Nell came to the bank to borrow some money. It was then that I discovered she had very little income. When we were kids, she had the Christmas tree farm, but other than that, all she had was what the State paid her for us kids. Now, she doesn't have that.

"The balance on her mortgage is over five hundred thousand dollars. The payments are almost eighteen hundred per month, and the taxes are not escrowed. Plus she let the homeowner's insurance lapse. The bank has had to secure a policy and has added the amount to the monthly payments."

Wade loosed a low whistle. Addison touched a hand to her cheek. "I'm shocked. How did this happen? I always assumed she was mortgage free."

The banker cleared his throat, forced a cough, and finally said, "She was. About ten years ago, Nell didn't have money to pay the taxes. She took out a small mortgage. Shortly afterward, Idaho had a particularly hard winter, with a terrible snowstorm that collapsed the roof on her barn. She borrowed more money to replace the roof, and more money to pay the taxes.

Shortly after, she purchased the two Percheron geldings at twenty-five hundred each."

He drew a deep sigh as if the explanation left him deflated. "Then, two years ago, the kitchen caught fire due to old, worn-out wiring. The house, after all, is over a hundred years old. The damage was extensive. Thank God Nell only suffered from minor smoke inhalation, though that didn't help her heart condition, either."

Addison didn't reply at first. She drew back and stared at the banker. "Let me guess. Nell added to the mortgage with every one of those situations. That explains the new kitchen and some of the other renovations to the house. What I don't understand is how Emmett Oxbow, who owns as much property as Nell…where does he get his income? He and Nell are about the same age."

J.T. leaned forward on his elbows. "Normally the business of our clients is confidential. In this case, Aunt Nell is family. Still I'm bound by ethics."

At the banker's hesitation, Wade cut in. "Addison, Emmett grows soybeans and corn. Both are marketable crops. He raises beef cattle for market, and he has his Christmas tree farm. Additionally, he has a small pension from the military, and since he was employed by the State as a deputy sheriff, his Social Security is probably much larger than Aunt Nell's. You've been at the ranch long enough to see what she has and doesn't have, which equates to no viable income."

Addison tried to absorb all she had heard. Her arm ached and the stitches in her forehead itched almost to distraction, and finding a solution to Nell's financial situation left her feeling cranky.

J.T. cupped his hands together. "Even if you

assumed responsibility for the monthly payments, the taxes alone would eventually erode your income; plus you'd be making payments on property you don't own. If Nell were to suddenly die intestate, you would be out a great deal of money."

There was a slight pause. His voice was all business. "Setting emotions and old friendships aside, as a banker, I'm advising against such an impractical move unless Nell is willing to refinance the mortgage and add you as co-payee." He cocked his eyes toward the plastic bag holding the survey stakes. "If a lucrative offer comes along, she might be tempted to sell Hope Ranch. Her gain would be your loss."

Addison touched the bandage on her forehead. The tightness in her chest was giving her a headache. "Nell wouldn't do that. She's devoted to the place, and besides, she's too honest."

Addison stood to indicate the meeting was over. She extended her good hand. "Then I have two months to come up with a plan." She offered an exotic smile. "By the way, does your wife work?"

J.T. blustered as if confused. He came instantly to his feet. "With four girls…yes…well, she is a stay-at-home mom."

"Good. I'll give her a call. I'm recruiting volunteers to help plan the Christmas festival."

Wade extended his hand. "Thanks for the information, J.T."

J. T.'s shoulders rose and fell. "Like you, Addison, I lived at the ranch until I was eighteen. Aunt Nell arranged funding for my college. I wouldn't be where I am today without her." Addison didn't miss the split-second judgmental change of stance behind his brilliant smile. He jotted something on the back of a business card. "My home number. My wife and daughters will be excited to help with the festival."

Sleep didn't come easily to Addison that night. Shortly after Wade dropped her off she had helped the twins write a letter to Santa. She didn't know if her wakefulness was caused by the contents of the children's letter beseeching Santa to bring their mommy home for Christmas, the shocking discovery of Nell's finances, or Wade's goodnight kiss.

How intimate could a kiss be when a blue cotton arm sling separated you? Standing on the front porch in the teeth-chattering cold, they had leaned toward each other slowly as if waiting for one or the other to change their mind at the last minute.

Their lips met lightly, passionlessly—a friendly goodnight peck on the lips that either of them could have ended with no regrets—until the texture of the kiss changed and his lips opened and she accepted the invitation knowing that, in the end, she might regret the aftermath.

Just this once, Addison warned herself. Still she'd known one kiss would never be enough. Not with a man like Wade Grey.

****

What the hell was he thinking? Wade had found himself pressing Addison against the hard, unyielding porch post. He had tilted his head and so had she, allowing the kiss to deepen. She had clung to him with her free arm…had nipped his bottom lip. Her mouth was soft, deliciously soft, and luxurious as it heated on his. She tasted hot and sweet. She made him burn. He had to hold back. Burns caused scars, and he'd been burned deep enough to last a lifetime.

He drew away, satisfied that his control was still intact although his mind wasn't perfectly clear. He saw the look in her eyes—the dreamy, take-me-anywhere-and-I'll-follow look. At the bottom of the steps, he looked up at her and quirked a crooked grin. "I'm still on duty, remember?"

She gave him a quizzical but disheartened smile. "Wade who is Gracie?"

"What?"

"Just now, you whispered her name."

Shit! If it were possible, he'd kick himself from here to kingdom come. "We all have our ghosts. You have the Hungarian prince, and I…" His voice trailed off. "Goodnight, Addison. I'll let you know when I hear from Ruby."

"Gracie must have really done a number on you, Wade. Maybe someday you'll tell me about her."

Wade's only response before he left the porch and walked toward his cruiser was to raise his dark eyebrows.

Later, in his office, he sat at his desk going through the pile of mail stacked there. The ache in his stomach had nothing to do with the hamburger and fries he'd eaten for lunch or the copious amounts of black coffee he'd consumed. What had happened with Addison had happened. He wouldn't allow her to become a complication, nor would he use her to satisfy his physical urges.

He told himself she was no different than his ex-wife. Just more sophisticated and a hundred times wealthier. After all, Addison James was the world's most beautiful woman and top model.

Wade bit back a frown. His lips still tingled from his and Addison's first kiss. Their first, because deep down he knew it would not be their last.

Chapter Ten

Sunshine and crisp air greeted Friday morning. The night before, Addison and the twins had helped Nell decorate the sleigh in green garlands, red silk poinsettias, and jingle bells. Nell had fashioned Santa hats for the Percheron geldings and draped red blankets trimmed in white faux fur over their broad backs. Excitement charged the air. Even Nell stepped a little more spryly.

Addison settled like a mother hen with a chick tucked under each arm, making sure the heavy quilt was tucked in tight around the six-year-olds.

Nell climbed aboard the sleigh's high seat and gathered the reins. She called over her shoulder, "You youngsters warm enough?"

"Yes, ma'am," Joey and Julie answered in unison.

"Good, 'cause here we go." She flicked the reins and encouraged the horses down the long drive to the main highway. "Step up, Chipper. Atta good boy, Bud."

The bells jingled merrily as the sleigh moved smoothly over the snow. They hadn't gone far before Joey bounced up in the seat and shouted with exuberance, "There's another one."

Ahead of them, a sleigh moved sleekly across the snow. "Lots of folks don't like driving their cars on icy roads. You just might see a few more sleds before we get to town."

Nell guided the horses alongside the smaller luge. She waved and called, "Howdy, Ethel. Good to see you out and about."

The older woman laughed and returned the greeting. "You, too, Nell."

Addison felt as if she had entered another dimension. The scenery was more beautiful than she remembered, or perhaps like most teenagers she hadn't bothered to notice limbs of spruce and oak trees bent low under the weight of snow that reminded her of huge tufts of cotton, or how long white ribbons of snow decorated miles of split-rail fences. So clean, so decent, so miraculously untouched by ugliness or pain.

How sweet the children are, she thought, watching them as they craned their heads and pointed and giggled.

The clip-clop of the large hooves and the jingle of the bells were right in sync with Addison's heartbeat. She had mixed emotions about the prospect of bumping into Wade. She hadn't heard from him in two days, not since the kiss. What had happened that night was simply one of those fleeting moments when two bruised people came together because the moment dictated it. She told herself it wouldn't happen again because she would be more in control next time. Her thoughts drifted to Gracie. Who was she, and what did she do to hurt Wade so deeply?

"Nell, who was Gracie?"

Nell sat tall and straight on the sleigh's high driver's seat. She held the leather reins in able hands. "I don't recall a child by that name living at Hope Ranch."

"I should have said who was Gracie to Wade—an

old flame, perhaps?"

Nell maneuvered the horses across a bridge and then again to travel on the road's snowy shoulder. "That's a question for him. Wasn't my business then and isn't my business now."

And that was that.

By the time Addison had finished thinking about Sheriff Wade Grey, Nell was saying, "Whoa!" as she pulled the horses to a stop in front of the doctor's office. "We're here, Addison. The twins and I will meet you at BB's Café after you're finished."

Addison climbed down from the sleigh. She glanced around. "Where will you park the horses?"

"Behind the sheriff's office." Nell pointed. "Which reminds me—I'll take the twins in and introduce them to Millie."

"Wait." Addison reached into her purse and withdrew the envelope addressed to Santa Claus, North Pole. "Would you give this to Sheriff Grey and make sure it gets delivered?"

"Sure will. When you're finished, don't forget to meet us at BB's Café. Maybe a cup of Brenda's special hot chocolate will put the smile back on your face." Nell urged the horses forward to leave Addison standing alone and feeling a little lost.

Addison glanced around. The town reminded her of a scene from a Norman Rockwell painting—almost too good to be true. Ruby's reminder not to be a grinch failed to bring a smile to Addison's lips. Disaster number four came to mind—*meeting Wade Grey!* She hoped meeting his twin sister wasn't about to be disaster number five.

A gust of icy wind drove her up the steps of the red

brick building and into the waiting room. A beautifully decorated tree stood in one corner. A myriad of Christmas decorations added to the room's cheerful ambiance. Curious patients glanced up from their magazines. Some openly stared, others went back to reading. The woman behind the desk greeted her with a warm smile. Addison glanced at the name plate: Lucy Grey.

"Hi, I'm Addison James. I have a one o'clock appointment."

A distantly familiar face stared at her. "Yes, we saw the sleigh. It's good to see Nell out and about. She's been a bit of a recluse lately." She handed Addison a clipboard. "If you'll fill out the forms, Doctor Montgomery will be with you in a few minutes."

"Excuse me for asking, but are you related to Sheriff Grey?"

Amusement seemed to glitter in the older woman's eyes as she squinted through thick glasses. "I'm Lucy Grey. You've made quite an impression on my son. You probably don't remember me, but I was the nurse who tended Ruby Raye when she jumped off the barn and broke her arm. You kept telling her not to cry."

Great! Disaster number five: giving Wade the wrong impression of me.

"I'm sorry. I sort of remember. I mean, I remember Ruby jumping off the barn." It was a long time ago.

The woman laughed. "It's okay that you don't remember me. Due to failing eyesight, I've given up nursing and now manage my daughter's office. Please be seated. Dr. Montgomery will be with you shortly."

Addison took a seat. She completed the paperwork

and returned the clipboard to Wade's mother. Minutes later, a nurse escorted her to a waiting room and helped her onto the exam table.

She flipped through a magazine while she waited. A quick rap on the door and it flew open as a petite young woman breezed in. "Good afternoon, Ms. James, I'm Ava Montgomery. It's nice to meet you."

Addison wasn't sure how much more of this gushiness she could tolerate. All she wanted was to get the stitches removed and leave Meadow Creek. She stared at the almost childlike face with a small nose and sweet mouth. "I thought you and Wade were twins."

Crap! Where did that come from? "I'm sorry, I—I..." She fumbled for words.

Ava washed her hands and drew on a pair of rubber gloves. "Don't worry about it. We get that all the time. We're fraternal twins. He's tall, I'm short, and while we have the same gray eyes, we really don't look alike." She winked. "Although Wade constantly reminds me that he is older by two minutes."

Addison's tensed shoulders began to relax with Ava's friendly banter. "Wade told us about the accident. You were very lucky. If you like, we can x-ray your arm through the cast to make sure the bone is knitting together properly. Fortunately, we can do it right here in the clinic."

"Of course. That would be great."

Ava reviewed the chart to check the date of the accident. Then she carefully applied a solution to remove the bandage over Addison's eye.

Addison's frown deepened. "The stitches are itching like crazy."

"Ah, that's a good sign." Ava pulled the dressing

free and tossed it in the hazard waste can. "Would you like to see what it looks like before I begin removing the sutures?"

Addison accepted the mirror. She gasped at the puckered line of stitches. Tears welled in her eyes. "I never dreamed it would look so terrible. There's so many of them."

"I'll be quite honest with you, Ms. James—"

"Addison, please."

"Addison—the surgeon did an excellent job with creating small, close-knit sutures." She patted the incision gingerly with the tip of a finger before clipping through the tiny knots. "However, once I remove them, the scar will look raw and unsightly for about a week."

Addison spoke through a flood of tears. "My career is over."

After the last stitch was removed, Ava measured the area and relayed into her voice recorder, "Ten point sixteen centimeters."

"What is that in inches, Doctor?"

Addison hated the sympathy she saw in Ava's eyes when she said, "Four inches. Addison, it won't look this bad once it's completely healed."

She sniffed. "You don't understand, Doctor. A model with the smallest flaw, much less a four-inch hideous scar on her face, is unemployable."

Leaning on all her emotional strength, Addison's voice still quivered. "My agent recommended a plastic surgeon who is supposed to be the best. He's in Las Vegas, and his name is Gustavo Reinhardt."

Ava removed the gloves and tossed them in the waste can. "A little medical advice—check his credentials and his reviews before assuming he's the best. In the meantime, keep the area clean and dry, and if you need me, please call."

Addison sat on the exam table. Her shoulders slumped forward. "Nell doesn't have internet, and my cell phone doesn't work at the ranch. How do you suggest I check Dr. Reinhardt's credentials?"

"The library has several computers, and most of the restaurants have wi-fi. If you like, I'll be happy to check and even do a referral to get you a quicker appointment if you decide to use him. I can assure you that with ten days before Christmas and then New Year's, it may be several months before you get an appointment, especially if he's as good as your agent claims."

Addison stood from the table. She collected her purse and jacket. "Of course. Thank you. Perhaps I should return to New York as soon as I can book a flight."

Ava escorted Addison down the hall to the x-ray room. She laid a hand on Addison's arm. "Please stay…for Nell. As her doctor, I can't divulge the extent of her medical condition. As a friend to someone I love as much as my mother, I know Nell's health is failing. She's had two heart attacks in two years. From what Wade tells me, your being here has been like a booster shot of happiness for Nell. He also told us about her financial situation, the survey markers, and that you plan to take over organizing the festival."

Addison shook her head. How was she going to keep her life from spinning completely out of control? She opened her mouth to object. Before she could speak, Ava smiled and said, "If that's a yes, then sign up my mother and me. We're glad to help wherever you need us. I'll be happy to put together a list of names and phone numbers of potential volunteers. And for the older ladies and men who don't want to drive to the ranch, my brother and my husband and I will act as taxi service. Okay?"

Ava waited in the hallway until the technician completed the x-rays of Addison's arm.

Addison's eyes burned with frustrated tears, and then she laughed. Even though she'd rather die than admit it, she was actually relieved not to spend the holiday alone. "Sure. Why not? Okay."

"Great." Ava walked her down the hall to the receptionist's window. "Mom, Addison is taking charge of organizing the festival, and I've volunteered both of us to help."

"Both of us?"

"Oh, Mrs. Grey, you don't have to. I'll understand if you—"

"I will only volunteer if I get first choice on location to set up my peach marmalade and candied praline booth." She laughed. "Had you going, didn't I?"

"Mom, you're so bad," Ava scolded. "My husband and I will gladly set up a petting zoo for the younger children. We have a couple of reindeer, alpacas, miniature ponies, a pair of donkeys, some geese, baby calves, and every year Emmet lends us his Shetlands for pony rides."

"It sounds wonderful. I can't thank you both enough." Addison pulled the sweater cap from her purse. "Will you help me with this?" She pointed to the scar.

As Ave assisted she said, "The bone in your arm has healed nicely. We can remove the cast in about a week."

Addison adjusted the strap on the sling. "That is great news." She touched the abrasion over her eyes. "It's been lovely meeting you."

Lucy Grey spoke up. Her advice was genuine. "Addison, scar or no scar, you're a beautiful young woman. If you show you are self-conscious about the scar, then people will gawk. If you hold your head high, people will still gawk, just not as long. Let us know when you schedule your first festival planning meeting."

"Thank you. I'm a bit nervous about undertaking this project." Addison stepped outside, bracing herself against the cold. She was genuinely confused about this new direction her life was taking.

She wanted to be happy and part of something other than looking glamorous. With all that had happened, she didn't know right now where she belonged. She didn't get to finish her thought because her phone chirped. Wade's name showed in the caller ID.

"Wade?"

"Come to my office. I've heard from Ruby." He opened the door and stepped out to the porch.

She waved as she crossed the street.

He held the door wide. "Millie is having lunch with Nell and the twins. Once Millie and Nell get together, it's like everything around them disappears." He chuckled. "I'm manning the office. Freddie is on a call, and unless there's an unexpected emergency, we'll have plenty of privacy to talk." He escorted her to his desk and handed her a paper sack. "I called Brenda and ordered lunch for us. Tossed salad with avocado and a dab of olive oil, no croutons." He grinned and added, "And one of Brenda's chocolate-covered spudnuts."

Addison smiled at him. "I take it all back, Wade Grey. You are not a good guy. You are the devil in disguise."

He grabbed the donut. "Just kidding! I know you don't eat sugar." He took a generous bite. "Still friends?"

The sincerity in his voice and the way he looked at her made her laugh, which oddly made her cry. "Always."

He walked around the desk. "Hey, need a hug?" He opened his arms wide, and she filled them.

It wasn't a sexy hug or even a suggestive hug. It was a feel-good embrace for a friend in need. He just hugged her and didn't let go until Addison pulled back and sat in the chair. She grabbed a napkin, brushed away the tears and blew her nose. Her hand trembled a little as she removed the plastic lid from the coffee cup. "Aren't you going to say anything?"

Wade opened his own container. He leaned back and propped his boots on the desk. "About what?"

"This!" She pointed to the scar.

He shrugged. "Just like any other war wound. Gotta wear it with pride." He swung his legs to the floor and leaned forward, his face serious. "Don't let me forget to tell you about Ruby's discovery."

All her rational instincts warned her not to misinterpret his indifference. She tried to laugh, even though she wanted to reach over and slap his handsome face with its perfect five-o'clock shadow. Instead she focused on the tank of colorful fish. "An aquarium? I haven't visited many law enforcement offices, but isn't this a bit unusual?"

He took a bite of his hamburger and chewed thoughtfully. "It was fish tank versus red-and-white polka-dot curtains trimmed with lace. Fish won out. Actually, it was Millie's idea. With days on end of nothing much to do except watch the traffic go by, Millie gets a bit bored. She says the gurgling sound of the pump and watching the fish swim is comforting."

"I can understand why. Meadow Creek wasn't a real happening place when I was a kid. Seems like nothing much has changed."

They let the conversation meander while they ate.

Chapter Eleven

Addison nibbled at the salad. Tension and anxiety skipped around in her stomach. Her stay in Meadow Creek was only meant to be a brief reprieve from the paparazzi while she healed from the accident and a broken heart. She had led an envied life representing such auspicious brands as Verllarde, Previsé, Herminé, and Gumaní. She had traveled the world, dined with royalty, and danced with the President of the United States. She didn't even like Christmas. What had possessed her to suddenly take charge of a small-town festival, and to get involved in Nell's financial affairs?

Coming from lowly beginnings, she tried hard to appreciate all she had achieved. She fingered the tender ridge that marred her face. At the moment, she was certain that phase of her life was over. After breaking her engagement and then surviving the accident, instead of staying in New York, she had run to the only safe haven she had ever known—Nellie Hopewell and Hope Ranch—the very same place she'd hated and had run away from so many years ago.

Who could say…maybe it was time to close the chapter on the fashionable part of her life.

Shifting the direction of her thoughts, she perched on the edge of her chair. "From the look on your face, I'd say the news from Ruby is ominous."

"You could say that and more. Ruby's sleuthing turned up a couple of corporations who swoop in like a bunch of vultures and buy up the paper on overdue mortgages and property taxes that are in arrears, especially those with large amounts of prime land involved." Wade finished off the donut. "She also said these companies send representatives to small towns, usually the ones hanging on by a thread, with promises of job opportunities and putting the town on the map. Ultimately what happens is that all the mom-and-pop shops are forced to shut their doors because they can't compete with the commercial stores. By the time the town fathers figure out they've sold their souls, it's too late. The land has been raped, the rivers and lakes polluted, and crime that once rarely existed is on the rise."

Addison set the plastic fork aside and closed the lid on the to-go box. "Is Meadow Creek in financial trouble?"

He wiped his lips with a napkin. "Not to my knowledge. However, tempting local government with millions of dollars is like dangling carrots in front of a starving horse. All it takes is for one person to sell out."

"You mean like Nell?"

"Yep. Ruby emailed this link."

Wade opened his laptop and typed. He turned the screen for Addison to see. "Look at this."

The screen opened to a website for Megala Land Development. The banner showed an idyllic scene of hikers, a smiling couple in a ski lift, and a row of modern condos overlooking a pristine lake.

A vague sense of impending doom filled Addison. "Scroll all the way to the bottom. Let's see what names are listed."

Oh, no! Disaster number six. But why? She pressed her hand to her heart and willed it to not explode. Her eyes burned with angry tears. "He's the lowest of slimy slugs."

Wade put his hand under Addison's chin, forcing her to look at him. "Damn it, Addison. Do you know these people?"

Her voice hitched. "Muhammed Ahmed Aslum and Rukn el Saddiq are pseudo names for Prince Rowan Sarkozy." She drew a deep breath. "I asked him about it once, and all he said was not to worry my pretty little head over such trivial matters, that it was for tax purposes. I was always so busy and so focused on my career that I never gave it another thought."

When she risked a look at Wade's face, she saw that he was frowning. "He's doing this to get back at me for breaking off our engagement." She buried her face in her hands. "Why would he hurt a harmless old woman that he's never met, just to punish me?" She moaned. "This is my fault."

****

Leering faces of men with similar names flashed behind Wade's eyes. Men he'd encountered when working counterintelligence in Afghanistan and Iraq. Men who dwelt in human trafficking, who sold weapons to rogue countries, who started wars for financial gain, and who operated under the guise of honest business men.

He watched Addison intently. He reached out to take her hand and gave it an encouraging squeeze. "Bastard," he grumbled. He felt possessive, which was out of character for him. He understood some of what she was feeling. Maybe someday, when the time was right, he'd tell her about Gracie. Or…maybe not…

"Don't beat yourself up, Addison. Men like Sarkozy are unconscionable. Don't let him win by blaming yourself." He leaned closer. "You've pulled the rug out from under him—at least temporarily."

He studied her for several long seconds and could tell she was conflicted. "Tell me what you're thinking."

She laughed without mirth. "I didn't come here to create problems for Nell." She stood and crossed her arms. "Ava told me about Nell's heart problems, and that she's in congestive heart failure."

She paced about the office and stopped to stare out the window. Meadow Creek was a town of about seventy-five thousand and depended on tourism dollars from the yearly bass tournaments, the gentle ski slopes for the less brave skiers, the hiking and horseback-riding trails, and the family-friendly annual Christmas festival. Meadow Creek was a true haven for the middle class without competing with the ultra-wealthy. "I owe Nell so much. Part of me wants to do whatever I can to save the ranch and make sure she lives out the rest of her life in the only home she's ever known. The other part of me wants to catch a flight to New York and never look back. Tell me what to do… What would you do, Wade?"

When he didn't say anything, she glanced over to find him watching her with a look that made her a little nervous. She said softly, "What will happen to the ranch when Nell…you know?"

"I expect she's made a will and has named an heir. Don't count Nell out so soon. She's a tough ol' gal and has a lot more miles left in her. As far as what you should do…only you can decide that." He scowled. "Stay in Meadow Creek or return to New York? Whatever your decision, you have to be prepared to live with it long term."

Addison pressed her lips together. "It seems running away has become a pattern in my life. I ran away from Hope Ranch, I ran away from Rowan, and now I'm considering running away again. Sometimes I think I have no true purpose in life." She continued, trying to keep her tone light, "Okay, I'll stay…for a while…just long enough to keep Rowan from getting his sleazy hands on Hope Ranch and Meadow Creek. After that—no promises."

Wade gazed studiously at Addison. With that tone she might just as well have said, *"See ya…bye."*

Her beauty was remarkable even with the raw scar that creviced over her eye and down to her cheekbone. It wasn't her beauty that attracted him—it was a sweet shyness about her. She probably didn't know how smart and capable she was, and if he wasn't careful she would steal his heart. "I admire your honesty, Addison. In the meantime, let's put our heads together and come up with a plan to keep Megala Corporation from gobbling up Hope Ranch."

A gust of wind chilled the office. Freddie Sumner bounced in waving a white envelope. "It came, Wade. Thanks to your recommendation, my transfer came through." The deputy rattled on. "Mother sent me a text that I had an important letter." His voice squeaked, "I only took five minutes of company time. I didn't think you'd mind."

Freddie glanced at Addison as if surprised by her presence. He snatched the cap off his head. The enthusiasm in his voice wilted. "Sorry, ma'am, I hope I didn't interrupt something important." He cut his gaze toward Wade.

Wade responded in a calm, indifferent voice. "Freddie, meet Ms. Addison James…Addison, my deputy, Freddie, uh, Fred Sumner. He's transferring to Maryland's Crime Unit."

She smiled. "Congratulations, Deputy Sumner. I hope the big city meets all your expectations."

The office filled with polite silence until Addison said, "I'm sure Aunt Nell thinks I've forgotten about meeting her and the twins for hot chocolate." She held her hand out to Freddie. "It's nice meeting you, Deputy. Just remember—there's no place like home."

Wade escorted her to the door. He gave her an easy smile. He leaned forward and touched her shoulder. "I'll come by tonight. Nell needs to know. We'll tell her together, and then we'll devise a plan."

****

Her heart jolted at the feel of his strong hand touching her. She could feel the heat of it through her shirt, and it distressed her in every possible way. "When I was a kid and would ask where I came from or who my mother was, Nell would say, *'What you don't know won't hurt you.'* The same is true for this situation. There's no need to embarrass her or to give her false hope. Let's use what little time we have to come up with a solid plan. We could each make a list and then compare them to see what we think is workable and what to rule out. Also, Ruby's fiancé is a corporate lawyer. He might have some ideas, too. "

He gave her an appreciative look. Not that the *look* mattered. Nonetheless, it warmed her insides. To divert attention from her emotions she said, "Did you read the twins' letter to Santa?"

"I did. The Red Cross is still waiting to hear back from the Army. I sure hope this is one gift my dad—um, Santa—can fulfill."

A twinge of sadness seeped into her heart. Her voice brimmed with commiseration. "I wonder if it was a difficult decision for their mother to go off and leave them."

"Like it or not, people do what they have to do, Addison."

She stared directly into his eyes, a hint of bitterness in her voice. "Sure, like abandoning your child in a bus station." She jutted her chin forward. "I use to believe in all that fairy tale baloney. Every Christmas until I was about eleven I wrote to Santa, pleading with him to bring my mother to me."

She gritted her teeth, hating the hot flush creeping up her neck. "I'm sorry. I don't know why I said that."

The sense of sexuality that had seemed so apparent moments ago had slipped away. Certainly Wade's manner was empathic now.

She threw him an apologetic look. "One more thing before I go—Nell promised to take us all to the woods tomorrow to cut down a tree for Christmas. Wade, with her heart condition, she doesn't need to be wielding an ax or even a chainsaw." She held out her sling. "I'm of no use. Will you or Emmett help?"

Amiable, he pulled the door open. "It's been a while since I went tree hunting. I'll give Emmett a call, too." His dark eyes settled on her face. He brushed her cheek with his thumb. He moved closer.

She told herself to remember that she wasn't ready

for another relationship, that she wasn't ready to trust another man with her heart.

She hurried outside and down the steps toward BB's Café. Foolish hope flared to life. She did her best to squash it, but it refused to die.

Chapter Twelve

Wade's frown deepened. His lips pressed together. "I hope you're giving a thirty-day notice, Freddie."

"Actually, I'm glad you asked, Sheriff. The letter states that I'm to report for duty on January second." The deputy fumbled with his words. "I honestly didn't think I'd get the job. I need to find an apartment, pack my stuff, and rent a moving van. Gosh, and with only three weeks left, I'm afraid next Friday'll be my last day." He shuffled his feet around while staring down at the tip of his spit-polished boots. "I hope you won't hold it against me…my leaving you in a lurch. I mean, if things don't work out in Maryland, I'd like to be your deputy again."

Millie set her book aside, her glare less than friendly. "Freddie Sumner, you've got some nerve. If things don't work out, what do you expect Wade to do, fire the new deputy just to give you your old job back? Humph!"

Freddie clenched his fist, his dark brown eyes bright with wounded pride. "Aw, shucks, Millie. You and my mother, you're both alike. Can't either of you be happy that I'm stepping up in the world?"

Wade hid his skepticism regarding his deputy's new position with a big city crime unit. "Don't mind Millie. She's scolding because she's quite fond of you and hates to see you go. In fact, we'll all miss you." He stood up and clapped the bumbling deputy on the back. "Don't worry about taking early leave. My dad is still a certified law enforcement officer. I'm certain he'll be more than happy to fill in until I can hire a permanent replacement."

"You're a stand-up guy, Wade." Freddie seemed at odds with himself. He thumbed over his shoulder. "I'll empty my desk and clean out my locker."

Later that evening, Wade helped his dad clear the dining table and load the dishwasher while his mother loaded a plate with homemade pecan balls and perked a pot of fresh coffee. Lucy Grey said, "Wade, add an extra log to the fireplace, and Ward, please bring the coffee and mugs?"

Wade plopped a cookie into his mouth and washed it down with a slug of coffee. His mother laughed. "Just like when you were a little boy with confectioner's sugar on your mouth."

Wade ran his tongue around his lips. "Mom, I have a question that I think only you can answer."

Lucy lifted her eyebrows. "You've piqued my curiosity. What is it you want to know?"

"The subject of why Emmett and Nell never married came up this morning. Emmett's comment was, 'Who says I never asked her?' It's plain as day the man loves her—so what gives?"

Lucy brushed at powdered sugar that had drifted to her son's shirt. Her cheeks reddened as she crossed her arms over her chest in a hug. "I suppose after all these years it no longer matters." She heaved a heavy sigh. "Viet Nam is what gives. You see, Emmett loved Nell more than any woman deserved to be loved, and the feeling was mutual. Poor Emmett was so bashful he could hardly speak to Nell without nearly fainting, much less ask her out on a date or propose marriage.

"Lester Hopewell and Emmett were best friends, almost inseparable. Emmett deployed before Lester and was immediately sent to Viet Nam. Lester's unit remained stateside. About a month later, Lester came home on leave, and he proposed to Nell. She accepted. I guess she got tired of waiting for Emmett to ask. Six months later, Lester was sent farther to Viet Nam. While the men were away, Nell opened Hope Ranch and began fostering children. I think she did it more to cope with the fear and loneliness than for the money. Long story short—Emmett came home. Lester didn't. War changed Emmett from a shy boy to a stalwart man. He took over his dad's ranch and worked as a deputy for your dad. Nell being a widow and him still loving her, he proposed. Before all that, she'd suffered a miscarriage and developed some female problems that resulted in a hysterectomy. In her mind, I suppose, she feared if she couldn't give Emmett children he wouldn't want her. Once, in a rare weak moment, she admitted she hadn't loved Lester and said she loved Emmett too much to deny him the chance of being a father. Even though they've been on shaky terms for years, Emmett has always taken care of Nell, whether she wanted him to or not."

Wade said in a quiet voice, "Kind of selfish on Nell's part."

Lucy kept her face resolute. "Maybe. Times were different then. The way of thinking was also different. There was a lot of social stigma against women who couldn't bear children. Still is, I suppose."

After a few minutes of small talk, Lucy excused herself. "It's time for *Murder, She Wrote*. I do enjoy clean, wholesome mysteries without all the blood and gore." She sighed. "Freddie...I can't help but worry about him. He's a grown man, but so naïve." She cast a pensive look toward her son. "It's like when you joined the Marines. I don't think I slept a wink the whole time you were deployed."

Wade reached over and clasped his mother's hand and brought it to his lips. "I never meant to worry you, Mom."

Ward finished off his coffee and set the cup on the tray. "Here's the thing...Baltimore has one of the highest crime rates in the nation. The crime unit he's assigned to will either grow Freddie into a good cop or send him home in a pine box."

Lucy gathered the tray of mugs and the plate of leftover cookies. "It's the pine box part that concerns me. I can't imagine how his poor mother is coping. He is their only child, after all."

After she'd left the room, Wade said, "Pop I'd like to discuss one of your old cases." He removed a folded copy of a news article from his shirt pocket and opened it. The headline read: Do You Recognize This Child?

Ward pulled on his glasses and read. "Ah, yes. Your mother told me Addison was back in town. I hope she doesn't step all over Nell's heart like she did years ago."

He cleared his throat and seemed to be lost in thought for a moment. "Best as I recall, she was found in the Boise bus depot. After Child Protective Services brought the child to Nell, she asked me to see what I could find out. As you've read, the details of her abandonment are sketchy." He removed his glasses and leaned back in the recliner. "She was an exceptionally pretty girl, but Addison wasn't the most pleasant child—threw temper tantrums, skipped school, and gave Nell a hard time. As I recall, Ruby Raye was about her only friend. Those two girls were pretty much inseparable, but nothing alike in temperament. Ruby was a star student and excelled in sports, even won a scholarship to college. But I digress.

"Even though it was out of my jurisdiction, I made a trip to Boise and paid a call on my old buddy Detective Stu Chatsworth. He'd worked the case, and he filled me in on what he knew. The bus depot's security camera had been broken for a couple of months, so that was a dead end. The woman who found Addison sitting alone on a bench and sobbing had come in on a different bus than the child and whoever was with her. She took the girl to the station master, who called my buddy, Stu, who called CPS."

Wade leaned forward, his hands dangling between his knees. "Did he check the departure depots of each bus?"

His dad replied, "Yep, and noted them in his report. Stu even interviewed as many passengers as he could locate from each bus that had arrived that day. No one remembered seeing anyone with a child or a toddler or anyone leaving a child alone in a seat. Same with the drivers—nothing."

Ward scratched the end of his nose. "The *Boise Times* posted articles in all the border states' major newspapers, and it was on all the nightly news channels. After a while, with no results, the case went cold. At seventeen, Addison packed a suitcase and left the same way she arrived—on an out-of-town bus."

Wade pushed off the sofa. He walked to the fireplace and laid another log on the fire. He stirred the embers with the poker, then stood warming his backside. "In one sense of the word, she's been running ever since. Without her actually knowing why she runs, I think it's because subconsciously she's searching—trying to find who she really is."

"You could be right, son." Ward Grey harrumphed. "And ironically, she's right back where she started."

"How did she get her name? Was there a piece of paper with her name on it pinned to her?"

Ward shifted his gaze from the fireplace's flickering flames to his son. "Nothing that simple. When a doctor examined Addison, he estimated she was about eleven months old. Of course, she didn't know her name and was barely talking. No, there was no note." Ward Grey chuckled. "The bus station sits at the corner of Addison Boulevard and James Avenue. CPS decided it was as good a name as any—thus, Addison James."

Wade gave his dad a quizzical smile. "Pop, it seems everyone assumed Addison was brought in on a bus and left inside the depot. With all you've told me, doesn't it make sense that the mother simply walked inside and left Addison on a bench? I mean, a bus station is usually filled with people. The mother probably figured someone would find her baby and give her a good home."

Ward stretched his long legs toward the fire. "Uh-huh. We thought of that, too. Stu canvassed the surrounding businesses and apartment complexes, looking for witnesses. 'Course, it brought a lot of loco yokels out of the woodwork, claiming they'd seen this or that and then asking if there was a reward. All of it just led to one dead end after another."

Wade smiled wearily. He wished he had better news from his father. He fought against feelings he didn't understand and wondered why he felt the need to protect Addison. "She's ready to run again. In fact, she's fighting hard to stay in Meadow Creek. I think that's why she volunteered to take charge of the bazaar. Hell, she even admitted she hates Christmas."

He snapped his fingers. "Wait..." He lifted the article from the coffee table and read, "...found on Christmas Day." He raked a hand through his hair. "My God, Pop, what kind of mother abandons her child on Christmas Day? Even though Addison was barely a year old, she probably innately remembers things like decorated trees and Christmas carols. The day I picked her up at the airport, I turned the radio on and "Jingle Bells" was playing. She asked me to turn it off. No wonder she dislikes Christmas."

He paced back and forth in front of the fireplace until his father beckoned him to sit. "Son, that was thirty-odd years ago. Things were different then for young mothers, especially if they were unwed and destitute or married to some sorry-assed no-good."

A husky timbre filled Wade's voice. "Ava and I were so fortunate. At least we knew our parents loved us. When they were killed, it was a real scary time, with us having no known relatives and being afraid Ava and I would be separated. We're mighty thankful for you and Mom, and we love you more than we show. I'm just sorry Addison wasn't that fortunate."

Ward stood and embraced his son. "Your mother

and I are the fortunate ones, and don't you ever think otherwise." He patted Wade on the back. "Besides with you and me having names like Wade and Ward, we took it as a sign that you and Ava were meant to be ours."

"Thanks, Pop." Wade heaved a sigh. "It's late. I'll say goodnight to Mom on the way out."

Ward waited by the front door. His gaze slowly met his son's. "I just had a thought. No one ever thought to take a DNA sample from the little girl and run it through the databases. 'Course back then, DNA testing wasn't all that reliable." He shrugged his shoulders. "If Addison is serious about knowing who she is, it's something to consider. Good or bad, she has to be prepared to live with the results."

Wade gave his dad another quick hug and a pat on the back. "'Night, Pop. You're the best. If or when the time is right, I'll consider mentioning it to her."

Chapter Thirteen

Saturday reminded Addison of a picture-postcard, a perfect morning with cloudless blue skies and a blanket of snow. The two Percheron geldings stood patiently while Emmett showed Joey how to harness the horses and then hitch them to the sleigh. Addison and Julie had helped Nell in the kitchen. The girls loaded egg salad onto homemade yeast bread, wrapped up the sandwiches they made, and packed them along with a container of gingersnaps and two thermoses each of hot chocolate and hot coffee into a large wicker picnic basket.

Julie scampered toward the sleigh. Addison helped Nell tote the wicker basket. Emmett rushed forward to relieve them of their burden. "Good day for picking out a Christmas tree, wouldn't you say, Nell?" He handed her into the sleigh while tucking the basket of food under the seat.

Nell drew a deep breath as she settled under the lap blanket. "It's a good day, for sure."

Addison suspected the tinge of pink that colored Nell's cheeks had nothing to do with the crisp air. She was careful not to let her cool exterior crack. "Too bad Wade couldn't make it."

Emmett shrugged as he lifted Julie into the sleigh. "That's the way it goes when you're the sheriff."

She didn't respond. Instead, she accepted his help getting in the sleigh. She settled next to Nell, with the little girl tucked between them. She hoped Wade wasn't avoiding her.

Emmett climbed up on the driver's box, with Joey seated next to him. "Wanna help me drive the team, son?"

The little boy's voice squeaked, "Me?"

"You're the only boy here, aren't you?"

Addison listened with interest as the man gave an easy explanation on how to hold the long set of reins between his fingers. At the boy's skepticism, Emmett said, "Don't worry. I'll have hold of the reins too."

Joey fretted. "I don't know what to do."

Emmett adjusted his hat a little tighter on his head. He lifted the youngster to his lap, his arms wrapped around him. "All you gotta do is flap the reins, call 'em by their names, and tell 'em to walk on. These ol' hosses are good boys. They'll obey."

Joey's little voice trembled when he flapped the reins and ordered, "Walk on, Chipper and Bud."

At the command, the wagon moved forward. Julie squealed and clapped her hands. "You're doing it, Joey!"

Joey giggled with delight as he flicked the reins again.

Conversation was spare, leaving Addison time to mull a plethora of thoughts. There was something appealing about the wide expanse of country, the miles and miles of snow-covered terrain without honking horns, neon signs, and the crush of crowds all bustling to get somewhere fast. Along the way, Nell pointed out a black-capped chickadee, a couple of rabbits, and a herd of deer.

Addison had a vision of herself never leaving Hope Ranch. The thirty-minute ride gave her time to think about ways to save Nell's home. Lost in thought, she almost didn't hear Nell say, "I can't remember the last time I tended to the trees. My mind says I can still do all the things I did when I was young." With a voice gruff from suppressed emotions, she added, "My body and my mind are often at war with each other."

Emmett glanced over his shoulder. "That's the plain truth, Nell. One thing for certain, gettin' old isn't for the faint of heart." And then he added, "Haul up on the reins, Joey."

Emmett helped the youngster pull the team to a halt. "All right, little man. A gentleman always helps the ladies, and you and I are gentlemen. Give your sister a hand down while I take care of Aunt Nell and Miss Addy."

Nell sighed as she licked her lips. "If you don't mind, Emmett, I'd like to wait in the sleigh."

The concern in Emmett's voice matched his furrowed brow. "You all right, Nell? We can do this another day."

"And disappoint the young'uns? Not on your life." She made a shooing motion with her hands. "Besides, it'll be nice to decorate the house again after so many years."

"Can we pick out a tree now?" the twins chimed.

Addison said, "Don't worry, Emmett. I'll stay with Nell. If we need you, I'll yell."

Emmett nodded. He grabbed the chainsaw from the rear of the sleigh and cautioned the twins to stay where he could see them.

Youthful chatter and giggles, mingled with Boomer's excited yips, drifted back to the sleigh. Addison opened the thermos of coffee and poured two cups. She handed one to the woman across from her. Meaningless chitchat passed between them until, no longer able to contain her concern, Addison blurted, "I know you're in financial trouble and on the verge of losing the ranch."

An incredulous scowl settled on Nell's face. "You have no right snooping into my business."

"I wasn't snooping, not exactly. That day in your office when I telephoned my agent, the letters from the bank were there. Nell, if you needed help all you had to do was ask."

"Who was I to ask…you?" Nell harrumphed. "Not a word from you in all these years. Every one of my kids calls me Aunt Nell. Not you. Why is that, Addison?"

She called me Addison! Not Addy. Disaster number seven: sticking my nose where it doesn't belong. Shocked to the core at the reality of Nell's words, she didn't blame her foster mother for being upset with her. She was angry at herself for starting a conversation like this one here in the middle of a snow-covered field. She wanted to move to another topic. A happier topic.

The cold was damp, causing her arm to ache, and Addison drew the coat more tightly around her. She was overcome with a conviction of possible irreparable loss. Searching for the proper explanation, she stared out at the mountains, thinking the ridges resembled purple and gray crushed velvet. She lowered her gaze. In spite of the cold, her cheeks burned hotly.

Addison offered a lopsided smile at her foster

mother. "I'm sorrier than you will ever know that I've hurt you so deeply. You can be upset with me all you want. The most important issue at the moment is to figure out how to save your home. As I see it, you have two choices: flaunt your stubborn pride and become homeless, or be the sensible woman that I know you are and let me help you."

The buzz of the chainsaw chewing through wood and then its silence signaled the perfect Christmas tree had been found and that this conversation was over—temporarily.

Nell's stiff composure and reluctance to express any of her feelings was beyond reserved or constrained, as if she denied the gravity of her situation. The silence between them became excruciating.

Exuberant shouts intensified the moment. "Aunt Nell…Aunt Nell…look at our tree!"

Addison's voice brimmed with commiseration. "Aunt Nell?"

Nell tossed off the lap blanket and stood. "Not a word of this to Emmett. I'm not his or anybody else's charity case." She stepped down from the sleigh. "I just have to—think about all of this."

Addison noted the rise and fall of the older woman's chest. It pained her to cause the only mother she had known such stress. "*Thinking* about it and procrastinating has brought you almost to the point of no return, Aunt Nell."

Nell glowered. "Stop with the *Aunt Nell*. All of a sudden it sounds like a…a mockery."

Addison wasn't about to apologize. She continued. "All right. Nonetheless, let us help you, and that includes Emmett. It's as obvious as the nose on your face that the man would walk through fire for you. Besides, Wade is coming out tomorrow. If we put our heads together, we can formulate a solid plan before it's too late."

Boomer raced toward the women. He jumped up, placing his large, snow-covered paws on Nell's chest. She scratched his head and crooned that he was a good boy. The sight of two six-year-olds struggling to help drag a blue spruce through the snow released the pent-up tension in Addison.

With little effort, Emmett loaded the six-footer in the back of the sleigh and secured it with rope. "The young'uns and I have worked up a powerful appetite gettin' this beauty."

Joey's red-cheeked face overflowed with pride. "Uncle Emmett let me help with the chainsaw."

"And I picked out the tree. It's taller than me." The words practically bubbled out of Julie's throat.

Emmett walked from the rear of the wagon. He gazed, bewildered, at the two women. "Something goin' on I should know about?"

Nell handed him a cup of coffee and an egg salad sandwich while Addison tended the children. Nell glanced at Addison with a tight-lipped, humorless smile. Relief washed over Addison when Nell said to Emmett, "Come for lunch tomorrow or not. Suit yourself. Seems Addison and Wade have some business to talk over with me."

Emmett lifted his bushy eyebrows skeptically. "By the looks on your faces, whatever is going on must be mighty serious."

Nell offered a doleful look. "Serious enough, I reckon."

The little boy wolfed down his sandwich. "Aunt Nell, can we decorate the tree as soon as we get home?"

Julie clapped her gloved hands together. Through chattering teeth she chimed in, "Can we...can we?"

Nell started to say something, but Emmett abruptly lifted Joey and then Julie to sit next to him on the driver's seat. "I expect we'll have to climb up to the attic to find the decorations. Maybe later in the afternoon, after Nell has rested a bit, you can decorate the tree. For now, you and your sister can help me drive the team back to the house."

****

When Emmett guided the team across the yard and halted them at the front porch, Nell took in the dismal-looking old rustic two-story ranch house. She sighed deeply and, as though speaking to herself, said, "It's in sad need of repair and a paint job."

She leaned forward and touched Addison on the arm. She smiled, her voice steady. "You know, the meeting tomorrow might be just the ticket. Can you forgive a foolish old woman for acting like a sore-tailed she-bear?"

Addison's smile was genuine when she squeezed her foster mother's hand. "It's me who should ask forgiveness. Don't worry. Together we'll come up with a great plan, Aunt Nell."

Nell blamed the stinging wind for causing tears to puddle in her eyes. "*Aunt Nell*...has a nice ring to it."

Chapter Fourteen

It took less time to find the two large blue plastic storage bins filled with Christmas decorations than it did to get Joey and Julie out of the attic.

"Did you see the rockin' horse, Julie? I wonder if Aunt Nell will let us bring it down from the attic so we can ride it."

"I bet if Uncle Emmett asks she'll say okay." This was followed by Julie's frightened squeal. "Sp...i...der!" She ran to Emmett and hugged his leg. "Don't let it get me."

"Here, now, little girl, hush up that screechin'. You 'bout scared ten years off me. It won't hurt you if you don't mess with it." Emmett removed his hat and gently encouraged the hobo spider to move along. "Let's get these decorations downstairs. Julie, help your brother with that smaller bin."

The children followed Emmett down the stairs to the living room, where they deposited their burdens. Emmett removed the lid and dug around until he found the tree holder and secured the blue spruce in it, then set the tree in front of the large window.

Nell lamented, "I haven't put up a tree in several years—don't know if the twinkle lights still work."

Emmett assured her. "Don't fret, Nell. We'll get it figured out."

After an hour of untangling cords, stretching them out, and testing to make sure all the bulbs were screwed in, Emmett pointed and said, "It's the moment of truth. Joey, there's the wall outlet. Plug 'er in."

Addison held her breath. Nell crossed her fingers. Julie scolded, "Hurry up, Joey."

Much to everyone's delight, the strands of red and green, blue and white lights twinkled. Nell helped Emmett wrap the strings of light around the tree. Addison's heart twanged when the couple's hands touched and Nell's cheeks flamed when Emmett winked.

"Let the decorating begin," Nell stepped back and declared.

Addison reached into the bin and drew out a miniature crocheted wreath. She sucked in her breath. A fat tear squeezed from the corner of her eye.

"Why are you crying, Addison?" Julie's childlike voice was a mixture of sympathy and curiosity.

Addison held up the teal wreath adorned with a red bow for the twins to see the picture glued to the wreath. "Aunt Nell crocheted one for each of us. This is me when I wasn't much older than you. It was my first Christmas at Hope Ranch." She lovingly placed the ornament on a bluish-green sprig.

Nell peeked around from her side of the tree. "If you dig around, you'll probably find one with Ruby's picture, and a lot of others, too."

"This is fun." Joey pulled a spotted rocking horse from the box and hung it on the tree.

Addison searched until she found a plastic bag filled with ornaments that were Nell's creation. She recalled most of the names as she hung other colorful crocheted wreaths. She held up a blue wreath with a green bow. "Who is this cute guy?"

"Oh, my goodness, that's Wade. I think he was about eleven years old. He and Ava didn't live here very long before Ward and Lucy adopted them." She ran a finger over the picture. "He grew into a fine man."

Addison found a place for the wreath. "Yes, he certainly has."

"Look, isn't she beautiful?" Julie crooned as she held up an angel tree-topper that wore a green coat with white faux fur trim and a green plaid dress with gold trim. The angel held a gold cross in one hand and a harp in the other. Her wings were snowy white feathers.

The little girl's happy face crumpled, tears rimmed her eyes, and she sniffled. Addison knelt. "Why are you crying, Julie?"

Joey came and draped his arm over his sister's shoulder. "She's sad because the angels took our gram away."

Addison used the tip of her shirttail to wipe away the tears. "Your gram wouldn't want you to be sad. In fact, you and Joey come with me."

Nell and Emmett exchanged curious glances and followed Addison as she led the twins outside to the front porch and down the steps. It was almost as if all of them had forgotten it was dark and cold.

Addison pointed to the inky sky littered with stars. "Stars are angels that watch over us and make us feel happy and safe. Look carefully for the star that glitters the brightest. That will be your gram smiling down at you."

As if of one mind the twins pointed and said, "There…see, Addison? That's the brightest star."

Addison swallowed the welling in her chest. "I do see it. Remember, any time you feel sad or lonely, you can always find your gram."

"How do you know this, Addison?" the twins asked.

Addison turned to see Nell wearing a misty smile. "A very wise woman told me." She shivered. "Let's go inside where it's warm."

Emmett lifted Julie in his arms and clasped Joey's hand. "I'll hold you up so you can place the angel on top of the tree. That way she can smile down at all of us."

Nell wrapped her arm around Addison's waist. "After all these years you still remember."

"I've truly missed you, Aunt Nell. It's good to be home."

After admiring the tree and declaring it was the most beautiful Christmas tree ever, Nell tucked the sleepy-eyed children into bed while Addison helped Emmett clear the clutter from the floor. Even as he lifted the bins, saying he'd stick them back in the attic, he pierced Addison with a no-nonsense gaze. "I may be gettin' on in age, but I'm nobody's fool, Addison. What's all this cloak-and-dagger stuff about me comin' for lunch tomorrow?"

At Addison's hesitation, he squinted hard at her. "I'm an old man, and my patience ain't as long as it used to be."

Keeping her voice hushed, Addison moved close to Emmett. She made a tick-a-lock motion against her lips as a way of asking him to keep quiet. "Nell is on the verge of losing the ranch. The meeting tomorrow is for putting our heads together and creating a plan that's more than a Band-Aid solution to her finances."

"What the hell…"

"Shh…you promised!"

"Why didn't she come to me?"

Addison lifted her eyebrows. "Same reason she didn't come to me or any of the others."

He grabbed his hat. "Yeah—same reason she refused to marry me—stiff-necked, stubborn pride."

The expression on Emmett's face told her that he was as surprised by his admission as herself. She touched his arm. "Don't leave, please. We're all treading on the same thin ice with Aunt Nell. Let's not give her a reason to make a decision that could leave her homeless and put this beautiful ranch in the hands of money-grubbing land developers. Don't forget your property adjoins hers." She drew a breath. "At least stay for a goodnight cup of coffee."

At that moment Addison made a decision to get in touch with Ruby Raye as soon as possible. She had made a decision that, good or bad, would affect her future and possibly the rest of her life. Not to speak of putting a huge dent in her savings account.

Emmett followed Addison to the kitchen and helped her set out the cups. In a few minutes, Nell joined them. She settled on her usual stool at the large island with its white quartz countertop. "I sure will miss those young'uns when they're gone. Until today it hadn't dawned on me how empty and quiet this house has grown over the years."

Addison realized she couldn't remember the last time she had felt the sense of family. How sad that she had allowed those opportunities to slip away by not visiting Nell, especially on special occasions like

Christmas and Nell's birthday.

Emmett's voice awakened Addison from her reveries. "Reckon I'll mosey on. See you tomorrow for the…um…meeting."

She remained at the kitchen island while Nell showed Emmett to the door. Once she returned, Addison said, "Has the festival ever held a fashion show?"

Nell lifted her eyebrows. "Not as long as I've served as chairwoman, and that's been over twenty years. Activities have gotten stale after all this time, and the crowds have dwindled. Tell me more about this idea of yours."

Addison was filled with renewed energy. "A fashion show with children—the twins would be adorable. T.J. Elsworth has daughters, and surely you know of others with children. To keep it cute and fun, we'd set the age limit at anyone between six and twelve years old. Maybe several store owners will donate outfits, and of course, it would be great advertisement for them."

Nell's brown eyes twinkled. She clapped her hands like an excited child. "By jingles, I love the idea and know the others will, too. What else you got?"

Addison took a sip of coffee, her mind whirling. "Hmm, here's another idea. Have you ever auctioned off dinner with a bachelor…say, start the bidding at twenty-five dollars, with donating a portion of the proceeds to a worthy cause? We could ask the restaurants if they'd be willing to donate the dinner. It could be a tax write-off for them."

Nell winked. "Smart girl, and another fun idea. Maybe we can recruit Wade and Emmett, and then there's Lars Johansson, Howard Fedderman... I'll make a list. With only two weeks before Christmas, we need to get clicking. When's our first committee meeting?"

"We can meet at the library, to make it convenient for everyone. What about Saturday at one o'clock?"

"Saturday should work. One suggestion—Brenda has a private dining room in the back of her café. We could meet and eat at the same time."

"Great idea, Aunt Nell."

Addison helped Nell clear the kitchen before excusing herself for the night. She peeked in to check on the twins, then headed upstairs to her room. She removed the sling from her arm and managed to undress herself and then slip into a pair of flannel pajamas. She climbed into bed and reached to turn out the lamp. Lying in the dark, she thought if the festival committee approved of auctioning off an evening with a bachelor she would definitely bid on Wade. She admitted part of her wanted him, and wanted him to want her. Her skin erupted in icy prickles merely thinking about him—his gray eyes, the way he stood, the sound of his voice, and the sensual scent of his cologne.

Addison gently rubbed the healing scar on her forehead to ease the itching. Sighing, she questioned her judgment. Unfortunately, Rowan had taught her a bitter lesson that all men were not what they seemed. In her mind appeared the image of her matron of honor, mauve silk gown shoved up to her shoulders, and Rowan with his tuxedo trousers and suspenders puddled around his feet, his hands squeezing the woman's hips while he pumped furiously in and out, and the damned bitch, her best friend, begging for more.

She had stood there, watching in shock, her brain not registering what she was witnessing, and her first inclination was to laugh because the scene reminded her of a television commercial where a guy was vigorously using a plunger to clear his clogged toilet. Then she remembered screaming, *"You bastard—it's our wedding day! For God's sake, we're in the church!"*

Addison covered her head with a pillow trying to obliterate the vision that seemed permanently branded in her brain. The pillow muffled her cries. "How could you…damn you…damn you both to hell…how could you betray me? Why…why…why!"

She reminded herself that she was no longer a gullible young woman and had to stifle thinking about Wade in a romantic way…or was it purely sexual yearnings? *If I know what's good for me, I need to throttle these fantasies and never let them get away from me. Besides, he called me Gracie. I won't be duped again.*

Lost in misery, she didn't hear the bedroom door open.

"Addy, honey, are you having a bad dream?" Nell stood silhouetted in the moonlight.

Like a dam that had burst, Addison sobbed, "Oh, Aunt Nell. I will hate him forever."

"Who? Tell me."

Propped against the headboard, in the light of the moon, between sobs and hiccups, Addison released her pent-up anguish and anger and the reason for her broken engagement to Rowan Sarkozy.

Chapter Fifteen

Addison had applied her makeup with extra care to hide the telltale evidence of last night's sob fest. She was thinking of today's meeting and how to save the ranch and the work to be done afterward. She wondered if she should forget the entire business and fly back to New York—perhaps start her own agency. After all, she wasn't without knowledge about the world of fashion. She knew how to book modeling gigs.

She stood at the kitchen sink and stared out the window. A herd of elk ambled out of the forested mountain slope and toward the river. I could live here, she thought, staring out at the graceful animals and the vast blue sky. Maybe I belong here.

She smiled a little as she watched Nell stir a simmering pot of hamburger soup. Strands of gray mingled with auburn hair pulled back in a bun, faded jeans, a blue plaid flannel shirt—Addison didn't recall ever seeing Nell in a dress. She wore a smidgen of makeup and yet, at age seventy-five, was an attractive woman.

The telephone interrupted Addison's musing. She listened to the one-sided conversation and watched the moods on Nell's face shift from mild to angry and then mystified. Nell said, "On a Sunday?"

She nodded, and the conversation ended with,

"What're we supposed to do with the twins?"

And then, "Okay, if you think it's for the best. We'll be ready."

Nell's frown concerned Addison. "What's happened?"

Nell hung up the receiver on the old-fashioned wall phone and turned off the gas burner. "That was Wade. Apparently something drastic has happened concerning my mortgage. He said Emmett is on the way to drive us to the bank and that we're to go to the rear entrance. Let's get the young'uns ready. T.J. said to drop 'em off at his house."

Addison listened as the woman grumbled almost under her breath, "People messing in my business. Don't like it. Don't like it at all."

Addison's heart plummeted to her stomach. "It must be dire for T.J. to give up his Sunday. I'll help you get the twins ready."

Minutes later, Boomer's whining yips echoed and his toenails scratched against the wooden floor as he raced to the front door to greet the visitor. Emmett called, "Hello."

Nell herded the twins down the hall. She groused, "Let's get this show on the road so we can get it over with." She pointed to the black lab and commanded, "Stay and guard the house."

Two concerned voices said, "Won't he get cold outside, Aunt Nell?"

Her face softened. "Boomer's a smart boy. He'll go to the barn and bed down with one of the horses."

Emmett whistled a Christmas tune as he assisted everyone inside the cab of his pickup. Addison wasn't feeling the spirit of yuletide and good cheer any more than any cheerfulness about the meeting with T.J.

Julie sat in Addison's lap with Joey tucked tightly between herself and Nell. She slanted a look at the woman who sat rigid as a rock next to Emmett. She was saying, "It'll be a treat for the two of you to visit with someone your own age. Kassi is seven and Kelli is five. There are two other girls, Kali and Karli. They're a little bit older."

"All girls!" Joey whined.

Addison ran her hand over the thick mop of the boy's blond hair. Her lips curved into a smile. "Remember what Emmett said about being a gentleman. Besides, I'll bet the girls have a lot of games and coloring books that you and your sister will enjoy."

She settled back and during the rest of the ride tamped down unease about the bank's vice president calling an emergency meeting.

Emmett maneuvered the truck up a circular driveway decorated with tall wooden candy canes. Before he could switch off the engine, the front door opened. An attractive woman in her early thirties raced to the truck, hugging a sweater close to her body. Addison rolled down the window.

"Hi, I'm Kate, T.J.'s wife." She peered inside. "Joey, Julie, we have hot chocolate. We're also going to toast marshmallows in the fireplace." She looked at Nell. "I hope that's okay, Mrs. Hopewell."

"They'll like that, Kate." And then to the twins as they jumped down from the truck she said, "Remember to mind your manners."

"I won't keep you. T.J. is waiting." Kate took each twin by the hand and rushed them toward the festively decorated front door.

****

The large conference room was totally silent. Nell toyed with the cup of coffee. She could feel Addison and Emmett both watching her, waiting to see her reaction to whatever T.J. had to tell her. The door opened, and Wade walked in and apologized for being late.

Nell merely nodded. She crossed her arms as if for protection. In reality she knew there was no one to blame but herself for getting head-over-heels in debt and then sticking her head in the sand like a damned ostrich, hoping that by some miracle the loan would pay itself off. *Foolish and stupid. I'm a foolish and stupid old woman.* She berated herself for not swallowing her pride and asking Emmett for help. Instead she swallowed back the silent scream stuck in her throat, refusing to allow such frailty to show. Beneath the table, where no one could see, her hands twisted into sweaty knots.

Her voice cracked when she spoke. "If the meeting is so all-fired important, then where did T.J. disappear to?"

The door opened again. T.J. held a laptop in his hands, while behind him followed a lanky man of about fifty. Donald Plough apologized as he set his briefcase on the table and then shrugged out of a brown jacket and removed his brown toboggan hat. He shook hands with Wade and Emmett.

Nell's breath came hard. She needed to be home, to bury her head under a pillow. She glanced from T.J. to the man who reminded her of an underfed scarecrow.

For her benefit, the banker introduced the man. "Aunt Nell, this is Donald Plough. He's a real estate lawyer."

Plough took a seat and removed his laptop from the briefcase. While the lawyer set up his computer, T.J. said, "It's easy to see the anxiety on all of your faces, so I won't bandy words. The reason for this urgent meeting is that late Friday the board of directors met to discuss a new offer from Megala Land Development Corp. Their CEO, a Mr. Rukn el Saddiq, has offered to buy Nell's mortgage, and he is also interested in the adjoining property." He drew a breath. "That would be your ranch, Emmett."

Emmett skewered the banker with a go-to-hell look. "That explains the black limousine with its tinted windows that was spotted driving back and forth in front of the property a few days ago. That jasper Saddiq was scoping out my place. Well, I'll tell you this—he'll play hell getting it."

The banker said, "Simmer down, Emmett. I assured Mr. Saddiq there were no liens on your ranch and that he'd have to deal with you personally."

Emmett banged both fists on the table like two thunderbolts. "He'll do it at the business end of my shotgun."

Wade reached over and laid a hand on the old man's arm. "I'll pretend I didn't hear that, Emmett."

Emmett hissed, "All right, then. Let's get on with it."

T.J. cleared his throat. "Mr. Saddiq also requested that, since the loan has been in arrears for nearly a year, once the account is cleared Nell is to vacate the property within twenty-four hours. He feels she's had adequate time to make other arrangements and will request an eviction notice be served if necessary." T.J.

cleared his voice. "Nell, if it hadn't been for Addison bringing the loan out of arrears plus paying it two months ahead—"

Nell burst out, "You did what, Addy? How many times do I have to say that I'm not a charity case? With a little time I could've come up with the money."

Emmett rolled his eyes. His voice firm, he said, "Shoulda, woulda, coulda, *didn't*. It's a little late to get all indignant, Nell. Be thankful Addy saved your bacon. Now hush your mouth and listen."

Nell covered her face with her hands. She was in mental pain. She had been pierced clean through.

The attorney spoke. "The plain truth, Mrs. Hopewell, is that even with Ms. James bringing the account current, the bank's position is that you are a bad risk and thus your mortgage is officially in foreclosure. With Megala dangling the golden carrot, unless you come up with the full five hundred thousand in the next seventy-two hours…" His voice trailed off. "It's out of his love and loyalty to you that T.J. called this meeting. Because of your deliberate lack of compliance, the bank has no further obligation to you."

Nell gave a long, exhausted sigh.

Addison slapped her hand on the table. "Please, stop. Can't you see how painful this is for her?"

Plough said, "It's not personal, Ms. James. It's business."

She narrowed her eyes to angry slits. "Then let's get down to business. Aunt Nell, I'd like to purchase Hope Ranch. Name your price. I'll pay whatever you ask and satisfy the loan in full—today!"

The silence in the room was mud thick. A nervous smile quivered Nell's lips. And then with a little catch in her throat, she replied, "Mr. Plough, T.J., Emmett and Wade, you are my witnesses…Addison James, I will sell you Hope Ranch and all that goes with it for the total sum of one dollar, to be paid in cash, today."

Addison reached into her purse and withdrew her wallet. She pulled out a dollar bill and laid it in front of Nell. "Mr. Elsworth, will the bank accept my personal check to satisfy Nell's loan?"

Nell sucked in her breath. "Addy, do you have that kind of money?"

"I've done well for myself over the years." She cocked an eyebrow. "Mr. Elsworth?"

The bank's vice president cleared his throat. "Actually, for such an amount, the bank will require a wire transaction from your bank to ours." He hesitated, looking intensely concerned. "However, since these are extenuating circumstances, yes, I will accept a personal check and hold it in good faith until you contact your bank to wire the funds. Once those funds are received, we'll void your check. Mr. Plough is prepared to have all parties sign a real estate contract for sale. Am I correct?"

Plough opened his laptop. "In anticipation of this, we've already completed the title search. Give me ten minutes and I'll have a contract ready. To expedite the sale, we'll do an electronic signing, and due to the mitigating situation, we'll forego the usual thirty-day closing period."

After what seemed like an eternity, the contract was signed and the transaction was completed. T.J. said, "I will drive out with the satisfied deed and personally hand it to you, Aunt Nell."

He wrapped her hand in his and held it. His eyes

were warm, his voice soft. "It's a good thing you've done, Addison."

Addison softened her features. "Thanks, T.J. I'm glad you were on our side."

Chapter Sixteen

Wade offered to drive Addison home while Emmett and Nell collected the twins. "You're awfully quiet. Not having buyer's remorse, are you?"

Without revealing a change of heart, Addison simply sighed. "If I can't make the ranch pay for itself, I'll have to sell it and hope to recoup most of my investment."

He stared at her. "I take it you have a plan or you wouldn't have stuck your neck out like you did."

She waved away his words. "I have a few ideas. Let's wait until Emmett and Nell get to the house so I can share with all of you."

An hour later, with lunch out of the way and the children down for a nap, the adults gathered in the living room. Comments passed back and forth about the great job everyone did decorating the Christmas tree and whether or not Wade had any word from the Red Cross about the twins' mother.

When the chit-chat died out, Addison said, "Nell, the ranch is still yours. I hope you know what happened at the bank today was purely a formality to keep Magala Land Development from getting their grubby hands on the property." Addison went on to explain that her ex-fiancé was the actual CEO and the money force behind MLD. "With Rowan, it's all about the money.

He doesn't care who he steps on to get what he wants."

Addison blinked rapidly to hold hot tears at bay.

Nell sounded dubious. "But you do have ideas about how to keep this place afloat?"

Wade raised his eyebrows. He'd removed his jacket and gun holster. There was a solidness about him that made Addison feel as if he could handle any situation that arose. Her heart fluttered. They looked at each other and then away. She had to take a steadying breath as her stomach tipped again.

"As a matter of fact, I'd like to form a corporation, an LLC with me as the CEO and Nell as the vice president. It will take most of a year to do all I've planned, and I hope we can be ready with the first phase by summer."

Anxiety tinged Nell's voice. "Do what, Addy? Stop talking around your tongue and get to the point."

Addison opened a manila file folder and pulled out a sketch. She held it up for all to see. Its title was Hope Ranch…Your Destination to Adventure.

She explained, "Hope Ranch will become a vacation resort. We will build a gazebo for wedding ceremonies. Couples will have optional packages to choose from, one of which will include a honeymoon cottage down by the river. We can add a couple more cottages accessible to the river for renting during bass tournament season. We'll get the Christmas tree farm up and running again, and offer sleigh rides to the farm so customers can cut their own trees, with hot chocolate afterward to warm them up. We'll also open a gift shop and sell honey, cider, and jellies, plus T-shirts and other items on consignment from local crafters. We'll have hiking trails and horseback-riding trails.

"I've crunched the numbers. Depending on the package clients choose, we can get at least two thousand a week for each cottage, and more if we stock them with food. For the cottages alone we're looking at a possible eight thousand dollars per week. In two years, I'll have paid myself back and more."

"Addy…slow down…you're boggling my mind. All of this sounds wonderful." Nell shrugged. "We're two women. I'm old, with a worn-out body. We can't do this by ourselves."

Emmett spoke up. "This is a fine idea, Addy. I'll help out as much as time allows, and I'm sure Wade will, too."

Wade winked. "You can count on me."

Feeling a bit flushed from her own unexpected excitement, Addison said, "Thanks for the offer, guys. In the beginning, we may need you for physical labor."

She focused on the woman sitting across from her. "Aunt Nell, during school holidays and the summer, we'll hire high school kids and kids from the community college. They'll work part-time, and with competition for jobs, I don't think we'll have any problems in the employment department."

She pondered for a moment. "We will need one full-time employee—a handyman. We'll convert that old shed behind the barn into living quarters. Part of his salary will include a place to live, utilities, and maybe two meals per day. And by the way, the house will be off-limits. No bed and breakfast. The house will remain our private residence. However, I'm sure your wonderful pastries will sell like hot cakes at the gift shop." Her excitement had increased with each explanation. "What do you think?"

For a few minutes they sat in stiff silence.

Emmett slapped his knee. A grin spread across his face. "Sounds like a dang good plan to me."

She stared blankly at Wade, waiting for his answer, and then a smile warmed his face. "I think you are a genius, Miss Addison James."

With his and Emmett's encouragement, she felt her own courage and fortitude rising, only to collapse when Nell asked, "Where are we going to get all the money it takes to fund your plans?"

She hesitated a moment, staring at the Christmas tree's twinkling lights. Part of her was annoyed that Nell had interrupted her moment of victory, and her other part saw the practical side of the question. She drew a deep breath and slowly let it out. "I'll telephone Ruby in the morning. After New Year's, I'll place my apartment in New York on the market. Except for making a trip to pack up my things and tie up a few loose ends, I'll have no reason to keep the place and will have no plans to return to New York except for pleasure. Don't worry, Aunt Nell. I've covered all the bases."

Secretly, Addison hoped this wasn't an unrealistic fantasy about turning Hope Ranch into a money-making enterprise.

Emmett declared it was time for him to get back to his place and see to a few chores. Nell claimed the day had exhausted her. She saw Emmett to the door and then escaped to her bedroom.

Wade checked his watch. "It's about time for me to relieve Freddie."

"I'll walk you out." Addison grabbed her cloak, and Wade helped wrap it around her shoulders.

Outside, standing next to his cruiser, Wade sent Addison a soft look out of guileless gray eyes. "You're not a very good liar, you know."

She narrowed her eyes and said sweetly, "I'm not sure I understand your meaning."

"Yes, you do. We both know you've dug yourself into a deep financial hole."

She looked down and kicked a small tuft of snow. Her shoulders rose up and down. "It's for a good cause." She jabbed a finger against his chest and leaned forward. "Have a little faith, Sheriff."

He tightened his grip on her arm to bring her a step closer. Warning signals cautioned. She stiffened. "What are you doing?"

"Nothing illegal." With his free hand he cupped the back of her head. "I'm going to kiss you."

"No. I'm not the kissing sort." She was terrified of her response.

His mouth was soft, gentle, coaxing her to taste him. Warmth and ropes of tension tangled together to slide through her belly. She made a sound, something perilously close to a growl. She whirled away. He grabbed her arm and held her in place. "Don't play hot and cold with me, Addison."

Her head was spinning. This was not a sensation she enjoyed. "My heart was ripped to shreds by Rowan... He mangled my soul and then had the audacity to laugh. So you'll forgive me if I've closed the door on my *trust* department. I won't be your latest fling."

He snarled. "My latest... What the hell are you talking about?"

"Oh, don't play coy, Wade. The other night, when

you kissed me, you called me *Gracie.* She must be some deep, dark secret. Even Nell wouldn't talk about her when I asked."

When he didn't answer, Addison arched a brow. "Whoever she is, I won't compete with her, and I won't let you use me to hurt her." Her heart was knocking against her ribs.

Casually he lifted her hand and turned it to kiss the palm. "It's not what you think, Addison."

She harrumphed. "No, it never is."

The radio in his cruiser crackled. A voice said, "Sheriff, everything a 10-17?"

"Shit." Wade hissed between his teeth as he opened the car door and leaned in to grab the radio's mic. "Freddie, it's a 10-4. I'll be in shortly."

Overhead, the sky was brooding and turgid with snow clouds pushed by the wind. Addison hugged the cloak closer as chills raced up and down her spine. Her teeth threatened to chatter.

He stepped forward, and she stepped back. The lines that bracketed his mouth might have been carved with a knife. "Things are a bit hectic, especially with Friday being Freddie's last day. I'll be in touch."

Her lips formed into a thin smile. She strode to the porch and up the steps. She turned back and watched the cruiser disappear down the long driveway.

Chapter Seventeen

Emotional storms besieged Addison that night. All that week they raged. There had been no word from Wade since their parting. She sat on the sofa with a notebook in her lap, wondering what she might do about it, tossing out one idea after another because each was impractical. She didn't want it to seem like she was offering herself.

She had known him barely a month. Very likely she was reading too much into their brief encounters, far more than he meant, anyway. All she had succeeded in doing was making a fool of herself and pushing him away.

Yet what she felt for Wade was entirely different from what she thought she had felt for Rowan. This is insane, she fumed. I am not falling in love with Wade Grey. A little voice bedeviled her... *Oh, yes, you are falling in love with him.*

Something inside her wanted to pick up the phone and call him. Inhibition stopped her, and so she sat there staring out the window with an ache of helplessness in her heart.

Nell set a teapot and two cups on the glass coffee table. "You look like you've lost your best friend. Anything I can do to help?"

Addison uncrossed her legs. She didn't want to

bring up the painful subject of her broken engagement again, or her mixed-up emotions about Wade. She reached across the table to accept the cup Nell had poured. She tapped a pen against the tablet. "The cable company is coming tomorrow to install wiring for the internet." She pointed to a room across the hall. "How often do you use the parlor?"

Nell chuckled. "There's probably ten years of dust in there, if that tells you anything. Why do you ask?"

"Bring your cup and follow me." Addison unfolded from the sofa. Inside the parlor, she said, "We will need a place to check the guests in and out. Originally, I was thinking of putting it inside the gift shop. I haven't completely abandoned that idea. However, that would mean one of us would need to be at the gift shop every day, or trust one of the students we hire to check the guests in and out. Then I thought if you didn't mind, we could convert this room into an office, which might work better since one of us will always be here. What do you think?"

Nell placed her hands on her hips and furrowed her eyebrows. "I'm not completely sold on the gift shop idea either." She pursed her lips. "Although you did say the house would be off-limits to guests."

Addison set her cup on a dust-covered table and walked to a window. "What if we installed a door to replace this window, to give direct access to the office from the front porch?" She walked around the space, pointed out where the file cabinets would sit, a desk with a computer, two chairs for the guests, and finished with, "This door to the hallway would be our private entrance to the house. No guests allowed unless invited."

Nell gave one of the faded blue drapes a vigorous shake, raining dust into the room. She expelled a series of sneezes. "As the young'uns today would say, 'Let's go for it.'"

A flash of dimples revealed Addison's excitement. She jotted a notation on the sketch she'd drawn. "Great. Moving on to the next project. Let's finish our tea while I run some ideas for the festival past you before the committee meets tomorrow."

****

Deputy Freddie Sumner's farewell party ended on a sour note with a telephone call from Wade's dad. "I sure am sorry, son. I actually looked forward to wearing my uniform again. Damned gout's got me laid up. Ava has me on medication. She said it might be a week before I can comfortably stand on my foot."

"Don't sweat it, Pop. Your health comes first. Besides, things are fairly quiet. If something does come up, Millie can handle the office while I take care of business."

"Say, did you tell Addison about the DNA idea?"

Wade expelled a mirthless laugh. His conscience gave a faint prick, but thankfully the feeling lasted no more than a few seconds. His fingers curled around the leather arm pad on his office chair. "'Fraid not, Pop." His voice dipped low. "Haven't given it much thought, especially with Freddie leaving sooner than expected."

"I hear the commotion in the background. Give Freddie my best regards and let him know why I didn't come to his farewell party. Talk to you later, son."

"Will do, Pop. If you or Mom need me, give a shout."

Wade's gaze flitted around the office several times.

The party had wound down, leaving Freddie and Millie in the room. The innocence of youth had it drawbacks. Except for his naivety, Freddie was in his thirties. The deputy turned toward him wearing his usual smile and sunny disposition, his hand outstretched.

"Guess this is it, Wade. I have to admit I'm both excited and nervous. Sure do thank you for all the years of experience I've gained working as your deputy."

Wade clasped the deputy's hand. He offered a slight smile. "Good luck to you, Fred."

The deputy's grin grew. "Gosh darn, Wade, you called me—Fred."

Wade issued a cheery farewell. "Maryland Crime Unit isn't for sissies. You're a man, Fred."

After the final goodbyes were said, Wade told Millie to go home for the rest of the day.

Millie settled back in her office chair and stretched her feet forward. "I'm not upset over Freddie leaving. Why're you sending me home?"

Wade sighed. How did he say that he wanted—no, needed—some alone time? "That was my dad on the phone earlier. He's down with the gout and may be out of commission for a couple of weeks or more."

"Aha. In other words what you're saying is to take the time off while I can because a few overtime hours might be in my future."

"You're a smart woman, Millie."

"Yeah, well, don't let it get around. Somebody might tempt me with a higher-paying job."

It was an old joke between them. For a few minutes the two of them watched the fish placidly swimming back and forth in the aquarium.

Millie opened the bottom desk drawer, collected

her purse and latest romance novel. Wade held her coat open while she slipped it on.

A worried smile wreathed her weathered face. "I hope Freddie has more sense than God gave gophers to keep his gun loaded and his fool head down if he gets in a shooting scrape."

Wade didn't want to admit that he was at all bothered by what might happen to his bumbling friend in a life-or-death situation. "Baltimore is a tough city. Maryland Crime Unit accepted Freddie's credentials as a qualified officer of the law. Otherwise, they wouldn't have hired him. It was his decision. We have to accept it and move forward."

Wade opened the door for Millie. "I don't want to see you until Monday morning. That gives you plenty of time to read your romance novels."

She held up the cover of *Cloud Woman's Spirit*. "This one is about a Deputy US Marshal tracking four insane brothers who killed his wife. You should read it. Your job is cushy next to what Jim Sawyer is going through."

He raised his dark eyebrows in response. "Enjoy your time off."

After she was gone, he settled at his desk, and his thoughts returned, as they did with increasing frequency, to Addison.

Chapter Eighteen

The meeting went better than Addison had expected. Everyone who attended was receptive to her ideas. In addition to the fashion show featuring children, and bidding on a bachelor, the Mistletoe Market would include the usual food and craft vendors. Also new this year, horse-drawn sleighs would participate in the parade, with prizes awarded for the most creative, most beautiful, and most Christmasy decorated sleighs.

Brenda encouraged Nell, Addison, and Millie to remain at the café a little longer. "Addison, your ideas are what we needed to breathe new life into the festival." She motioned a waitress over for more coffee. "It's too bad about Ward having the gout. Kind of puts Wade in a tough spot, not having a deputy."

Millie broke off the edge of a chocolate-covered spudnut and popped it into her mouth. "Meadow Creek is a quiet town. Even though my primary job is dispatcher, I'm still officially a deputy. Wade and I will pull extra hours until he can hire someone. It's no big deal."

Addison's mouth curved into a secret smile as she stared off into Neverland. *So that's why he hasn't been around. Still, he could have called.*

"Addison, you look like the canary that just

swallowed the cat. Couldn't be the mention of a certain sheriff's name, could it?" Nell's eyebrows rose innocently at the deliberate question.

Suddenly, Addison felt out of sorts and on the defensive. "Actually, I was thinking it's getting late, and I know you don't like driving in the dark. Perhaps we'd better go to the library to collect Joey and Julie and then head back to the ranch."

Nell gathered the napkin in her lap and placed it on the table. "One last bit of business before we leave." She fixed her face in a cool mask of contriteness. "I have a little announcement." She cleared her throat. "I got myself into a bit of a financial mess, and I'd rather you hear this from me than through some bank secretary's overly inflated gossip. I must confess I am embarrassed to admit this."

"What in the world, Nell—" Brenda began, when Nell interrupted.

"It's nothing for any of you to fret over." Nell glanced around the table at her friends. "Luckily, Addison bailed me out with the bank and is the new owner of Hope Ranch. Some powerful foreign corporation was out to snatch up the ranch and turn it into goodness knows what. The point is Addison and I formed a partnership. We're converting Hope Ranch to a vacation resort where folks can hold family reunions, or a destination wedding-honeymoon, or whatever family event they want to plan. The sky's the limit."

A blush heightened Nell's face. "At first I was bull-stomping mad…until I realized the only person to blame for my financial pickle was myself."

She picked up a Santa Claus-shaped salt shaker and examined it as she spoke. "After giving it a lot of thought, it dawned on me that once Addison left for New York I'd be all alone."

Nell lifted her gaze, and in that instant Addison saw loneliness and fear in those faded blue eyes. Nell had always been resolute, strong, and independent. She had fostered numerous children of various ages and temperaments. She'd had responsibilities then: a ranch to run, children to feed and clothe, and she did it on a pittance, never asking for help. Now she was past her prime and in failing health.

Addison studied her for a second as if assessing the truth of Nell's statement. After the slightly awkward but nonetheless heartening confession, Addison kept her voice matter of fact. "We plan a grand opening in June, and a re-grand opening in December. You are all invited to both celebrations."

Nell stood. "And you'll never believe this—the cable guys were out yesterday to install internet connections, and Addison will teach me how to use a computer." She guffawed. "Who said you can't teach an ol' dame new tricks."

A bell's tinkle drew Addison's attention. The café door opened and closed. Wade strode in to the counter. The man looked good. Her mouth went dry while other parts of her—did not. Her brain supplied perfect memories of both late-night kisses and the searing touch of his hands exploring her body. Her heart fluttered, and a sensual sensation slithered all the way down to her womanhood.

"Afternoon," he said. He grabbed a large cup of coffee and a sack of spudnuts. "Nice seeing you, ladies. If you'll excuse me, I have to get going."

When Millie pushed back her chair to stand, he

held up his hand. "Nope, it's only Saturday. I don't want to see you in the office until Monday, remember."

With that he was gone. Addison inwardly groaned. He'd barely looked at her. How was she to interpret that? Never mind. She wasn't going to obsess over it, not that a lack of specifics ever got in her way. Still it was frustrating. Before she could really get into psychoanalyzing, Brenda heaved an exaggerated sigh. "That's one handsome hunk of a man. He's got a heart as big as all outdoors." She cocked an unabashed grin toward Addison. "And he's a bachelor. If I weren't old enough to be his grandmother, I'd bid on him myself."

A full-bodied laugh burst from Millie, and she kept laughing. "Brenda Brown, you are a shameless hussy."

"Yes, and at my age, I've been without the comforts a man gives a woman behind closed doors for too long."

Millie waggled her eyebrows. "Ah, come on, Brenda, what's stopping you? Hank Pierson is our age and available."

Nell guffawed. "That's the problem—*he's...our... age.*"

Millie continued to laugh and offered a wink. "Tell it like it is, sister. We can dream, can't we?"

This time Brenda nudged Millie in the ribs. She winked. "Nell, if Emmett agrees to participate, will you bid on him? I can see it now—you with Emmett and Addison with Wade on a double date."

Addison rolled her eyes. The more the woman laughed, the more disgruntled she grew. "To set the record straight, I have more important things on my mind than the sheriff."

A mischievous sparkle lit the café owner's brown

eyes as she gave Addison a "you poor girl, you are fooling yourself" expression.

Addison tamped down the rising tide of annoyance. What response did she give this woman who seemed to be able to read her mind? Eager to leave the conversation, she shoved back from the table. "We need to go. The children will think we've forgotten them."

****

At the sight of Addison in the café, his heart had taken off on a wild gallop. Her air had been one of total detachment. Every time he saw her it was a shock to realize how beautiful she was. Her intense blue eyes had cut straight through him. A frustrated gasp tore from Wade's throat as his fingers squeezed the paper cup so tightly that hot coffee surged upward to scald his hand and soak through his trousers. He yowled as he sprinted to the bathroom and grabbed a wad of paper towels.

What was wrong with him? He used to be better with people, women particularly. He used to enjoy charming them, making them happy, and he had always presumed they were honest and forthright. That was before Gracie.

Unfortunately, she had taught him that not all women were what they seemed. In all the years since, he'd filed most women under the same category as the woman who had forever soured him on true love. So here he was presuming the worst about Addison, a beautiful woman who had trusted her heart to a contemptible bastard.

He was tempted to call the answering service, put a Gone Fishing sign on the door, and drive out to his favorite fishing spot.

Dabbing at the wet coffee stain on his pants, he heard, "Hello…Wade?"

There in the office stood Ava, setting a basket on Millie's desk. She removed several bowls and a set of utensils. She offered a sisterly smile as she commanded him to sit. "I brought you some real food. A sheriff cannot live on coffee and donuts alone. It isn't healthy." She smirked. "Besides, how can you chase down bad guys if you're trying to lumber along with a pot belly?"

Wade kissed his sister's cheek. "In case you haven't noticed, Meadow Creek isn't exactly teeming with bad guys."

She poured two cups of coffee and handed one to Wade, followed by a bowl of beef stew. "Sorry about Dad. He was looking forward to wearing his uniform again."

Wade nodded. "I know. He told me." He chewed thoughtfully for a moment. "I've put in a call to Boise requesting a temporary deputy until I begin interviewing candidates for a permanent position."

"Great." Ava slapped her hands together. "I have other business to discuss. Today's meeting was awesome. Addison's ideas were off the chart, especially the bid-on-a-bachelor idea." She offered her brother a dimpled grin. "I'm in charge of recruiting bachelors, and naturally you are on my list. So, how 'bout it, big brother?"

"I don't know, Ava. I'd feel awkward standing on stage waiting…no, hoping some woman might bid more than a dollar on me."

"Just so you know, bidding must start at twenty-five dollars."

"Still, I'm not a hunk of meat to be auctioned off.

I'll let you know later."

"Um, no…you'll let me know before I walk out that door. Aw, come on. It's for a great cause. Half the proceeds go to fund the new children's story-time wing at the library."

He spread his hands wide. "Do you know how embarrassing it'll be if no one bids on me?"

Ave gave an impatient snort. "For your information, I've already signed up Hank Pierson, Tommy Jenks, and LaVar Studstill."

Distracted by the colorful fish in the aquarium Wade tried not to let his thoughts meander to how he'd spend the evening if Addison were to bid on him and win. "Okay, I'll do it on one condition."

Ava pursed her lips, her eyes filled with skepticism. "What is the condition?"

He finished off the last of his coffee and offered his sister a broad grin. He had this in the bag. There was no way he'd have to put himself on display. "I'll do it only if Emmett agrees to participate too."

Her face grew somber. She pulled a pout, and then she shouted, "Yes!" as she pushed the clipboard forward and pointed. "Read it and weep, brother." She hooted. "In his very own handwriting—Emmett Oxbow."

Wade sputtered. "That traitor! He… He…"

She cut her brother a sideways grin and handed him a pen. "Stop sputtering and sign on the dotted line." She snapped her fingers. "I have it on good authority that the ladies of Meadow Creek are already checking their bank accounts."

She gazed studiously at Wade as she gathered the dishes and repacked the basket. "By the way, what's your take on Addison James?"

"From a cop's point of view, she appears honest, with a hint of deceit behind those blue eyes of hers. From a personal point of view, she's intelligent, beautiful, sexy, snooty, and opinionated. Not my type."

"And you're falling in love with her."

"What…? No way, sis. You're out of your mind."

Ava let out a chuckle and lifted her brow in a smug stare. "Get over yourself, big brother. Gracie Howard happened eons ago."

Wade helped Ava with her coat. She collected the basket. "You might want to get that deputy as soon as possible. We've changed the festival venue to downtown. Vendors will set up on both sides of the street and in front of their stores. The sleigh parade will travel down Main Street with Santa and Mrs. Claus in the lead sleigh. On night two, we'll hold the children's fashion show and the bidding for a bachelor at the high school gym, with a dance to follow."

She stood on tiptoes to kiss her brother on the cheek. "If you keep brooding over Gracie, then you let her control your life. She wins and you lose." She patted his chest. "It's time to let go of the past. See you later."

"Yeah, later," Wade returned.

Ava left, and the office had never seemed emptier. With Millie and Freddie gone, the place echoed with loneliness. Just him and the fish. A constant reminder that he was all by himself.

Gracie.

Every time he thought of her, a chill raced through his blood. No, that wasn't it. His blood didn't run cold. In fact, thinking of her brought him to a boiling point.

He rolled his chair away from the desk and walked over to the double plate-glass doors. The view of the town was homey and festive. A great place to raise a family.

Family.

Yeah, Gracie had ruined that, too.

He returned to his chair, propped his feet on the desk, and stared at the fish tank.

Ava had told him to get a life, and in this case she was right. He had dug himself deeper into his rut. Hell, he'd fought in three wars and bore the forever scars. He'd faced down terrorists without fear. It wasn't that the past with Gracie held any allure for him. It was sheer terror of repeating with Addison the same mistake he'd made years ago, terrified of what it would do to him and to Addison.

For the remainder of the day, Wade was glad he was alone, his mood dark and brooding. Going over a pile of neglected paperwork, he was distracted by children's laughter. He pushed from his office chair and walked to the door. Addison and Nell strolled down the sidewalk holding hands with the twins. Addison looked happy—and maternal, which was mildly surprising. He'd never thought of her as anything other than a jet-setting, superficial, glamorous model.

Seeing her skipping down the sidewalk with the twins and laughing made him realize his feelings for her ran deeper than he thought. Not only because he wanted her in his bed but because he wanted her forever in his life. He remembered the abject hurt in her eyes when she'd told him about finding her fiancé having sex with another woman only mere minutes from walking down the aisle.

Addison deserved better than a quick tumble, no

matter how pleasurable or how explosive the experience. She deserved to be courted properly and with respect—even more so because he intended to claim her as his.

Chapter Nineteen

Addison noticed the light that shone from under the twins' bedroom door. She knocked, then swung the door wide. Two nearly identical faces pouted up at her. Joey and Julie sat propped against the headboard. The black lab that lay snuggled between them raised his head for a cursory look.

"It was lights out an hour ago. After your exciting day at the library, I thought you'd be fast asleep by now." It was the uncertainty in the children's eyes that brought her to sit on the edge of the bed.

Their questioning gaze met Addison's. She exhaled. "Are you hiding something under the covers?"

The twins shrugged and said nothing.

She kept her voice casual. "Whatever it is, you can show me."

Slowly the picture frame was pulled from beneath the quilt. The misery in the little boy's voice crushed Addison's heart. "What if she doesn't want us?"

Inwardly, she commiserated with the children. Although her experience had been different, her mother hadn't wanted her. And the question had always lingered—why?

"Will Aunt Nell send us away if our mommy doesn't want us?" Julie looked up at her imploringly.

Addison took the frame that held a picture of a

young woman wearing an Army uniform. She understood the twins' concerns. The unsmiling expression on the young soldier's face was less than endearing. She did a quick mental calculation and determined the twins' mother was probably no more than eighteen or nineteen years old at the time. She also understood that when the photo was taken the woman was probably directed not to smile.

"When was the last time you saw your mother?"

Joey and Julie looked at each other and shrugged. Their voices blended together. "We don't know. We only remember Gram."

Addison set the picture on the nightstand. She cleared her voice. "I suppose when a person is in the Army they don't get much time to visit family. Did she write you letters?"

Again, identical shrugs. Joey said, "Gram used to get letters. She would hug and kiss us and say it was from our mommy and that our mommy loved us."

"One time I got a dolly for Christmas and Joey got a…a…I forget."

"A flashlight. It didn't have batteries, and Gram never remembered to buy any. It's okay, though, 'cause she didn't have much money."

One time! She only sent them gifts one time! Addison's heart ached for these children. More and more she realized how fortunate she was to have spent her childhood at Hope Ranch, with a foster mother who gave each child a hug and tucked them in at night and encouraged them to say their prayers, and although it wasn't much, every child received a birthday gift on their special day and a present under the Christmas tree.

She said, "Scoot down under the covers." She

pulled the quilt up to their chins and then leaned forward and kissed each one of them. "Are you warm enough?"

Joey reached out and grabbed Addison's hand. "I hope Santa Claus got our letter. He'll make sure she comes to get us." Doubt dimmed the little boy's eyes and brought tightness to Addison's chest. "Won't he, Addison?"

Her eyes misted, and she blinked to clear them. How did she answer this question without giving him false hope? With a heavy heart, she said, "I'm sure Santa will do everything within his power to find her."

Julie gave Addison an anxious look. "Other kids at our school had daddies in the Army, and they came home for Christmas. Our mommy never did." She leaned close and kissed the black dog on the head. "I think only Gram loved us when we were little."

Addison offered a reassuring smile. "Aunt Nell and I love you, and Boomer, too."

Julie asked, "Will you be our mommy if she doesn't want us?"

Addison's brow furrowed with disquiet. She didn't want to commit with a promise she couldn't keep. "I believe you don't have anything to worry about. Now, close your eyes and think good thoughts so you'll have sweet dreams." She kissed them on their cheeks and turned out the lamp.

Nell stood outside the door as Addison left the room. She whispered, "I'm going to be mighty angry if she doesn't want those sweet young'uns." She motioned Addison to the living room.

Nell switched on a lamp, then turned off the Christmas tree lights. "If Wade had heard from those children's mother, he would have already let us know. I can think of two reasons why he hasn't. Maybe she's wounded and in a hospital—or heaven forbid, worse—or it's possible she has decided she doesn't want the children."

"You don't really think their mother would abandon them…"

Nell lifted her eyebrows and pursed her lips in an "I guess you've forgotten" expression.

"You're right. I'm a living, breathing example, aren't I?" Addison's expression grew solemn. "What will we do if their mother doesn't show up?"

Nell turned her head in the direction of the bedroom door. "Those children will always have a home as long as I'm alive and kicking."

A fierce gust of wind rattled the kitchen door. Nell rushed to make sure the lock was secure. She returned and assured Addison the door was solidly locked.

After a moment of silence, Addison gazed at Nell. "Who am I?" She waved her good hand. "Oh, I know my name and how I got it. I know I was found in a bus station and no one ever came forward to claim me. All my life I've wondered—who am I? Who was my mother, and why didn't she want me?" She wiped a tear from the corner of her eye. "I've held people at bay for fear of letting them get too close…for fear of not being good enough to be loved. I'm not even sure I truly loved Rowan." Her voice trailed off.

Nell clasped Addison's hand. "I wish I had the answers about your mother. The box with the news articles about you is in the attic. You poured over those clippings a million times when you were growing up. I've kept them in case you wanted them. And, just so you know, that Rowan guy is a real bastard. Be glad you found out about him before you were married—saved yourself more heartbreak and probably a costly divorce."

Addison squeezed Nell's hand. "You are so endearingly practical."

"I'll take that as a compliment." Nell stood. She pierced Addison with a stern frown. "You are Addison James—smart, successful, beautiful, and a woman with a lot of love to give. And don't you forget it." She yawned and said goodnight.

Addison stood at the base of the attic stairs. Why not let the ghosts of her past remain inside a box? The lure of what secrets might lie inside led her one step at a time until she stood at the door and opened it.

She switched on the light and glanced around the chilled and musty interior at memories that belonged to many of the children who had called Hope Ranch home. A rocking horse, a guitar missing its strings, a doll with one eye, a birdcage, a dress form, an antique desk, a cedar chest, and shelves laden with jars filled with buttons of every size and color, books, magazines, and Nell's rocking chair with a reading lamp next to it. Her place of escape, she used to call it. Addison brushed aside a cobweb.

She let her eyes rove around the room. Searching among the shelves, she discovered a wooden box with her name painted in red letters. Almost with reverence she carried her prize to the rocking chair. Memories, so many memories, flooded over her as she lifted the lid. On top were pictures of her and Ruby Raye, two scrawny little girls holding hands, several of herself on one of the draft horses, and one of her sitting next to a

Christmas tree holding an unopened gift. Addison sifted through the photos and laid them aside. A certificate for winning the fifth grade spelling bee, along with a couple of blue ribbons, brought back forgotten memories. She opened a small sketch pad, amazed at the layout of the ranch and an almost perfect rendering of the house, created by a young Addison, and pages filled with dress designs. She sat back in the rocker and closed her eyes, wondering what had become of that young girl's talent. Carefully laying the mementoes aside, Addison lifted out a manila folder. She undid the clasp and emptied the contents onto her lap—newspaper articles yellowed with age. Reading each report with care left her disappointed. None revealed a clue as to who had left her at the bus station or why. There was even an old police report that stated her name as Baby Anonymous. It was dated December 25. She was no closer to discovering her true identity than she was years ago.

The eagerness that had warmed her had worn off and left her chilled. Suddenly weary, she thought about the twins downstairs who fretted about whether or not their mother would want them, and the big black dog that slept between them as if he were the children's guardian angel.

She determined that if she ever had a child she would never give it up, no matter the reason. A bit dispirited, she carefully laid the contents back inside the box and replaced the lid. She rose from the rocker and returned the box to the shelf.

By the time she left the attic and had gone to the bathroom to remove her makeup and apply moisturizer to her face, she felt so emotionally tired that she barely had enough energy to change out of her clothes and into her pajamas and crawl into bed. Her body tightened into a ball between the cold sheets. As she lay there, waiting for the bed to warm and her body to relax, she tried to take the same advice she'd given the twins—think happy thoughts so she'd have sweet dreams.

A soft rap on the door intruded into the quiet. Addison forced herself to keep from screaming, *Go away.* "Who is it?"

Tears welled in her eyes and her bottom lip trembled when Nell entered the room and quietly sat on the edge of the bed, a cup of steaming cocoa in her hand. Addison reached over and turned on the lamp. She scooted against the headboard. Neither woman spoke.

Addison broke the silence. "A long time ago, I remember you telling Ruby and me that nothing in life ever comes easy." She set the cup aside and allowed Nell to wrap her in a comforting hug. She heard herself say, trying to keep the bitterness out of her voice, "Why is life so damned difficult?"

Nell held both of Addison's hands. "If I knew the answer I'd tell you." She met Addison's eyes, seeming to feel her pain as well. "A while back I saw a commercial on the television advertising one of those DNA kits to test your ancestry. If you think it'd put your mind to rest about who you are, I'll gladly pay for it."

Silence filled the room again.

Nell inhaled deeply. "I'm just an ol' fool. What do I know?"

Addison wiped at a tear that threatened to fall. "Don't put yourself down, Aunt Nell. You're a wise and wonderful woman. In many ways, I know who I am and what I've become, and how hard I've worked to get to this point in my life. It's not so much that I want to know the name of the woman who gave birth to me, or the man who was my sperm donor, but the *why*… If she didn't want me, why didn't she give me up for adoption instead of abandoning me in a bus station? Why didn't she at least pin a note on my dress with my real name and age?"

She swiped the tears. "I can tell you one thing. If I ever have a child, he or she will always know who they are and that they are loved without measure." Her heart pounded with a mixture of emotions. "Aunt Nell, I appreciate your generous offer. I've also considered getting a DNA test. Part of me is afraid of what I'll learn about my biological parents and another part of me says what's done is done. Remember when you used to tell me to let sleeping dogs lie? Maybe someday I'll do the test that will specifically determine my biological parents."

"There's no rush. You'll know when the time is right and, good or bad, whatever the results, I'll be right here to support you."

In a choked voice, she managed to say, "Aunt Nell, you are my *real* mother and the only one that counts."

She brought Nell's arthritic hands to her lips and kissed them. Nell's voice hitched. "My dear sweet, Addy, you have filled my heart to the point of overflowing." She kissed the top of Addison's head and bid her sweet dreams.

Addison turned out the light and slid deep beneath the quilt. A heady sense of freedom filled her. She had gained a true sense of belonging.

Chapter Twenty

A week before the Christmas festival, a young soldier disembarked from a Boise State transit bus at the Meadow Creek bus station. Inside the ticket office she asked directions to the sheriff's office. Outside, the sun moved across the sky, doing little to warm the temperature or boost the soldier's confidence.

She was a bit embarrassed and at the same time honored, while striding along the sidewalk through the town, that people stopped and thanked her for her service. Four blocks later, she marched up the steps to the sheriff's office. In a moment's hesitation, she turned as if changing her mind about entering. She hated to admit how panicked and unprepared she felt for meeting the twins she'd birthed but didn't know.

Heaving a sigh and mustering her courage, she pushed open the double doors and walked into the office's warm interior.

Millie looked up from her book. "Can I help you?"

The young soldier said, "I'm Private J.J. Wallace, to see Sheriff Wade Grey. The Red Cross said he has information about my children."

"Oh, my lord, you're her! I mean, we've been looking forward to meeting you." Millie offered a contrite smile. "I'm rambling, aren't I? Sheriff Grey is on a call. I'll let him know you're here. Would you like some coffee while you wait?"

"How long?"

"How long, what...oh, sure, ten or fifteen minutes at the most." Millie pointed to the coffeepot and cups. "Help yourself." She picked up the shortwave radio mic and contacted Wade.

While they waited, Millie said, "I'm sorry about your grandmother. We were all friends in high school... Nellie Hopewell, Clare, me, and some others, but that was eons ago. Except for Nell, we lost touch with Clare when she moved to Seattle. The children are staying out at the ranch with Nell."

J.J. squared her shoulders. She had learned to close off her emotions. She was a soldier; who could blame her? "I didn't know my grandmother was sick. Didn't know she'd died until I got word from the Red Cross." For lack of something else to say, she stowed her rucksack in a corner and walked over to the aquarium. "Nice fish."

After she removed her jacket and hung it on the coat rack, she took a cup and filled it with coffee. The cup's warmth felt good to her cold hands.

For want of conversation, Millie said, "You're just in time for Meadow Creek's Mistletoe Market and the Jingle Mingle. Don't you just love the holidays?"

J.J. cut her gaze back toward the aquarium. "I don't give much thought to the holidays, ma'am."

"Yes, well, make yourself comfortable. Sheriff Grey should arrive any minute."

J.J. was grateful when the woman opened a book. She toyed with the idea of cancelling the rest of her leave and returning to Fort Riley. She closed her eyes for a moment, and when she opened them looked straight into Wade's.

She squared her shoulders and, from force of habit, almost saluted.

****

A corner of Wade's mouth twitched into a parody of a smile as he observed the woman wearing a man's-cut blonde hair, her blue eyes void of emotion. "Relax, Private Wallace." He indicated the chair for her to sit. "We were getting concerned that perhaps the Red Cross hadn't made contact with your unit. Allow me to express my condolences regarding your grandmother."

"Thank you, sir. It took a while for me to get stateside. I went to Seattle first to visit my grandmother's grave, and to settle some of her affairs. I have fifteen days before reporting back to base."

Wade kept his eyes on her face. He understood her lack of emotion. From the report he'd received, her detail had been deep in terrorist territory. She'd been deployed for more than a year in some of Afghanistan's most treacherous areas. "Understood. How much time do you have left before your enlistment is up?"

The question seemed to take her by surprise. "Thirty days, sir. I had planned to re-up. Now, I'm not sure."

"I'll come straight to the point, Private Wallace. What do you plan to do about your children?"

"That's the part I'm not sure about, sir." She cut her glance toward Millie. "May I speak candidly?"

Wade nodded.

She opened her mouth, then closed it again as if collecting her thoughts. "When I was a kid, my old man was a slacker. He couldn't stay sober enough to hold a job. We moved around. I lost track of how many trailer parks we lived in, how many schools I attended, all the new and different faces—I never got to make any real friends. When he and my mom died, I went looking for love and found it in all the wrong places. I was seventeen and pregnant when my grandmother took me in. I had no job skills and was basically illiterate. When the twins were nine months old, I was slinging hamburgers at a truck stop and hanging out with the wrong crowd. It was only a matter of time before I ended up pregnant again. Gram suggested I join the Army. It's been the worst and the best five years of my life."

She rubbed her hands down the legs of her fatigues. "Most of my five years I've been deployed." She pierced him with a frank gaze. "I don't know my children, and to be honest, I'm scared to death to meet them."

She swiped a hand under her nose as a couple of tears welled in eyes that held a light of defiance. "I'm a damned good soldier, sir, but I'm not at all certain that I'm mother material."

Wade stood and walked over to Millie's desk. "Hand me the letter to Santa."

Millie opened her desk and removed the envelope. She gave him a questioning look as she handed it to him. He returned to his desk and sat, toying with the red envelope. He leaned forward. "Read this."

J.J. removed the letter and unfolded it. Her eyes darted back and forth across the page.

When she looked up, she saw the emotions that stormed in Wade's eyes when he ordered, "Out loud, Private. Read it out loud."

She cleared her throat, "Dear Santa, all me and my

sister want is for our mommy to love us. We promise to be extra good and collect the eggs, even if that old hen pecks us, and we'll feed the horses, and make our beds. We like living with Aunt Nell. She's nice, but can you bring our mommy home from the Army?"

Her bottom lip trembled, a sign that she struggled to hold the tears at bay. "What kind of life can I give my kids, huh? If I reenlist, who will take care of them when it's time for me to redeploy? If I separate from the Army, I'm unemployed and with no place to live."

She didn't cry. Soldiers didn't cry. She raised her chin and spoke with as much dignity as she could muster. "You got an answer for that, Sheriff?"

Wade sighed deeply, as if he resented being cursed with this assignment. "Joey and Julie are temporarily guests of Nell Hopewell at her ranch."

She swallowed hard and sat up straighter. "So why can't they continue to stay there? I'll send money for their support."

Wade kept his eyes on her face. "Nell Hopewell is seventy-five years old and with a bad heart. Does that answer your question?"

The realization that she was backed into a corner was a slap of surprise. Like a caged animal looking for an escape, J.J. paced back and forth, stopping occasionally to look at the fish and then at Wade. "I apologize, sir, for coming across as a hard-assed bitch. The truth is I don't know what to do. One thing is for certain—I refuse to give the children false hope."

An unexpected voice filled with anger said, "I was abandoned by my mother, and even after all these years, I've never understood why she didn't want me. How *dare* you even entertain the idea of leaving the twins wondering why they weren't good enough for you to want them."

Addison stood there, shocking them all with her presence. She continued, "Joey and Julie are bright and precious and already fear you don't love them. Instead of slinking off like a coward, the least you can do is explain why you're choosing the Army over them."

Wade wasn't certain whether he was glad or frustrated at Addison's arrival and her outburst.

J.J. rose from the chair, her arms stiff at her sides and fists clenched. "Ma'am, my children and what happens to them are none of your business."

The expression on Addison's face and her rigid stance reminded him of a she-grizzly ready to attack anyone who messed with her cubs. He positioned himself between the two women. "Private Wallace, this is Addison James. She's the owner of Hope Ranch. The children have become quite attached to her."

A slow smile spread over his face, and he stared at Addison for a long moment. His manhood itched, and he wished he could throttle the sensation. "I see you've got the cast off."

Her voice softened. "About ten minutes ago. I rode in with Emmett. He's down at the feed store." She shifted her eyes back to the woman in uniform. "Private Wallace—"

"Please, call me J.J."

Addison tried to keep her tone light. "J.J., I...we've all promised the twins the best Christmas ever. In fact, they are models in this year's children's Mistletoe fashion show. Bottom line—there's a spare bedroom at Hope Ranch. I'm personally requesting you give the children three days of your time. Get to know them, and…and let them believe Santa Claus answered their wish. After Christmas, if you choose the Army, I'll pay the airfare back to your base." She extended her hand. "Deal?"

A hush fell over the office. Only the soft whirring of the fish tank's pump interrupted the silence. For a moment, Wade was certain the young mother would ignore the olive branch Addison was extending, and walk out the door.

J.J. accepted Addison's hand. "It seems the sensible thing to do."

A horn beeped. "Grab your belongings, J.J.—Emmett doesn't like to be kept waiting."

Chapter Twenty-One

The wind chilled J.J.'s cheeks as she followed Addison down the steps and to the red vintage pickup. She tossed her gear into the back of the truck and climbed in next to Addison.

After the introductions were made, J.J. sat in silence, taking in her surroundings. Emmett said, "I was a Marine, myself. Thirty years. So was our sheriff. In fact, he retired just three years ago. He served a lengthy stint in Afghanistan, too."

She glanced over at the man. He didn't look like a Marine. He just looked old. He was tanned and lean, and his hair was streaked gray. His jeans were worn and his denim jacket faded blue. The hands that gripped the steering wheel were calloused. From years of hard work, she guessed. So unlike her worthless father. "Good to know, sir."

She squeezed her hands into a ball and fell silent, not encouraging further conversation. She found it difficult that she was actually on her way to meet her children. Gazing out at the countryside, she marveled at the cows and horses that lifted their heads in curiosity to watch the truck pass by. At one point she watched a squirrel shimmy along a wooden fence to leap onto the bough of a tree.

She peered through her sunglasses at the rolling,

snow-covered expanse that stretched out before her. This beautiful land. She could easily see herself settling here, if only she had a way to support her children.

An uneasy feeling coursed through her.

Emmett maneuvered the truck up a gentle slope, and then up another hill before turning into a tree-lined driveway that led up to the two-story house, barely making it to the porch before a young boy and a big black dog came racing out to greet them.

J.J.'s heart beat like a wild thing against her chest. It reminded her of her first firefight with a group of terrorists. Except this six-year-old child wasn't the enemy. It had been a lifetime since she'd seen Joey and his sister, and if circumstances and places had been different she wasn't sure she'd have recognized him.

She opened the door and climbed down from the truck.

He smiled up at her. They were the bluest eyes she had ever seen. The blood rushed to her head, and her knees threatened to buckle.

Nell and Julie walked out onto the porch. The little girl grabbed blindly at Nell's sleeve and whispered, "Is that her?"

"My word," was all Nell said.

Fighting the crippling sensation that had taken over her legs, J.J. stood rooted. *Dear God, they are beautiful children.*

Nell hugged the sweater closer to her body. "Well, don't just stand there. Come in out of the cold. Wade called to let us know we'd have a special visitor. Emmett, can you stay for a bit?"

He hauled the backpack from the truck and handed it to the young soldier. He glanced at J.J. rather indifferently before giving his attention back to Nell. "Gotta take a raincheck, Nell. Call me if you need anything." He climbed back into the pickup, tooted the horn, and drove down the long drive.

Joey grabbed Addison's hand. "You got your cast off. Did it hurt?"

She ruffled the top of his blond head. "No, Dr. Ava was very careful." She smiled down at him. "I was a little bit afraid."

His eyes widened. "Gosh." He followed her up the steps and into the house. "I'm glad it didn't hurt."

Nell invited everyone into the kitchen. "It's about our dinnertime. I hope you like bacon-and-potato soup."

"And homemade gingersnaps. Aunt Nell makes the best," the twins said in unison.

Nell's gaze fell upon J.J. again, a little more attentively this time. For a long moment, she studied the young woman's face.

J.J. suddenly felt self-conscious in front of all these onlookers. She opened her mouth to say, "Thank you for inviting me to stay," but before she had a chance, Joey drew his brows together with a look of concern.

Doubt laced his cherubic voice. "Are you really our mommy?"

J.J. felt the color drain from her face like a slow, painful torture. No one spoke. There was only the uncomfortable sound of the spoon ladling soup out of the pot and into the bowls.

Her whole body went numb. Her eyes turned to Addison and pleaded for help.

Addison came to the rescue. "Joey…Julie…didn't you write Santa a letter asking him to bring your mother home for Christmas?"

Two identical heads bobbed up and down.

"Go to your bedroom and get the picture on your nightstand and bring it to the kitchen."

As soon as the twins left the kitchen, Nell glanced from Addison to J.J. "Wade gave me the short version of your doubt about the children." She pointed the spoon forward. "Don't you dare leave those precious young'uns with broken hearts, do you hear me?"

J. J. bristled at Nell's gritty tone. "Yes, ma'am. Loud and clear."

"Good. Now that we've got that straight, you're more than welcome to stay as long as you like. We'll talk more tonight."

Gasps at the doorway were followed by, "It is her!" Joey held up the picture. He looked at his sister. "See, I told you if we were extra good Santa would give us our wish."

Julie's face lit up at that. "Are we going to live with you?"

The little girl's question struck J.J. hard. She stood there, saying nothing, feeling depleted and exhausted and manipulated. She settled on a stool at the long white countertop, trying very hard not to look at the twins because every time she did it seemed to invite another question she couldn't answer.

Nell set bowls of soup at each chair. "Your mother has had a long and tiring trip. I'm sure after she's rested she'll answer all of your questions. Besides, we're all hungry." She cut a look toward J.J.

J.J. focused on her bowl for a minute. She cleared her throat. "Your letter to Santa said you collected eggs. Tomorrow I'd like it if you'd show me the chickens and the horses."

Julie lifted her sweet gaze toward J.J. "Is it okay if we call you Mommy?"

Joey shoveled a spoonful of soup into his mouth. "I know how to hitch up the horses to the sleigh. Uncle Emmett showed me."

Addison was curious all of a sudden about the twins' father. If J.J. couldn't or wouldn't take care of the twins, then what about the father? She made a mental note to ask.

Julie giggled. "We're going to model clothes at the Mistletoe Fashion Show. I get to wear a fancy dress."

Joey's enthusiasm topped his sister's. "And we're gonna help Aunt Nell decorate the sleigh for the parade, and Uncle Emmett is gonna let me help him drive the sleigh. Are you coming to the parade?"

Both twins begged, "Please, Mommy. Please."

J.J. turned her attention back to the soup. After a long pause, she said, "It sounds like fun."

When dinner and dessert were finished, the twins were excused to play in the living room. They invited their mother to see the Christmas tree they had helped cut down and decorate. The beauty and warmth of the home filled J.J. It felt like a welcoming hug, from the twinkling lights on the brightly decorated tree to the landscape pictures on the wall and the artful curtains on the windows, and most of all the flickering fire in the fireplace.

She sat cross-legged in front of the fire. The twins settled on either side of her. Joey tugged at her arm. "Mommy, why did you go away and leave us with Gram?"

J.J. drew in a bracing breath to keep from bursting

into tears in front of the children. She was a seasoned soldier, and no crying was allowed.

"When I was young, my mama and daddy died in a terrible accident. We were already living with Gram, but she was old and didn't have a job. Instead of finishing school and getting a good education, I made poor decisions which…landed me in trouble…and you guys were born. Gram couldn't work, and without a good education I couldn't get a job making enough money to take care of all of us. That's why I joined the Army."

Julie scooted around to face her mother. She leaned forward, her expression serious, and placed tiny hands on each side of J.J.'s cheeks. "You don't like Joey and me, and you're going to leave, aren't you?"

"Yeah." Joey sighed. "It's okay, 'cause we have Aunt Nell and Addison, and Uncle Emmett, and Sheriff Grey."

J.J. drew her bottom lip between her teeth. Thick despair choked her. "Of course I like you. Why would you think I don't?"

The twins' silence filled every corner of the room. The silence dragged on for several moments.

No one saw the shock that rippled across the faces of Addison and Nell. The children stood when Nell said, "Tell your mother goodnight, and come along to bed. We have a busy day tomorrow."

Addison hugged each of the children as she met J.J.'s troubled gaze. When they were alone, J.J. paced about the room. She placed her hands in the back pockets of her fatigues. "I don't understand why they'd say such a thing. I mean, they should know I love them."

Addison settled on the couch. "Joey and Julie are quite astute for six-year-olds. Not once since you arrived have you hugged them or touched them, or offered any semblance of affection."

"Well, I—"

Addison held up her hand. "Let me finish." She repeated what the twins had related about other military parents visiting their children at school. "You can't tell me that you didn't have enough leave time when you could have visited. Those babies don't remember receiving telephone calls or birthday cards from you, much less gifts. You stand there with your face looking like a piece of carved stone...not even a genuine *I love you* smile for your own children. And you dare ask that they should know you love them?"

Before J.J. could answer, Addison rushed on, "What about their father?"

Nell joined them. She sat in her favorite chair next to the fireplace and waited.

J.J. gave each woman a critical look. "Don't judge me until you've walked in my shoes." Just as quickly, she apologized. "I do love my children. Maybe not like mothers who've been with their kids for more than just a few months after giving birth. Don't ask me why I stayed away. I can give you every excuse in the world and it would still be an excuse. I figured if I wasn't in their lives and I got killed during a raid, it wouldn't be as hard on them. That's why I stayed away and why I didn't send gifts. Gram tried to tell me." She shrugged and spread her hands wide. "I don't know why I didn't listen."

Addison shook her head in disbelief. "And the father, why isn't he in their lives?"

J.J. cursed under her breath. "I'm ashamed to admit that I don't know who the father is. Back then I wasn't particular about who or how many I slept with. I guess that's another reason I stayed away. Eventually, the twins will ask that same question. What am I supposed to say—your mother whored around and you're mutts because she doesn't know who's your daddy?" She hastened on. "I've changed. I'm not like that now. The Army has taught me values and self-respect. The thing is I don't know how to be anything other than a soldier."

A sudden creaking of the old house let them know the wind was picking up. It was almost ten, and Nell suggested they call it a night.

J.J. followed Addison up the stairs. At the door to the spare bedroom, Addison said, "What is your job in the Army?"

"I'm a member of the field artillery team. We're a combat unit, ma'am."

"If you had a job, would you leave the Army?"

"I refuse to live hand to mouth, Ms. James. I want my children to have better than I had when I was growing up."

For several seconds the two women stood in silence. J.J. had hedged around the question. This was not the answer Addison had hoped for.

Addison locked gazes with the young soldier. "I meant what I said about paying airfare back to your base if you decide to choose the Army over your children. Goodnight." Addison quietly left J.J. standing outside the bedroom door and made her way down the hall to her own room.

Chapter Twenty-Two

Thankful for the recently installed internet and wi-fi at the house, Addison opened the screen of her cell phone and speed-dialed Wade's number. The mere thought of hearing his voice sent her heart thumping into overdrive.

"Addison, is anything wrong at the ranch?"

"How did you—oh, caller ID, of course. There's no emergency, and I know it's late, but I want to run an idea past you. I'm too excited to wait until morning."

"Okay, you have my attention."

"I may have a solution for your deputy problem."

"And that would be?"

"Would you consider hiring a woman for a deputy?"

"You're not considering trading your career as a ranch resort owner for law enforcement, are you?"

Addison tsked. She could tell by the tone of his voice that he was joshing. "Don't be a smart ass. I'm serious."

She imagined his smile when he said, "I would consider hiring a woman if she was qualified. Do you have someone in mind?"

"Actually, I do. J.J. Wallace told me she is assigned to a field artillery team. It seems that with her military training she'd have the discipline and mental fortitude to transition into law enforcement. I was thinking that with her combat experience, maybe you'd consider hiring her?"

"Have you talked to her about this?"

"Not exactly. I asked if she'd leave the Army if she had a job." Addison repeated the conversation and J.J.'s response. "Wade, if she chooses to remain in the military, it sickens me to think about what will happen to Joey and Julie. Six-year-olds—and especially twins—are considered almost unadoptable, and the chances only get worse as a child gets older. I'm the voice of experience."

"Yeah, Ava and I were eleven when we were adopted. We were lucky."

A rush of new emotions coursed through her as she sat waiting for Wade's response to her suggestion. Suddenly she trembled with grief for the twins' uncertain future.

"Addison, I'm not opposed to your idea. As long as she doesn't have a criminal record and receives an honorable discharge from the Army, I could hire her on the condition that she completes the academy."

"That's wonderful. Would you mind presenting the idea to her? She seems to view me more as an enemy than a friend."

"You did come across like a tough sergeant." Wade chuckled. "It'll have to wait a few days. With the festival ready to open, the town is filling up with tourists. Being short-handed, I need to stick close."

"I understand. We're in need of decorations for the sleigh competition. It will give me an excuse to drive to town for supplies. Maybe J.J. would like to do a little Christmas shopping for the twins. Would it be inconvenient for you to accidentally bump into us at BB's café around noon?"

"Noon at BB's. I'll try to act inconspicuous. "

Addison said goodnight and set her phone aside. A smile curved her lips. The idea of seeing Wade tomorrow lifted her mood.

****

For a woman who'd openly voiced her dislike for Christmas, Addison's seeming change of heart was genuinely pleasing to Wade. He wanted her in his life. He couldn't force her to let him into her life if she didn't want him there. He thought about the stupid son of a bitch who had never deserved her.

Was he any better? He hadn't told her about Gracie.

In an effort to veer from unwanted feelings toward Addison, he opened a drawer and removed a manual to brush up on hiring standards for a new deputy.

There was something about J.J. Wallace's demeanor that had impressed him. Other than morally, she was under no obligation to come to Meadow Creek. For her to do so clued him that deep down a spark of maternal love lay waiting to be fully ignited. He'd grown fond of Joey and Julie, and he commiserated with the uncertainty of their future.

He contacted his answering service to let them know he was clocking out. At the stroke of midnight he locked the office. Tomorrow would be another long day. He sprinted through the cold toward his cruiser. The more he thought about offering J.J. Wallace an opportunity to remain with her children and become gainfully employed as his deputy, the more his mood lightened. He switched on the radio and sang along with

Burl Ives' rendition of "A Holly Jolly Christmas."

Chapter Twenty-Three

Christmas carols and noisy chatter filled BB's Café. Addison scanned the room for an empty table.

"Merry Christmas, Addison. Who's this you have with you… Nope, don't tell me." Brenda Brown touched the side of her nose and with a rouge-cheeked jolly smile said, "Let me guess—you must be Joey and Julie's mother. They are two of the most precious little dumplings. I'll bet they're excited to have you home. Are you staying in Meadow Creek? Of course not, silly me. You're in the Army." Brenda prattled on as she led Addison and J.J. through the maze of tables. She handed them a menu. "I'll return in a jiff to take your orders."

J.J. seated herself and scowled over the open menu. "Is she always that yappy?"

"Brenda means well." Addison lifted her brows. "Look around. There are other restaurants in Meadow Creek. BB's is always the most crowded. Her food is outstanding, and she mothers everyone."

Brenda returned and took their orders. While they waited for the food to arrive, J.J. said, "That's one wicked scar. How did you get it?"

Powerful emotions welled up inside Addison, mostly anger. She touched the line of healing tissue. "In another life I was a model. During a show, a poorly constructed runway collapsed."

"*Was?*"

"I retired. Aunt Nell and I recently became business partners. After Christmas we plan to restructure Hope Ranch into a vacation resort."

J.J. gave Addison a questioning look. "I'm curious. You said you were abandoned as a child. How does an orphan become successful enough to buy a ranch?"

Addison cocked an eyebrow. "Hard work and perseverance, plus a boatload of tenacity."

Brenda returned with a tray and unloaded the food. "Whew, by the time I close tonight, these dogs will be barking for relief." She laughed at her joke and bustled off.

J.J. smiled. "I waited tables once. She's right about her feet hurting."

"That's nice."

"What…about my feet hurting?"

"No. It's nice to see you smile."

A flush of pink tinged J.J.'s tanned cheeks. "Yeah, I guess. When you've seen the things I've seen, there isn't much to smile about."

"I'm sorry, J.J. You're awfully young to have experienced so much."

Addison glanced over the young soldier's shoulder, and there he stood. He wore a heavy coat over his tan pants. He removed his cap and tucked it inside a pocket. Seeing him made her remember the night he'd held her in his arms, and the way his lips had tasted. It wasn't the blast of cold air that caused her to shiver.

It was as if a magnet had drawn his gray eyes to hers. His heated gaze warmed her. What she wanted to feel was admiration for a handsome sheriff. Not love.

She didn't want any part of that particular emotion. Not anymore. She donned a polite mask as he approached.

A muscle in his jaw jumped. "Afternoon, ladies, mind if I join you?"

Addison extended her hand toward a chair as an invitation to sit. The scent of brisk winter air lingered on his clothes.

A waitress bustled over with a cup of coffee and a bowl of steaming venison chili topped with shredded cheese and a slice of garlic toast. "Brenda saw you come in, Sheriff. She figured you'd want your usual." She set the food in front of him and rushed to take an order from another table.

Addison arched her eyebrows at him and grinned. "With the festival and all the people it's drawing, now doesn't seem like a good time to be shorthanded."

Returning her smile, Wade loaded his spoon and enjoyed a mouthful of chili. He shifted his attention to J.J. "Actually, Private Wallace, you've been on my mind."

J.J. stiffened. "How so, sir?"

Wade toyed with his spoon. "I did a little checking, and with your field artillery and combat experience, have you considered transitioning from the military to law enforcement?"

He went on to explain about his deputy leaving to take a position in Maryland. He also explained that he'd retired from the Marines, and with his dad being the former sheriff, it only seemed logical that he chose law enforcement over other career choices. "Even though Meadow Creek depends mostly on tourist dollars, it's a good place to live and raise children. We have excellent schools, a community college, and a hospital. The bottom line is, Private Wallace, I need a deputy. If you're interested, the pay is good, and mostly the job is dull. That's the primary reason Deputy Sumner transferred to a crime unit. He craved excitement."

The question seemed to take J.J. by surprise. "I have no experience, sir, but it's certainly something I'd seriously consider. What kind of schooling is required?"

Wade filled her in on the requirements and other job-related details. "In the meantime, you could work with me on the condition that you successfully complete the training at the academy. You'd be on the payroll." He finished off his coffee and wiped his mouth with a napkin. "There's no need to make an immediate decision. Think about it."

"What's the first step, sir? I mean do I fill out an application?"

"The first step is to obtain an honorable discharge from the Army."

J.J. furrowed her brow with incredulity. "I don't need to think about it, sir. My answer is—yes! Thank you for this opportunity. I won't let you down." She swallowed hard. "This is going to be the best Christmas ever. I can't wait to tell Joey and Julie." She drew a deep breath and grinned. "Addison, will you help me select gifts for my children, and a couple of new outfits for myself, and something for Mrs. Hopewell, too?"

Addison didn't try to suppress her own smile. "It'd be my pleasure. And she prefers to be called 'Aunt Nell.' "

Wade situated the cap on his head. "Duty calls, ladies." His eyes glinted with humor. "My dispatcher and her sister shared a house that's a duplex. Cora moved to Florida last week to be closer to her daughter and grandchildren. I know for a fact that Millie plans to rent out the side her sister lived in. It's two bedrooms, two bathrooms, and located across the street from the elementary school, only two blocks from the office. I'm sure the rent is reasonable. If you're interested, stop by the office and talk to Millie."

J.J.'s voice hitched. "My head is spinning. I don't know what to say except...thank you."

Something that was definitely the faint stirrings of Christmas spirit filled Addison. She couldn't remember the last time she'd witnessed this type of generosity.

Night was closing in by the time Addison turned the car off the main highway and up the lane. Smoke curled from the chimney of the ranch house. Christmas tree lights twinkled from a living room window.

The sight brought a smile, reminding Addison of innocent, long-ago days as a kid. What Nell couldn't afford in material gifts, she'd made up for in love. Pleasant memories of snowball fights and making snow angels with the other foster kids brought a surprising sense of nostalgia.

J.J.'s voice interrupted Addison's musing. "I hope Julie and Joey like their walkie-talkies and story books, and the extra special surprise."

"They're good children, J.J. The best gift you've given them is yourself."

"I can't wait to tell them that we're staying in Meadow Creek."

"Why don't you give them the news tonight as an early Christmas gift?"

J.J.'s laughter mingled with Addison's as they entered the house. Two exuberant children, one excited black lab, and a smiling Nell acted as the welcoming committee. Nell said, "Supper's waiting."

At the table, J.J. clapped her hands together in glee. "I have an early Christmas present for Joey and Julie."

The twins giggled. "Is it under the tree? Can we unwrap it? Did Santa bring it?"

J.J. glanced at Addison who gave an encouraging nod. J.J. grinned. "No, it's not under the tree, and no, you can't unwrap it because it's not a thing, and yes, in a way Santa did bring it. Now, hurry and finish your supper. Aunt Nell, do you mind if we have hot chocolate in the living room by the fireplace?"

"You betcha. I'm as excited as the twins."

A vast happiness permeated the kitchen. During the evening meal there were unexpected lapses in the conversation until after the meal was finished and the dishwasher loaded. With a carafe of hot chocolate in Nell's hands, the twins carried the cups and saucers to the living room.

Nell sat in her favorite chair by the fire and proceeded to fill each cup with hot chocolate. The twins settled on the floor next to Boomer.

Almost whispering, doubt shining on her face, J.J. said, "Joey, Julie, how would you like to live in Meadow Creek and go to school here?"

Their eyes filled with tears. Julie's face crumpled into a picture of sadness. Joey wrapped his arm around his sister's shoulders. He sniffled. "I guess you're going back to the Army."

J.J. scooted off the couch and gathered the children in her arms. She kissed the tops of their blonde heads. "I didn't mean to make you cry. Please don't…don't cry. I meant this to be a happy surprise. I'm *leaving* the

Army and I'm going to work for Sheriff Grey as his deputy. And I already have a house for us. It's right across the street from the school you'll attend."

The twins hugged their mother. "For real, Mommy?"

J.J. explained to the children that after Christmas she'd have to return to her command base to officially leave the Army. "I'll be back to enroll you in school. When I return, we'll go shopping for furniture to fill our new home."

Joey continued to stare down at his shoes.

J.J. lifted her son's face to look at hers. "What's wrong, Joey? Aren't you happy about living in Meadow Creek and going to a new school?"

He sniffed. His eyes filled with tears. "The kids at our old school didn't like us. Maybe the kids here won't like us either."

Julie chimed in, "No, they didn't like us. They said bad things about us."

A muscle in J.J.'s jaw ticked as she shifted a puzzled glance toward Addison and Nell. Her words dripped with compassion. "What kind of bad things did the kids say about you?"

The little boy looked at his mother with tears in his eyes. His chin quivered as he spoke. "'Cause we didn't have a mama or a daddy, and Gram was really old, and 'cause…'cause of our clothes, they said we were *throwaways* and nobody wanted us. Then Gram died and some people came and got us and brought us here." His voice trembled.

Julie wiped her nose on her sleeve. "Yeah, they said only trash got thrown away."

The words stung, causing J.J. to flinch. She lifted

her son's drooping chin with her finger. "It was mean of those children to say such ugly words to you and your sister."

She opened her arms and gathered the twins close. "*I* want you, and *I* love you. Together we're going to make a wonderful new life in Meadow Creek."

Nell lifted her shirttail and dabbed at the tears in her eyes. She lifted her cup. "I propose a toast to—family." She added, "I'm sure Clare is up there in heaven wearing a great big smile."

Chapter Twenty-Four

The next few days were busy, with everyone helping Nell bake gingerbread men and a variety of cupcakes for the festival. Hours of mulling over ideas on how to decorate the sleigh for the parade ended with the twins standing in a corner whispering to each other.

Joey timidly stepped forward. "We have an idea."

"Yes, we have an idea." Julie smiled.

Nell dusted flour from her hands. "Don't keep it a secret. Tell us."

Joey pointed to his mother. "Mommy's in the Army, and Uncle Emmett was a Marine. They could wear their uniforms, and Julie and me and Addison and Aunt Nell can ride in the sleigh and wave flags."

Not to be left out, Julie said, "Yes, and with a Christmas tree, too."

When no one said anything, Joey hung his head and looked down at the tips of his shoes. "It's okay. It was just an idea."

Nell clapped her hands together, sending up a cloud of flour dust. "It's a grand idea. We can string red, white, and blue lights and tinsel, and I can whip up a couple of blankets that look like flags to drape over Chipper and Bud's backs. Somewhere in the attic is an old artificial Christmas tree that we can decorate to match the sleigh."

J.J. bent down and planted a kiss on her son's cheek and hugged Julie. "The two of you are geniuses."

Joey giggled and brushed at his cheek. "Aw, Mommy."

Addison grabbed her cell phone and dialed a supply warehouse to place an order for all the supplies needed to decorate the sled. "Yes, you heard me correctly. Overnight delivery. I need this order tomorrow."

Nell used the landline to place her own call. "Hello, Emmett…Nell. Listen, I have a favor to ask, and it's important." She explained about the children's idea to use a military-patriotic theme for their sleigh. "So will you wear your uniform and drive the sleigh?"

Four pairs of eyes and ears waited for a response. Even Boomer sat quietly as if he, too, was waiting.

Nell nodded. "I owe you one, Emmett."

She cradled the receiver. A wide grin spread over her face and crinkled the corners of her eyes. "He said, 'You're danged tootin' I'll do it.' "

The twins pumped their little fists up and down in victory. "Yippee!"

"Let's pray the weather holds." Nell expressed her concern.

Addison checked the weather app on her phone. Her eyes lit up. "Clear skies the entire weekend."

****

The next afternoon, a half hour after lunch, Boomer's toenails clacked across the floors and his frenzied barks notified everyone in the house that a strange vehicle approached the yard. Joey raced ahead of Addison, down the hall, and into the living room. He peered out the window. "Addison, it's a delivery man."

Addison rushed to the door. She ordered the black lab to stay while she opened the door and walked out to the porch. She pointed and shouted to the driver, "Would you mind driving your truck to the barn? We'll unload the boxes inside there."

She grabbed her jacket and pulled it on while trotting down the steps. She heard J.J. order the twins to put on their jackets and caps. "C'mon, we'll help, too."

J.J. held Joey and Julie's hands as they skipped across the snow. After Addison signed for the packages, an assembly line was formed, with the delivery guy handing out boxes. The twins toted smaller and lighter packages inside the barn.

Finally, the driver wished the group a Merry Christmas, climbed into the truck, and drove away.

The sled sat in the barn's wide aisle. Curious barn cats and the horses added their own excitement with meows and nickers. The chickens clucked, and Boomer raced up and down the aisle.

"Can we start decorating now?" The twins bubbled with enthusiasm.

Nell answered seconds later, "I'll keep the hot beverage and snack line going while all of you work your creative magic."

Shortly before eight o'clock that evening, Emmett and Nell entered the barn. Emmett held a plastic container. "I've brought over a small generator. Let's hook 'er up and see if the lights work."

Shouts of glee filled the drafty old building as red, white, and blue lights twinkled around the sleigh and lit up the Christmas tree. The twins declared, "It's really beautiful, isn't it, Mommy?"

J.J. gathered the children to her side. "Yes, it really

is."

"Once the horses are hitched, I'll run a string of lights along their harness." Emmett tucked Nell's hand in the crook of his arm. "I vote we go to the house and toast marshmallows in the fireplace and make s'mores. All this hard work calls for a celebration."

Emmett's intimate gesture wasn't lost on either Addison or J.J. and brought a smile from each of them.

Nell grumbled, "But Emmett, I don't have the marshmallows or the fixin's to make s'mores, and it's too late to drive to town."

He tossed a conspiratorial look at the twins. "There's a big paper sack in the front seat of my truck. I brought marshmallows, peanut butter, chocolate, and graham crackers. Why don't you young'uns fetch the bag and meet us in the house."

A smile lit the little boy's face. "Race you, Julie!" Joey sprinted ahead of his sister toward the truck, with Boomer hot on their heels.

J.J. laughed out loud. "Thank you, Addison."

Addison scrunched a puzzled look at the young woman. "For what?"

J.J. expelled an audible sigh. "For making things happen. I think you know what I mean." She, too, dashed to the truck.

After satisfying themselves with ample toasted marshmallows and treats, the twins lay in front of the fireplace with Boomer snuggled between them. The fire crackled and popped in the quiet as the adults sipped steaming cups of hot chocolate.

Emmett rolled the cup between his hands. "J.J., I'm glad you're gonna live in Meadow Creek. Wade's as good a sheriff as they come. I don't think you'll regret becomin' a deputy."

"Thanks." J.J. finished off her cocoa. "I'm looking forward to a new start and providing a promising future for my children." She set her empty cup on the coffee table. "If you'll excuse me, it's time to put these two sleepyheads to bed. They've had a busy day. I think I'll turn in also."

Joey and Julie rose from the floor and yawned as they hugged Nell, Addison, and Emmett. "G'night."

The old man stared after the young soldier and her children. He scratched the end of his nose.

"You got something on your mind, Emmett?"

"What would make you think I've got something on my mind, Nell?"

"Because you always scratch the end of your nose when you're troubled, or trying to make a decision, or both."

Addison uncrossed her legs. "If you'll excuse me—"

Emmett cleared his throat. "Uh, would you mind stayin', Addison? This concerns you, too."

Addison and Nell exchanged curious glances. She settled back on the couch. "It sounds serious. You're not ill, are you?"

"Nothing so drastic, although I am gettin' a little long in the tooth." He pursed his lips and furrowed his brow. "Those fellas in that black limo, the ones I told you had driven back and forth in front of the house, paid me a call yesterday mornin'." He whipped a business card from his shirt pocket and handed it to Addison.

The easy atmosphere was gone. A disquiet settled over the room.

Addison gasped, making her anger evident. "They didn't threaten you, did they?"

"Not exactly. They said their boss wanted to make me an offer I couldn't refuse. I didn't exactly take kindly to the tone of their voices. I did call Wade and let him know."

Nell frowned. "My gosh, Emmett, what're you going to do?"

"I'll tell you what I'm not goin' to do. I'm not cowin' down and I'm not accepting any offers from this Megala Corporation. I've got me a plan. It involves Addison, now that she's the new owner of Hope Ranch and the two of you are partners. Thing is it's late and I don't see so well at night anymore. Maybe I should wait until I've worked out all the details."

"You ol' coot, that's like dangling a steak in front of a starving dog! Why'd you even bring it up if you don't have all the details worked out in your head? I won't sleep a wink tonight."

He stood and grabbed his hat and coat. He huffed. "Guess that's what gettin' old does to you, Nell. My apologies. I didn't mean to worry you."

Nell's voice held little patience. "Sit down. The rest of the week's going to be too busy for any of us to have a spare moment, and then it's Christmas. You're not going anywhere until you've told us what's on your mind."

Emmett squared his shoulders and hung his coat and hat back on the rack. "I swear, Nell, you are one bossy woman." The crevices on both sides of his face deepened with his smile as he settled on the sofa.

The question again crossed Addison's mind as to why Emmett and Nell had never married. Even at his age he was a ruggedly handsome man and with an old-fashioned respect for women that most men no longer possessed.

"I'm sellin' the Oxbow." He held up his hand to stop any comments or questions. "Just hear me out. The only heir I have is a nephew who was born with dollar signs in his eyes. He'd sell the ranch in a heartbeat. I've worked too hard and too long to see the land ripped into little lots with crackerbox-sized houses built on them." He drew a breath. "Couple of weeks ago, the university contacted me about sellin' them two hundred acres. They plan to expand their agricultural science and animal husbandry departments. I told them to give me time to think it over."

Emmett stood with his backside toward the fireplace. "The ranch is free of debt." He heaved a hefty sigh. "Even so, the taxes increase every year. Not only that, the men who work for me are my age and ready to ride rockin' chairs. It takes young men to run a ranch the size of Oxbow."

He twisted the tip of his white mustache, a rascally glint in his aging blue eyes. "Those rapscallions with their implied threats made up my mind. Right after they left, I called the university and offered them the entire four hundred acres. They accepted my offer and my price with no hagglin'. Then I drove over and signed preliminary sale papers."

He drew a breath and rubbed the back of his neck. He gave a light laugh. "From the looks on your faces, I reckon I've surprised the daylights out of you."

Shaking her head in disbelief, Nell huffed, "For gosh sakes, Emmett. I don't know what to say. I understand your reasoning, but I never in a hundred years thought you'd sell the ranch."

Addison was as surprised as Nell at the man's declaration. She fixed him with a questioning stare. "You said this involved Nell and me."

Emmett returned to the sofa. "Addison, you mentioned that Hope Ranch will need a handyman. I'd like to apply for the job."

At her expression, he shook his head. "Nope, hear me out. The university will convert my house to offices and livin' quarters for the staff. A couple of the barns will become dorms. That way the students get hands-on experience and earn credits without havin' to leave the ranch."

His voice became a little raw and husky. "I'm not much on livin' in town or in an apartment, and I'm dang sure not ready for a nursin' home. I'll remodel that ol' tool shed behind the barn into suitable livin' quarters, and with what I'll receive from the sale of the ranch, plus my retirement, I won't need a paycheck. Like I said, I'm gettin' too old to run a ranch, but I'm still young enough to do odd jobs and the like."

He shifted a wary glance from Nell to Addison. "Of course, I'll understand if—"

Addison remembered all the times Emmett had been around when she was a child—helping Nell with chores, taking the kids on hiking trips, even taking them to task when they got a little out of hand. He'd been a positive male role model for all the children at Hope Ranch. How could she say no to this man who'd been like a father or an uncle to her? The answer was easy.

She couldn't stop the twitch at the corner of her mouth. "Nell?"

The older woman answered with a smile and a nod.

Addison stood and offered her hand to Emmett. "You've got yourself a deal on one condition."

With a reluctant look, he accepted her hand. "What is the condition?"

She smiled. "That you let me design the floor plans for the tool shed."

Emmett's eyes twinkled, and Addison could see his delight.

Chapter Twenty-Five

The town was packed on opening day of the festival. The aroma of roasting chestnuts filled the air. At the petting zoo, Joey and Julie squealed with delight as they petted baby goats and pleaded with their mother to get them a puppy.

J.J. explained that she'd need to get permission to have a dog at their new home. "Taking care of a puppy is a big responsibility. I don't want you to be disappointed if Miss Millie says no."

"That's okay," the twins chimed. "We can always visit Boomer."

She checked her watch. "We'd better hurry. It's almost time for the sleigh parade to begin."

By dusk, the decorated sleighs and prancing horses had lined up for the parade, and spectators stood waiting on both sides of Main Street. Mayor Dorothy Clark stood on the podium in front of the massive, twenty-foot, brightly lit Christmas tree. She tapped the microphone.

"Welcome, everyone, to Meadow Creek's sixtieth annual Mistletoe Festival and, thanks to Ms. Addison James, our first annual sleigh parade. The leader of our parade, of course, is Santa and Mrs. Claus."

She addressed the sleigh drivers. "Drivers, you will guide your sleighs once around the town square, keeping your horses to a walk, and then on to the parking lot at the elementary school."

She added, "Judges, do you have your score sheets ready?"

A committee held their clipboards high and answered, "We're ready, Mayor."

"All right, then. Folks, don't forget—as soon as the parade is over, head to the school's auditorium for our first annual Mistletoe children's fashion show. Winners of the sleigh contest will be announced right after the fashion show. And I promise at the Mingle and Jingle there will be plenty of delicious refreshments loaded with calories."

She nodded to the high school band leader. "Maestro, strike up the band and let the parade begin."

The crowd cheered and clapped and laughed. Elmira Cosgrove's black horse pranced by wearing a pair of red flannel pajamas with his ears sticking through a red nightcap. Elmira had created her sleigh as an old-fashioned bed with her grandchildren pretending to be sound asleep.

Dickie Drummond's theme was candy cane lane, followed by a nativity scene, and then the music changed to "God Bless America." Emmett, dressed in his Marine uniform, saluted as he guided the horses wearing their red-white-and-blue-striped blankets with matching twinkling lights. J.J., dressed in her uniform, stood at attention and saluted the crowd. Joey and Julie stood on each side of a Christmas tree decorated to match the sled. They both waved little American flags and mimicked Emmett and their mother by saluting.

Nine more sleighs, all with unique and fun themes, circled the town square and made their way to the school parking lot.

Nell wiped tears from her eyes as Emmett winked and saluted her. "It's been a lot of years since I saw him in his uniform. He still cuts a handsome figure of a man."

Addison clapped and returned the twins' wave. "It's as clear as the nose on your face, Aunt Nell, that he's crazy about you."

"Do you think it's too late for an old woman to admit she's in love?"

"It's never too late, but I'm not the one you should be telling."

Nell patted Addison's arm. She sighed and changed the subject. "I don't envy the judges having to choose winners."

Addison hugged her foster mother. "Every sleigh is a winner in my book. Will you be okay if I leave you to get to the school by yourself? I promised J.J. to help dress the twins for the fashion show."

Wade's baritone voice spoke from behind. "Don't worry, Addison. I'll personally escort one of my favorite ladies."

Addison's stomach flipped as a shiver that had nothing to do with the weather shimmied down her spine. "We looked for you. Did you miss the parade?"

"I caught the beginning." He kissed Nell's cheek. "If it were up to me, I'd pick your sleigh."

"What happened?" Addison wanted to know.

"Right after Aunt Nell's sleigh passed I got a call from Leo, down at Smitty's. A couple of tourists had enjoyed a little too much holiday cheer, tangled with a couple of rowdy locals, and they all decided to take it out on each other."

"I haven't seen a good fisticuffs in years." Nell chuckled as Wade helped her skirt around a group of sightseers. "Did you arrest them?" Nell asked.

"Yes, ma'am."

"Shouldn't you be at the jail guarding the prisoners?"

Wade scanned the crowd while he escorted Nell and Addison. "Pop happened to drift in about the time I had locked the cell doors. Though he'd never admit it, his gout is still painful. He volunteered to keep an eye on the overnight guests while I do crowd control."

Addison said, "I hope the prisoners don't give your father any trouble."

Wade laughed. "When I left the jail, those four were snoring like buzz saws. The only danger Pop's in is trying to filter out the noise."

Before excusing herself and hustling through the crowd, Addison said, "See you at the fashion show. Save me a seat, Aunt Nell."

She offered Wade a dimpled smile before bustling down the sidewalk.

"I'd offer to give you a ride in the squad car, Aunt Nell…" Wade observed the throng of people and sleds all making their way in the same direction. "The streets are too crowded. It's faster to walk. There's no rush. We'll go slow."

"I'm old, Wade, not decrepit. Lead the way. I'll keep up."

Nell chattered as she held tight to Wade's arm. "I guess Emmett told you he's selling Oxbow?"

"Yes, ma'am. It's a smart move on his part. Selling to the university is an excellent decision. The ranch will benefit students for years to come, and the land will continue to thrive." He glanced down and asked Nell if he was walking too fast. She assured him he was not.

Nell said, "I suppose he also told you that he more or less hired himself on as Hope Ranch's handyman?"

Wade shook his head and grinned. "He didn't exactly put it that way. It was more like an offer and a mutual agreement between the three of you."

"Uh-huh," she replied, with a good-natured laugh.

In less than ten minutes they strolled through the front doors of the elementary school. Refreshment tables lined the festively decorated hallway walls. High school students dressed as elves greeted them with a program of events.

Wade stopped at one of the tables and ordered three hot chocolates and at a different table for three cookies decorated like ugly sweaters. He winked as he handed Aunt Nell a cookie. "I'll bet these aren't nearly as good as yours."

She harrumphed with a smile. "You sure know how to fluff an ol' gal's ego."

Strolling down the hallway and wishing people "Happy Holidays," Nell followed Wade into the auditorium, where they spotted J.J. waving to them.

An excited glow lit the young soldier's face as she greeted Nell and Wade. "Emmett will join us as soon as he's taken care of the horses, and Addison is backstage helping with the children." She thanked Wade for the hot chocolate and cookie. "I can honestly say this is the most exciting and fun day I've ever experienced."

Nell settled in a chair next to Wade. "Oh, and it's not over yet."

She turned in her seat when a male voice said, "It's dang cold outside."

Emmett seated himself on Wade's opposite side. Wade asked, "You need any help getting the sleigh home in the dark?"

"I appreciate the concern. Yesterday I brought the sleigh over on the flatbed, and then trailered the horses today. J.J. and I've already removed all the decorations and loaded them in the truck. I'll get the horses home the same way I brought them. Then tomorrow I'll drive over to get the sleigh."

"Do you need help loading it?" Wade wanted to know.

Emmett shucked out of his jacket and laid it across his lap. "Sure. You can help steady it while I winch it up and on."

Addison rushed to where her friends were seated. Her excitement at the sight of Wade was tinged with a bit of disappointment that Emmett and Nell sat next to him. She met their happy faces. "I can't wait for you to see Joey and Julie! Of course, all the children look so sweet in their outfits."

J.J. squeezed Addison's hand. "It's a proud-mama moment. It's been an extra special day."

The conversation was interrupted when the mayor walked to the front of the stage with a microphone in her hand. Once again she introduced herself.

"We meet again, ladies and gentlemen. If you thought the sleigh parade was spectacular, you are in for another treat." She pointed toward the spectators. "Addison, please stand and take a bow." She went on to praise Addison for organizing the children's fashion show and the department stores for helping to sponsor the event by lending the outfits. "When you came in, you should have received a program. If you'll look inside, there are discount coupons from each sponsoring store for the outfits you'll see tonight and for other items, too."

With an exaggerated flourish of her hand, Mayor Clark continued, "Tomorrow night is our first annual Mistletoe Bid on a Bachelor event. All you single ladies out there, bring your checkbooks. And the evening isn't just for single ladies. No-no-no! There is the Mingle and Jingle dance afterwards for everyone to enjoy, and more refreshments. And remember, once the fashion show is over, don't leave, because we'll announce the winners of the sleigh contest. Now…on with the festivities."

The crowd oohed and aahed as children dressed in flannel pajamas to summer play togs to fancy dresses and suits showed off their outfits. Proud parents and grandparents clapped and cheered. Then there was hilarious laughter as one five-year-old stood in the middle of the stage, crossed her legs, and announced very loudly, "I need to go potty."

One of the backstage mothers rushed across the floor to grab the little girl's hand and hurry her through the exit curtains. Mayor Clark used the incident to say, "Out of the mouths of babes."

She then announced, "For our last models, we have adorable twin brother and sister Joey and Julie Wallace, wearing outfits perfect for Easter Sunday—which is closer than you think."

The twins held hands as they walked across the stage to the X taped on the floor. As practiced, they stopped and turned to reward the audience with bright smiles. They waved and said, "Hi, Mommy."

J.J. pressed her hands to her chest. "I wish Gram

were here to see our babies." She turned sad eyes toward Addison. "Due to my selfishness, I've lost so much time...no...thrown away...precious moments that I'll never get back."

Addison leaned close and whispered, "Don't beat yourself up. We all make mistakes. The important thing is to learn from them. Besides, you and the children have a lifetime together. Your grandmother would be proud."

Mayor Clark blared through the microphone, "Let's bring all the children back on stage and give them a great big round of applause."

After she'd settled the crowd down, she reminded everyone again about the bachelor bidding and the Mingle and Jingle dance. "Okay, are you ready to hear the winners of our first—and I hope not our last—sleigh parade?"

A hush fell over the auditorium. Mayor Clark delivered each category winner's name with a flourish and presented each with a blue ribbon. "And the award for the most creative sleigh goes to Hope Ranch for their patriotic theme."

She pointed toward J.J. "We would also like to thank Private J.J. Wallace for serving our country. And to all our military men and women, whether retired or on active duty, we thank you, too, for your service. God Bless, and Merry Christmas!"

She bade the audience a goodnight and safe travels home.

Chapter Twenty-Six

"If you don't mind, I'd prefer spending the evening with my children. I'm sure the bidding on a bachelor and the dance will be fun." J.J. shrugged. "Neither interests me. Besides, the day after Christmas I need to head back to Fort Riley. It'll take a week to get there by bus."

Addison searched through the closet for an outfit appropriate for tonight's events. "As my Christmas gift to you, let me pay your airfare."

J.J. sighed. "It's a generous offer, and I'm tempted to take it. Please don't be mad that I'm declining. Here's the thing, Addison—it's my desire to begin this new phase of my life paying the way for my children and me. Does that make sense?"

Addison held up two outfits—a green pants suit and a long red dress. "Which one?"

J.J. pointed to the green. "Save the red for the night you go out to dinner with the bachelor you bid on."

Addison hung the dress back inside the closet. "No offense taken, J.J. In fact, I admire you for wanting to stand on your own two feet. Tell you what—I'll use the money to start a college fund for the twins."

The springs creaked as J. J. rose from the edge of the bed. "You're a generous person, Addison."

Addison slipped out of her robe. "I see a lot of

myself in you, although it's taken me years to learn the difference between true generosity and generosity with strings attached." She made a shooing motion. "I need to hurry. I promised to help Aunt Nell with her hair and makeup."

An hour later, Addison gave herself a critical look in the mirror. She had fashioned her hair into a neat chignon. Using a curling iron, she had coaxed tendrils of curls gracefully around her face. She dabbed perfume behind her ears and down her cleavage, and finished by applying an iced mauve lip gloss that enhanced her fair complexion and blue eyes.

Satisfied with her appearance, she bustled downstairs to Nell's bedroom. She had forewarned the older woman that she'd better not walk in and find her dressed in a flannel shirt, jeans, and boots.

Nell whistled as Addison walked in. "You look beautiful. I'll bet my last bottom dollar that Wade will be disappointed if someone besides you wins him."

Seeming to ignore the older woman's comment, Addison arched her eyebrows at the array of clothing piled on the bed. "You haven't decided on an outfit."

Nell fussed, "It's been years since I dressed up. I've got all these clothes and don't know what to wear. Some of them are probably outdated."

Addison sorted through the pile and held up a black chiffon pants suit. The blouse was beaded in a Native American design. She held it toward Nell. "This one is perfect."

She applied a pop of strong color on Nell's lips, with a rosy blush on her cheeks that looked gorgeous against her graying French braid.

Boomer raised a fuss before the knock sounded on

the front door. "I can tell by the way he's whining that it's Emmett." Nell turned to Addison. "I'm as nervous as a June bug on the tip of a toad's tongue." She peered closer to the mirror. "I hardly recognize myself."

In a minute they heard J.J. greet Emmett and invite him into the living room.

"I'll die of embarrassment if that ol' coot makes one snide remark."

Addison was surprised at her foster mother's nervousness. "You're the one that's beautiful. I truly think Emmett will be at a loss for words when he sees you, and in a good way."

Nell blew out a long sigh. "We'll see in a minute. C'mon, let's get this over with."

Addison followed the woman down the hall and into the living room. Emmett stood facing the fireplace. J.J. said, "Wow!"

Emmett turned. The expression that lit his eyes when he looked at Nell needed no words. He stared for a moment. "Nell, you…you look pretty as a picture." As if he'd remembered that he and Nell weren't alone in the room, he didn't take his eyes off her while he said, "You, too, Addison."

Addison and J.J. exchanged winks. The twins said, "Gosh, you don't look like Aunt Nell."

Everyone laughed. Nell said, "Who do I look like?"

The twins giggled. "You and Addison look like movie stars."

Nell kissed each one of the twins on the head. "That's the best compliment I've ever had."

With that, Emmett helped the women with their winter wraps and led the way out the front door and to his truck.

****

Except for the glitter ball and loops of colored tinsel hanging from the ceiling, the elementary school's cafeteria looked the same as it had the night before. Women of all ages and sizes filled chairs closest to the stage. Couples seated themselves farther back. Small groups stood and chatted.

A decorated table sat between the doors. Two festively dressed women greeted Addison and her friends with a warm smile. "If you ladies are bidding, you'll need your bidding paddles."

Addison and Nell each claimed a numbered paddle.

Emmett worried the knot on his tie. "Dang thing feels like it's chokin' me." He glinted at Addison. "I wouldn't do this for just anybody."

Nell pushed his hand away and adjusted the tie. "Stop your grousing. It's for a good cause." She brushed at a piece of lint on his sleeve. Her voice softened. "I'd forgotten how handsome you are." She gave him a quick peck on the cheek.

He blustered as if at a loss for words. "There's two seats in the front row. You two'd better grab 'em. I'm going to see if Wade is backstage."

Addison spotted two women heading for the chairs. She muttered to herself, "Oh, no, you don't."

"Head 'em off at the pass, Addy. I'll catch up."

Addison smiled sweetly. "Sorry, ladies." She turned to survey the room and pointed. "There's a couple of chairs over there." As Nell arrived, she told her, "You save the seats, Aunt Nell, and I'll go get us a cup of coffee."

Addison stopped to chat with Brenda Brown and

then Wade's sister and mother.

The lights flickered to signal that everyone should be seated. Chatter quieted as Mayor Dorothy Clark took the stage. After her usual welcome speech, she said, "To add a little intrigue to the bidding, we asked each bachelor to select a sealed envelope which isn't to be opened until he meets with his date. Inside the envelope is the name of the sponsoring restaurant." She clapped her hands together in glee. "As a special treat, Darla Hill, our very own auctioneer, will conduct the auction tonight."

She added, "Remember, this is all in fun, and the proceeds go toward funding a children's wing for the library." She gave the event over to the auctioneer.

The lights dimmed enough to add a special ambiance to the room. "Welcome, ladies. I'm honored to be your auctioneer for this special occasion. I've been asked to remind you that bidding starts at twenty-five dollars. All bids afterward are in five-dollar increments. Are you ready to have some fun?"

The crowd responded with woots and clapping.

The auctioneer offered a huge grin. "All right, then, bid big and bid…bid…bid."

The red velvet curtains opened, showcasing the bachelors seated on high stools. Wolf-whistles sounded, accompanied by several oohs.

"Ladies, we'll begin with bachelor number one: LaVar Studstill. Mr. Studstill is our local pharmacist. Who will open the bid?"

An attractive African-American bachelor in his mid-forties stepped to the front of the stage. Wearing a wide smile, he pirouetted and then stood with his legs slightly apart, hands on hips.

A woman's voice rang out, "Twenty-five dollars."

Another woman yelled, "Thirty."

A third woman shouted, "Sixty-five dollars."

A sigh wafted through the auditorium as the auctioneer announced, "Going once, and going twice." She pointed her gavel. "The bid is closed at sixty-five dollars to bidder number thirty-three."

The auditorium was abuzz by the time Emmett sauntered to the front of the stage. The auctioneer announced, "Mr. Emmett Oxbow, rancher and owner of Oxbow Ranch."

He turned and looked straight at Nell, offering a wink. Before the auctioneer opened the bidding, a woman shouted, "Sixty dollars."

The auctioneer guffawed. "My, my, aren't we anxious! Ladies, the bid is open at sixty dollars. Do I hear sixty-five?"

The surprised look on Emmett's face was priceless. Addison laughed, and Nell stammered, as she turned to look in the direction of the voice, "What the jingles is Brenda up to, offering a bid like that?"

Addison nudged her on the arm. "What difference does it make? Bid a hundred."

Nell's eyes widened. "But I don't have—"

"Call it an early Christmas present. Hurry…bid before someone else does."

Nell held up her paddle and called out, "One hundred dollars."

It was the auctioneer's turn to look surprised. "Ladies, we have a one-hundred-dollar bid. Who will make it one hundred five?"

It was if an anxious aura hovered over the crowd waiting to see who would offer the next bid and how big.

Nell reached over and gripped Addison's hand. Addison leaned close and whispered, "If we have to, we'll up the bid. I want this to be your and Emmett's special time together."

Nell glanced over her shoulder, only to have Brenda shrug with a good-natured wink.

The auctioneer said, "One hundred dollars going once…twice…" She grinned. "The bid is closed at one hundred dollars. Congratulations to the lady holding paddle number twelve."

The cool weather outside did not match the steamy atmosphere inside the school's cafeteria.

****

It made no sense. It was crazy. He'd only known Addison a short while. Yet the impression she made on him was undeniable. Wade tried not to think about the kiss they had shared or how beautiful she looked tonight. Thoughts of holding her in his arms at the dance after the auction kept pestering him despite all attempts to prevent them. He'd only known her for a short while, and for some crazy reason knowing her reminded him of all the wrong decisions he'd made in his life.

A tense silence followed while the auctioneer shuffled a stack of papers.

He was the last bachelor, and the idea of women bidding on him like a bull at auction made him antsy.

Emmett resettled on the stool he had vacated. He leaned close to Wade. "Makes you feel like a danged sacrificial lamb gettin' ready for the slaughterhouse. Sure am glad to get it over with."

"Yeah, I hear you. I'd rather wrestle a grizzly than

face this group of women for the next minute or two. My palms are actually sweating." Wade heaved a sigh and walked to the front of the stage. He turned in Addison's direction and greeted her with a crooked smile.

They stared at each other for a heart-dropping moment. Wade gazed into her smoldering blue eyes, and his heart thudded faster. Never had he felt such a sharp need to hold a woman in his arms, to kiss every inch of her silken skin until she was breathless. To—

The auctioneer's voice interrupted his lustful thoughts and drew everyone's attention. Her speech was punctuated with dramatic pauses and exaggerated hand gestures. "Ladies, our last bachelor is none other than Meadow Creek's very own Sheriff Wade Grey. Dig deep into your purses and bid big. Who will start the bidding?"

"One hundred dollars."

Wade searched for the bidder. He groaned inside when he spotted the wide grin of Mrs. Turley, better known as "the cat lady." She was old enough to be his grandmother.

Another bidder shouted, "One hundred fifty."

Wade's six-foot-two frame craned forward, searching the crowd for a voice he didn't recognize. He arched an eyebrow toward Addison. Why didn't she bid?

Bids ping-ponged back and forth from every direction in the room. He didn't have time for this.

Relief weakened his knees when Addison smiled and held up her paddle. "Three hundred twenty-five."

Wade felt like doing a happy-dance shuffle. He held his breath. *Surely no one will top that amount.*

Wrong!

A five-hundred-dollar bid rang out.

Someone from the audience loudly exclaimed, "Holy crap!"

Wade felt his neck growing red beneath his collar, and his body heated with discomfort when a female voice chortled, "He can put his shoes under my bed anytime. Five hundred twenty-five."

He prayed his cell phone would ring with Millie on the other end telling him there was an emergency and he was needed asap!

Thirty seconds seemed like a lifetime to Wade. His stomach muscles tightened when Addison's lips quirked into a mischievous smile. Her blue eyes piercing his seemed to say, "Oh, if only you could see the expression on your face."

Her hand lifting the paddle moved in slow motion, and her sultry voice purred, "One thousand dollars."

Wade mustered a fresh smile when the auctioneer finally called the bidding closed to the woman holding paddle number seven. At that moment he wanted to kiss Addison with every ounce of the pent-up emotions he'd suppressed for the last few minutes.

Chapter Twenty-Seven

The auctioneer closed the bidding and welcomed Mayor Clark back to the podium. The mayor thanked all the participating bidders and the bachelors. She encouraged everyone to enjoy refreshments while a crew of volunteers moved chairs against the wall and the band set up for the dance.

The crowd dispersed into small groups. Wade and Emmett meandered over to where Addison and Nell stood.

Emmett handed Nell a white envelope. He waggled his eyebrows. "Let's see where we're to have our date."

Nell accepted the envelope and ran her finger under the sealed flap. She withdrew a certificate. Her cheeks pinked. "The Dockside, that new place out by the waterfall. Maybe we should wait until the weather warms and we can sit outside."

Emmett agreed.

Clamping down on his wayward thoughts, Wade handed his envelope to Addison. She opened it and held the certificate forward. "Le Chalet. Sounds very French and *very* romantic."

The lights dimmed, and the band struck up its first number, a waltz. Wade offered his hand and swept Addison into his arms. He held her close. She looked more beautiful than anyone had a right to look.

"Le Chalet is the sort of place a man takes a special woman," he said.

She drew back a little, gazing into his eyes. "Did you know the woman who bid five hundred on you?"

Wade whirled Addison around the floor. The lilt of her voice caused his belly to do a flip-flop. "I know most of the locals pretty well. With so many tourists at the auction, I didn't see anyone I recognized."

As her body molded perfectly against his, sparks of awareness ran through him. Everything inside him grew still and quiet. Everything except his heart. He drew back to appreciate the bold but feminine lines and curves of her face, focusing on her lips for longer than he should—long enough to cause a stirring sensation below his belt.

His breath feathered the top of her hair. He inhaled the subtle sweetness of her shampoo. Her fingers toyed with the nape of his neck, sending sensual slithers of desire to places that were responding with a sweet ache.

He bent closer as she tilted her face, her lips slightly parted, inviting, and then just as his mouth took hers, his phone whirred and vibrated. A rueful annoyance flashed in her eyes, replacing the dreamy glint.

He scowled, pulling his phone from his pocket and looking at the caller ID. "It's Millie." He blew out an aggravated breath as he escorted Addison off the dance floor.

The song ended. Emmett led Nell over to where Wade stood with Addison.

Wade's jaw clenched when he disconnected. "There's been an accident. Car and a moose collided. I'm sorry, Addison." He placed his hands over hers and kissed her knuckles. "This isn't the way I'd hoped the evening would end."

"Don't you worry, Wade. We'll see to it she gets home," Nell declared.

Addison sighed and patted Wade's shoulder. "Such is the life of a lawman. Truly, I hope no one is badly hurt. Go, and if I don't see you before—Merry Christmas."

He bent and lightly brushed her lips with his. Addison watched him wend his way through the crowd, stopping only to speak to his sister and mother. Both women grabbed their coats and followed him through the double cafeteria doors.

****

Dressed in flannel pajamas and heavy robes, Addison and Nell regaled J.J. with comments and quips about the auction. Nell giggled like a young girl when she said, "I almost peed myself when Brenda yelled out a sixty-dollar bid. She was the first bidder. And the expression on Emmett's face was priceless."

"Speaking of surprises—Nell, did you recognize the voice of the woman who bid five hundred on Wade?"

J.J. sputtered. "Someone actually bid five hundred dollars?"

"We're not joking, J.J." Nell elbowed Addison. "You have to admit Wade is one handsome hunk and a prize catch, if a woman can rope him and put her brand on him."

J.J. remarked, "Sheriff Grey seems like a stand-up guy, but my guess is he's no pushover." She finished off the cup of Nell's old-fashioned German Glühwein. "I still can't believe someone bid that much money on him."

Nell arched an eyebrow at J.J. "Don't forget all that money goes for a good cause. Not to speak of getting to spend the evening over dinner with him."

Nell sat pensive for a moment. "It almost seems like I've heard that voice before. The room was filled with lots of tourists. It could have been anyone."

"Yeah, well there's that." J.J. unfolded from the sofa. "By the way, who did have the winning bid?"

Addison cleared her throat and grinned. "Ahem, that would be me."

J.J. matched Addison's grin. "I'm not even going to ask what the final bid was. As Aunt Nell said, it's for a good cause."

Nell yawned as she stood. "Tonight was the most fun I've had since I can't remember when." She gave each woman a hug. "Tomorrow's Christmas Eve. Let's sleep a little late in the morning. For the remainder of the day, we have a lot of cooking to do."

Addison tipped her cup forward. "I'll turn out the lights. Goodnight, Aunt Nell, J.J."

Addison stood in front of the living room window watching snow feather down from the sky. Behind her the fire crackled, casting a warm glow around the room. A wave of nostalgia washed over her as she took in the twinkling lights on the tree, the garland, and the angel topper.

She felt content and happy. She thought about Wade and his sensuous lips against hers, his sexy smile, and how the aroma of his cologne mingled with his masculine scent. Desire stole through her. She tamped down a rush of emotions that she shouldn't be feeling. It'd been months since she'd had sex, and she refused to give in to carnal needs.

    She wanted more. She wanted to be cherished and loved by only one special man—Wade.

Chapter Twenty-Eight

Christmas Eve morning arrived with sunshine and blue skies feathered with wispy white clouds. Snow blanketed the grounds of Hope Ranch. Addison stood at her bedroom window, soaking in the scene that reminded her of a Christmas greeting card. Suddenly invigorated by an idea, she hurriedly shrugged out of her pajamas and into denims, flannel shirt, and boots. With nimble fingers she quickly plaited her hair into a French braid and applied a minimum of makeup.

She knelt down and, from the beneath the bed, pulled out a suitcase and opened it to remove her camera case and lens. She couldn't remember how long it had been since she'd had a desire to pursue her hobby as a photographer.

The aroma of coffee and blueberry pancakes wafted upstairs. Addison followed her nose to the kitchen, and J.J. and the twins stumbled from their bedroom and followed her.

Addison held up the camera. "Good morning. I have a fun idea to do after breakfast. Whatta you say…are you game?"

Joey and Julie climbed up on stools at the kitchen counter. Joey rubbed sleep from his eyes. "What kind of game?"

Julie scoffed. "Not a game, silly. Addison said she

had an idea."

Addison framed her face into dismay. "Oh, my, if you're too sleepy and would rather go back to bed—" Her voice trailed off when the twins protested.

"We're game, Addison. Really!"

Addison choked back a chuckle. "You are going to make snow angels while I take pictures of you."

"Yippee!" The cherubic voices shouted in unison. And then, "What are snow angels?"

Addison explained, and immediately the twins wanted to involve their mother, Aunt Nell, and Addison.

Addison set the camera on a shelf while she helped J.J. fill plates and cups. "Someone has to take the pictures," she said.

Excited pleasantries were exchanged around the marble counter, with the twins asking if they could leave cookies and milk for Santa and J.J. expressing excitement about settling in Meadow Creek and having a home for her and the twins.

The morning chatter was interrupted by Boomer's yippy barks and the patter of his paws on the floor as he raced to the living room to settle in his favorite spot on the sofa to look out the window.

Everyone in the kitchen raised their eyebrows in expectation. Nell pushed from her stool. "We're not expecting anyone until tomorrow. Wonder who it could be?"

The waiting group heard her say, "Well, this is a nice surprise, J.T. What brings you all the way out to Hope Ranch on Christmas Eve?" And then she added, "C'mon to the kitchen. Coffee's fresh."

J.T. Elsworth removed his coat and hung it on the

rack in the hallway. He followed Nell to the homey kitchen and greeted everyone, then asked the twins if they were ready for Santa Claus.

"Oh, he's already brought our Christmas." Joey smiled at his mother.

Julie followed with, "We wrote Santa a letter asking him to bring us our mommy, and he did."

J.J. stood and extended her hand. "I'm Jenny Wallace. J.J. to everyone."

J.T. returned the handshake. "Welcome home, Private Wallace, and thank you for your service. I understand congratulations are in store."

Her curious glance bounced from Nell to Addison to the banker. "How so, sir?"

"Meadow Creek is a small community. There aren't many secrets here. We need a good deputy, and Millie is excited that these little tykes will live next door. Just be careful that she doesn't spoil them rotten."

Nell handed him a cup of coffee. "You didn't say what brought you all the way out here, J.T."

The bank's vice president pulled a white envelope from the pocket of his cardigan. He smiled. "I promised that as soon as the deed to the ranch was satisfied I'd deliver it to you in person. I'm here to keep that promise."

Nell accepted the envelope then handed it to Addison. She used a napkin to blot the tears from her eyes. "This would never have happened without you, Addison."

The two women hugged. It was the banker's voice that interrupted them. "I'd better get going. Thanks for the coffee."

Addison laid her hand on his arm. "Wait. We need

another favor."

She explained about making snow angels with the children. "They insist that I be in the picture, too." She handed him the camera. "Would you?"

He grinned. "I'd love to do this with my family. Do you mind if I borrow your fabulous idea?"

"Free for the taking, J.T." Addison hugged him. "We owe you so much for going the extra mile when most bankers might have simply closed the door on us and sold Nell's loan for the payoff amount from a mega corporation."

While they all donned their jackets and knit hats and went outside, J.T. agreed with Addison that Nell was a special woman who had given hope to children who otherwise might never have had the opportunity to know love.

Outside, Addison demonstrated how to fall to create an impression in the snow that resembled an angel. Amid the giggles and the swooshing of arms and legs by almost everyone, J.T. clicked away, catching pose after pose with the camera.

After he bid them goodbye, Nell suggested they build a snowman. Addison showed her foster mother how to use the camera and proceeded to help J.J. and the twins roll snow into large balls. They huffed as they heaved the two top balls into place to create the body. Nell disappeared inside the house to return with a red scarf, an old red cap with ear flaps, a carrot, and some pine cones for the eyes and buttons for the mouth. The twins searched until they found a couple of sticks to be used for the snowman's arms. While Nell helped decorate the snowman, Addison clicked frame after frame. While she snapped pictures, she came up with an idea for last-minute Christmas gifts.

As an added unexpected surprise, Boomer sped down the long driveway. He returned trotting next to Emmett's pickup truck. Behind the truck was a long stock trailer.

"What's in it, Aunt Nell?" The twins wanted to know.

"I reckon we're about to find out." What she didn't say was that Emmett had telephoned a few days before.

Addison lifted her camera for a few shots before she followed the group to the barn where Emmett parked. He greeted them with a wave as he walked around to the back of the trailer.

Julie and Joey raced up to give him a hug. "Whatcha got, Uncle Emmett?"

He patted each one on the back as he released them. "Stand out of the way. It's a surprise."

He undid the latch and dropped the trailer's tailgate ramp to the ground. He unhooked the chain and stepped inside to lead out two horses, a sorrel with a white face and a palomino. "This is Baldy. He's a good ol' boy, and this one is Blondie. She's Baldy's best friend."

Nell walked over and took the lead ropes from him while he disappeared back inside the trailer.

Addison continued to click shot after shot.

Emmett led a brown-and-white pinto and a leopard appaloosa down the ramp. "This here is Patches, and the appy is Freckles."

"Can we ride 'em?" two excited little voices twittered.

"You betcha." Emmett lifted Joey up on Patches and Julie on Freckles to ride while he led the two horses into the barn and down the wide aisle to separate stalls.

Nell followed, leading the sorrel and the palomino.

J.J. sighed. "Every time I think my life can't get any happier, something like this happens."

Addison slung the camera strap over her shoulder. "Remember what I told you...this is only the beginning."

Emmett declared he had a lot of work to do and needed to get back to his place. He promised to return Christmas Day and bring his famous fruit cake. He climbed into the truck's cab, stuck his hand out the window, and waved as he disappeared down the driveway.

Nell laughed. "Emmett's fruit cake hasn't changed. It's still heavy enough to knock a grizzly out cold."

Addison hooked arms with her foster mother. "I remember. I also remember how you would threaten us within an inch of our lives if we kids didn't eat a slice and say how good it tasted."

"Yep, and I'm thinking I'd better put a bug in J.J.'s ear. I wouldn't hurt that ol' coot's feelings for all the money in the world."

Later that night, after the cookies and milk were placed on the coffee table and the gifts situated under the tree, Addison sat in her room printing out pictures on her printer and placing them inside the empty photo album she had bought for J.J.

"Perfect," she complimented herself as she yawned and finished up her picture projects for Nell and Emmett.

Her cell phone vibrated. The name on the caller ID elicited a smile. She answered, "Merry Christmas, Wade. I hope the people who hit the moose weren't hurt."

Wade apologized for the necessity of unexpectedly leaving her at the dance. He explained that unfortunately the moose was a fatality. From the tone of his voice, Addison could only imagine his somber expression. "It's never a pretty sight when an animal that big collides with a vehicle. A couple of the family members suffered serious injuries and will spend Christmas in the hospital. The good news is they are all alive."

There was a long pause before Wade said he wanted to see her. The sensuality of his voice flamed her desire. She almost wished she could reach through the phone and pull him to her. "J.J. is leaving the day after Christmas. I'll stop by the office for a few minutes."

She envisioned him holding her in his arms when he said, "That's not exactly what I had in mind."

He wanted her. It was the innuendo of his words that caused her stomach to clench. She was tempted to tell him that she wanted him, too. But she couldn't bring herself to do it. She would never allow herself to be a passing fancy to another man. She refused to warm his bed, to chase away his boredom, and when he got tired of her, he'd go on his merry way, leaving her broken, again.

"That's not what I had in mind, either, Wade. I'm looking forward to our dinner at Le Chalet, perhaps during the summer, before the grand opening of Hope Ranch as a destination place."

He exclaimed in mock shock. "Let's not wait that long. What about before New Year's? Pop and Millie will man the office for me. I'll need to work New Year's Eve and New Year's Day."

"Okay, when did you have in mind?"

"Tomorrow is Sunday. What about Wednesday? I'll pick you up at four."

"It's a date." She again wished him and his family a Merry Christmas and said goodbye.

Dancing down the stairs, she smiled as she placed the last-minute gifts under the tree.

Chapter Twenty-Nine

"He came! Julie, look at all the presents."
"Wow, Joey. Santa never left this many presents when we lived with Gram."
"Yeah, and look, he ate all the cookies."
"That's because Aunt Nell helped us add an extra pinch of love, 'member." The little girl rocked back on her knees.

Christmas morning at Hope Ranch was a flurry of excitement. Addison lifted her camera and clicked shots of the children on their hands and knees looking under the tree.

Their mother said, "Merry Christmas Morning! What are you looking for?"

Addison clicked a picture of the twins wearing sheepish grins as if they'd been caught snooping.

As usual, Joey and Julie answered in perfect sync. "We're looking to see if there are presents with our names on them."

Nell sauntered into the living room wearing a Christmas-themed apron over her jeans and red flannel shirt. Atop her head was a Santa hat. "Ho-ho-ho! Merry Christmas. Santa asked me to be his special helper and hand out gifts. Are you two buttons ready?"

Excited yeses rang out that included J.J. and Addison. As she settled on a stool next to the tree,

Boomer announced someone was in the yard.

Joey scrambled to look out the window. "It's Uncle Emmett, and he's carrying a red sack slung over his shoulder."

Julie joined him. "I bet Santa left his sack at Uncle Emmett's house."

Joey rushed to open the door to a blast of wintry air.

Emmett stamped the snow from his boots, then handed the red cloth sack to the twins with instructions to place the gifts under the tree while he hung his cowboy hat and jacket on the coat rack.

He declared, "It's colder'n a well-digger's... aahh..."

Nell nodded her head toward the children and cut him a sharp look that said, "Watch your language."

The tips of Emmett's ears turned bright red. He corrected himself, "A well-digger's freezin' hands."

The morning was spent with the twins unwrapping gifts of cowboy boots, building blocks, and coloring books, a doll for Julie, and a dump truck for Joey.

J.J. wept over the photo album filled with pictures of her and the children building the snowman, the children on the horses, and of course, of the entire group posing as snow angels. She declared it was the best gift ever.

Nell handed Joey a long, heavy box. She and the twins shared a conspiratorial wink before he said, "This one is for you, Mommy. It's from me and Julie. We made it with Aunt Nell's help."

J.J.'s cheeks flamed, and she blinked back the tears that blurred her vision. She laughed when the twins said, "Hurry. Just tear the paper off."

J.J. removed the box top, and lying on a sheet of red tissue paper was a framed picture of two green handprints, the thumbs touching to form a heart. Written in a child's hand was the phrase, *Even ten little fingers can't count the ways we love you.* In the palm of each hand was that twin's name and age.

Quiet sobs filled the room. The twins hugged their mother. "Don't you like it, Mommy?"

She held her children close. "I'm not crying because I dislike it but because it's the most precious gift I have ever received, and it will hang in a special place in our new home for all our visitors to see."

The twins patted their mother's face, and she smiled. "There're more presents to hand out. Don't keep Aunt Nell waiting."

Nell accepted a package and made a big production of removing the colorful paper. She cried out, "Oh, my stars, Addy, this is too much," when she opened a slender box that held a plane ticket to New York and a ticket to see the Rockettes. "It's always been my dream to see them in person."

Addison said, "There's an ulterior motive involved. You know that Ruby Raye is listing my penthouse as soon as I can get it packed up and completely moved out. I need your help."

Nell reached over and grabbed Addison's hand. "You betcha. It's the best deal ever."

Emmett's eyes misted when Addison handed him a large white envelope adorned with a red bow. "I didn't expect anything. I-I-I…"

Nell scolded. "Stop your blustering, ol' man, and open it."

The first item he slid out was a sepia-toned picture

of him and Nell standing together, holding the horses. He turned the photo over and read, "Two of my favorite people. You mean so much to me." It was signed, "Addy."

He choked and cleared his throat as if trying to find his voice. He said nothing as he removed a set of blueprints and a rendering of the old tool shed that was to become his new home as caretaker of Hope Ranch. He held the drawing up for all to see. "It's more than I expected, Addison. A front porch with a rocking chair, and nine hundred and twenty square feet is more livin' space than I need." He grinned widely. "Don't get me wrong, 'cause I ain't complainin', not one little bit. I sure do thank you."

Joey laughed as he lifted an odd-shaped gift from under the tree. "This one is for Boomer. It was hard to wrap."

The dog, hearing his name, left his spot in front of the fireplace. He sniffed the thing in the little boy's hand and gave a questioning look. Nell said, "Open it for him, Joey."

The little boy tore open wads of paper held together with long strands of scotch tape to reveal a large rawhide bone. Everyone laughed when Boomer waggled with excitement as he held the bone in his mouth and ambled back to his spot in front of the fireplace.

"He likes it," the twins declared.

"It's your turn, Addison. Hurry! We want to see what you got," Joey and Julie exclaimed over the pile of colorfully wrapped gifts next to her chair.

She asked the twins to take turns handing her a package. She gushed over the new pair of western boots, a gift from Emmett. From Nell, an afghan crocheted in red-and-white spirals that resembled peppermint candy. And from J.J. and the twins, an apron embellished with each of their handprints in a variety of colors.

Addison lifted the twins onto her lap. She hugged them and planted kisses on their cheeks. Her voice hitched, and her eyes brimmed with tears. And through the thickness of her throat, she managed to say, "Today has reminded me that family is not always blood kin. You are the best family ever!"

An aura of serenity filled the room. The fire crackled, and Boomer gnawed his bone.

****

Monday morning arrived and was the exact opposite of Christmas Day. Heavy snow clouds bloated an ominous sky. After Nell's old truck wouldn't start, Addison was thankful Emmett had been available to drive them to the bus station in what he referred to as his *grown-up* vehicle, a four-door sedan. She was glad on several accounts. There hadn't been enough room for three adults and two children in the front seat of Nell's truck.

He parked and popped the trunk to lift out J.J.'s duffel bags. "We're sure gonna miss you."

J.J. hugged him. He refused to let her carry the bags. "Nope," he said, "From Marine to soldier, this is the least I can do."

Dressed in her fatigues, J.J. walked to the ticket master and checked in. Several people spoke to her as she made her way back to where the others waited for her. A voice called, "Private Wallace?" She turned to see Wade approaching her.

He shook hands with Emmett, hugged Nell, and smiled at Addison. He turned to J.J. "Your paperwork is in and approved. If you change your mind about going to the academy, let me know asap. I'm sure hoping you won't—change your mind, that is."

"Don't you worry, Sheriff Grey. I have two good reasons to return." She extended her hand. "Thank you again. I won't let you down."

J.J. squatted and wrapped each of the twins in her arms. She hugged them close. Joey pulled back from his mother. He placed a little hand on either side of her cheeks and, with a very serious look, he said, "Promise you're not going to stay in the Army. You will come back, won't you?"

She slid her gaze over the two children. "You and Julie are the most important people in my life. It may take a couple of weeks or even a month, but I *will* return to you. That's a promise, and soldiers don't break their promises. As soon as I return, I'll enroll you in school and we'll move into our new house. Okay?"

The twins sniffled and nodded. Together they said, "We love you, Mommy."

An announcement blared over a speaker for all passengers leaving on bus number three-twelve to board.

Nell hugged J.J. "Don't you worry about the twins. We'll take good care of them."

Addison and Emmett added their assurances to Nell's.

It was a somber group who walked out into the cold to watch J.J. mount the bus steps. She turned and waved, then disappeared inside to sit next to a window. She continued to wave as the bus pulled out of the station.

Emmett suggested they all go to BB's café for a cup of Brenda's special hot chocolate. "Might help cheer us up," he declared.

A few minutes later, the group sat at a table sipping peppermint hot chocolate. The twins were unusually quiet. Emmett waved a waitress over and ordered an extra-large basket of French fries. He said, "I have it on good authority that French fries help put the smile back on sad faces."

Nell reached over and gave him an affectionate pat on the arm.

After a few minutes of small talk about Christmas and gifts, Wade said he needed to get back to the office. "I for one am looking forward to J.J.'s return. She'll make a good deputy, and we need the extra person."

He lifted Addison's hand into his and toyed with her fingers. "Are we still on for Le Chalet on Wednesday?"

She had been so lost in thought that she almost missed his question. Being inside the bus station had evoked a host of painful emotions. Her gaze rose to his eyes—deep gray, waiting for her answer until she broke contact. "I'm sorry, I guess I was daydreaming. Yes, of course, Wednesday is great."

Wade stood. He assured the twins not to worry, their mother would return to Meadow Creek as soon as she got her discharge papers.

Brenda bustled over with the basket of piping hot fries. Wade grabbed a few and stuffed them into his mouth. He winked at Addison. "Our reservations are for six. I'll pick you up at five."

The conversation centered on the sale of Emmett's

property to the university, and the aggravation of packing up years of accumulated things and getting ready to vacate his ranch.

It took mere minutes for the party to finish the fries and hot chocolate. Emmett suggested that since it would be getting dark soon and he didn't much like driving on slick roads in the dark, they should get on the get-go.

Brenda bustled over. "Hey, do you mind if I speak to Nell in private? I, um, forgot to tell her something important."

Addison held each twin's hand. "We'll wait for you in the car."

Nell shrugged. "I won't be long."

Chapter Thirty

"Okay, what's so all-fired important that you couldn't tell me in front of the others?" Nell followed her friend into a small office.

Brenda kept her voice low. Nell propped against the desk. "Why are you whispering, Brenda? The office door is closed."

"Because the walls are thin. I don't want anyone else to hear this, just in case I'm wrong." Brenda paused. "I've been wracking my brain over who would bid five hundred dollars on Wade. This morning a youngish woman was standing outside the café. She stood there peering in the window like she was trying to make up her mind whether or not to come inside."

Nell gave an impatient snort. "Lots of tourists look inside store windows trying to make up their minds. What's this got to do with the bachelor bidding?"

Brenda leaned closer, her voice even lower. "You have to swear not to tell anyone. I could be wrong. In fact, I hope I'm wrong, but I-I'm almost certain the woman was Gracie Howard."

Nell released a shocked gasp. "Brenda Brown, are you sure you haven't been knocking back a few too many spiked eggnogs?"

Brenda glared at Nell. "I knew I should've kept my mouth shut. Still, I have a niggling feeling it was her."

Nell paced about the office's small space. She tapped a finger against her lips. "Don't, and I repeat, whatever you do, *do not* tell anyone else. Especially Addison. It's as clear as the rouge on her face that she's falling really hard for Wade, and every time he looks at her he goes all moonified." She reached over and placed her hands on Brenda's shoulders and gave a little shake. "Promise on your grandmother's grave not to say anything until we're absolutely, positively sure it's her."

Brenda shook her head vigorously. "On my grandmother's grave…I promise."

"Good. May she come back and haunt you if you break your promise. I gotta go. It's getting dark out, and I don't like being on the road at night even if Emmett is driving."

Brenda walked Nell to the café's front door. "What are we going to do if it is her?"

Nell shivered when she opened the door. "Nothing. It's none of our business." She closed the door and rushed to the car.

****

Ava hugged her brother and father as her mother set out sandwiches of leftover turkey and cranberry sauce, along with slices of pumpkin pie. Ava filled four cups with coffee.

Wade and his father exchanged smiles. "I guess we're special, huh, Pop."

Ward Grey chewed thoughtfully on a bite of sandwich. "Yep. Your mother often brought me supper when I was working late." He winked. "I always enjoyed her company. Still do."

Small talk shifted back and forth. Silence fell.

Wade expected his sister and mother to pack up the dishes and leave, but they didn't.

Wade slid his eyebrows up. "Out with it! You both look like you're ready to explode."

Ave huffed out, "Something unexpected has come up."

Lucy shrugged. "*Maybe* it's something. We're not sure."

Wade squinted as he searched their faces. "If you're concerned about my relationship with Addison, don't be. She's been hurt as badly as I was. Right now she's vulnerable. We'll take it one day at a time."

He thought of Addison and how she'd felt in his arms. He also felt guilty for letting Gracie's name slip from his lips while indulging in the most sensual kiss he'd experienced in a long time.

"We're not concerned about Addison. Oh, that didn't come out right," Ava cried. "The truth is we are concerned about her and you. Because…because Mom and I are certain we saw Gracie." She rushed on, twisting her hands together. "And we know how deeply she hurt you and how long it's taken you to get over that hurt, and—"

"Whoa! You're talking about my ex…Gracie Howard?"

His sister and mother nodded.

Anger welled inside Wade. "That's crazy. Her parents moved to South Carolina fifteen years ago. After what happened, there's no one and no reason to draw Gracie back to Meadow Creek."

Ava tilted her head and expelled a long, fretful sigh. "There's you."

Lucy slammed the lid on the picnic basket. She

placed her hands on her hips as she faced Wade. "Son, we like Addison very much, and I for one would love to see the relationship grow beyond friendship and into forever happiness…and grandchildren. If you haven't told her about Gracie, then I encourage you to do so sooner rather than later. That is unless some part of you still loves that witch of a woman."

Wade struggled with how to put his mother at ease. Still he had doubts about his feelings for Gracie. He had loved her from the time he'd yanked her pigtails in first grade. But now? How could she have put him through hell and then, when it was all over, walk away like it was no big deal?

Apprehension filled Ava's voice. "You wouldn't consider getting back with her, would you?"

He honestly didn't know how to answer that question. He found it difficult to mention Gracie's name, let alone think about seeing her again.

He heard the plea in his sister's voice. "Wade, she almost destroyed you. How could you ever trust her integrity…her love?"

He turned the coffee cup in circles. "It's true I don't want to repeat the emotional wringer she put me through. Maybe she's changed. Maybe she deserves a second chance."

He raked his hands through his thick hair. "As far as I'm concerned, this is all private—between Gracie and me. And we don't actually know that she's back in town. It could be someone who resembles her."

Ward had sat quietly, taking in all the facial expressions, the exchange of words. Now he sat forward in his chair. "You're wrong, son. It isn't private. What that little bitch did to you she did to all of us, including the town. Why in hell do you think her parents sold their house and moved all the way across to the other side of the United States? They were embarrassed and ashamed. You're a grown man. Responsible." The timbre of his voice increased. "Last time, your mother and sister nearly made themselves sick watching you fall apart. Keep that in mind while you're making your decision about how to handle this."

Ward stood up and hobbled to the door. He scowled back at his son. "This has got my stomach in knots. Consider me off duty. I need a beer. Maybe two."

Lucy wrapped her arms around Wade. She hugged him tight. "Make the best decision for your well-being, son. And whether it's Gracie or not, *tell* Addison, all of it, and don't put it off."

Ava brushed tears from her eyes. "You're my brother. My twin. When you hurt—I hurt, too."

His family bundled up to brave the cold. Hours after they left, he sat watching the fish swim back and forth in the aquarium. "Right now I'd like to trade places with you and not have a care in the world."

One large goldfish turned to stare out from the tank. Its mouth moved up and down as if it were speaking.

Wade unfolded his six-foot frame from the chair and ambled to the coffeemaker to refill his cup. He returned to the chair and stared at the generous slice of pumpkin pie his mother had left, then pulled it toward him. He forked a large piece into his mouth and chewed.

He pointed the fork at the tank. "You know, fish, you and your buddies are pretty lucky. All you do is swim, eat, and poop. Me, on the other hand—" He shoved another bite of pie into his mouth. He tried to enjoy the dessert, but he knew if Gracie had truly returned to Meadow Creek it was because she had an ulterior motive and not because she loved him.

He decided that chances were slim he would see her before Wednesday. Relaxing a little, he would dress in his best suit, enjoy a fine dinner with Addison at Le Chalet, perhaps order champagne, even enjoy a sleigh ride around the lake. After a few hours, he'd drive her back to his place and over coffee fill her in on his disastrous love affair.

The thought of reliving a past he'd rather forget and possibly losing Addison caused the pie to sour on his stomach.

Chapter Thirty-One

The woman sitting across from Wade took his breath away. Even the scar over her eye enhanced her beauty. Her complexion was creamy smooth, with a pale blush to her cheeks and a deep rose to her lips, the black of her eyelashes and perfectly arched eyebrows, her platinum hair combed over in a flawless wave with her long hair pulled up into a fashionable do. He certainly wasn't an expert on women's styles, but there was no doubt in his mind that Addison James had earned her title as the world's most beautiful woman.

Addison seemed to glow as she took in the ambiance of the restaurant. "Le Chalet reminds me of Christmas in France's Central Square of Mègeve. The owners have created a lovely and homey atmosphere with the fireplace and all the decorations. Do they offer sleigh rides?"

Perfect, he thought. "As a matter of fact, they do, and I've arranged for a trip around the lake."

She rewarded him with a dreamlike smile that caused his heart to ratchet up a couple of beats. With a smile like that, how could he not be drawn to this woman? Being near her infused him with an energy that made him optimistic about a possible future together.

He reached across the table and wrapped his hand around Addison's. A kind of magic had entwined them.

Her gaze rose to his. Deep blue. Honest. Expectant. He was speechless, and for what reasons, he couldn't say except that he felt like the legs of the chair had been knocked out from under him. His mother and sister had nailed it. If he was to have a serious relationship with Addison, he needed to be forthcoming about Gracie.

"Addison…" He fumbled for the words. "There's something important I need to tell you. Maybe later tonight, at my place."

Her laughter reminded him of tinkling bells. "Please don't say you're going to propose. Neither of us is ready to take such an important leap this early in our relationship."

Before he could answer, a voice laced with mockery said, "My, my, my. Isn't this romantic."

Her words were met with stunned silence. "What are you doing here?" Wade finally managed.

Her dark eyes widened with mock surprise as she set her long-stemmed goblet of wine on the table and pulled out a chair and seated herself. "I'm sorry, am I intruding?"

Addison's brows furrowed as she looked at the petite woman with spiked brown hair and dark eyes.

The woman smiled as though she saw confusion and a hint of anger in Addison's face. She heard Wade's deep intake of breath and then the release. The two exchanged glances before she turned smug attention to Addison and held out her hand. "Forgive my rudeness. I'm Gracie Grey. Wade's wife." And then her belly laugh drew attention from guests at other tables.

Addison couldn't bring herself to look at Wade. With as much calm as she could muster she pushed from the table and stood. "This is obviously a shock. I had no idea Wade was married."

Before he could react, Addison had grabbed her coat from the back of the chair and wove her way through the crowded restaurant, intent on making her escape.

Gracie clutched Wade's arm and held it with a firm grip. "Let her go. She'll get over it." She purred, "As Mother Dear would always say, 'We mustn't make a scene.'"

****

Addison couldn't look at Wade. As she hurried away, she guessed he watched her. What he'd done was just more proof of her bad judgment in men. This time, however, she refused to come unraveled. She still had her apartment in New York. She'd sign the ranch over to Nell. Options raced through her mind. She'd open her own agency. Damn him. Damn!

The snow-covered landscape with its brightly lit firs and the old-style farmhouse had lost its charm. At the moment, her only thought was to escape. A man dressed as a French doorman held the door open. She asked, "Is there a taxi service available?"

"No, mademoiselle. There is only the sleigh driver and his horse. He doesn't go into town."

"How far is it into town?"

The doorman had lost his fake French accent. "Too far for those shoes."

Fueled by anger and oblivious of the cold, Addison had just whipped out her phone to call Emmett when a white paneled van stopped. The window rolled down. "Addison, everything okay?"

Although she'd only met him once, at the Mistletoe

Market, relief washed over her. "Dr. Montgomery. Can you give me a ride to Nell's?"

"Hop in."

As Layne Montgomery guided the vehicle down the brick drive, Addison glanced at the man dressed in navy blue coveralls. She wrinkled her nose against an odious stench. "What are you doing out here?"

"Sorry about the smell. Manure comes with the job." He gave an apologetic grin. "Mr. Bettencort, the owner, keeps a stable of draft horses to pull the sleighs. One of the mares was having a difficult time foaling. The better question is where is Wade, and why are you in my truck without him?"

Addison groaned at the memory of seeing Gracie sitting at the table with a death-grip on Wade's arm and a malevolent smirk in her eyes. Worse was learning he was married.

Wife.

That one word was a difficult blow. She wasn't just angry. She was furious.

The fact that it had come out of nowhere only made the entire situation worse. Had Wade planned it this way? Had the entire family duped her? Did Aunt Nell know about Gracie, too?

She gritted her teeth. "Let's just say I must be the biggest fool that ever lived."

Her phone vibrated.

—Addison, where are you?—

—Addison, I can explain but not in a text—

—The doorman said you left in a white truck—

The screen on her phone lit up again. Damn! This time she turned it completely off.

She curled her fingernails into the palms of her

hands. She thought back over the betrayal of her fiancé. She groaned at the memory, and then inexplicably she started to cry.

Lost in her misery, she was oblivious to the brief phone call Layne Montgomery made to his wife. It wasn't until he pulled into the ranch yard that she realized a strange car sat in the driveway. She didn't want to see anyone or answer any questions, and most especially she did not want to give details about her date with the not-so-honorable sheriff.

Layne opened his door, jumped to the ground, and raced around the front of the van to open the passenger door. He reached up to assist Addison.

She tried to smile. "Thank you for the ride. I'll telephone Ava tomorrow and explain. Now, if you'll excuse me, I have a terrible headache…no, wait. How rude of me. May I offer you a cup of coffee?"

A woman's voice called out, "Addison?"

She turned toward the porch. Ava skipped down the steps toward them. She kissed her husband and thanked him for the phone call. "I'll see you at home. Supper is in the warming oven."

Layne Montgomery hugged his wife. Inside the van he gave a last wave and drove off. Before allowing Ava to guide her up the steps and into the house, Addison stopped to watch the taillights disappear into the darkness.

"I am *such* an idiot," she muttered to herself. "The men in my life are like disappearing taillights."

Inside the living room, Nell sat in her favorite chair. Lucy Grey sat on the sofa nearest the crackling fire, a cup of coffee in her hand.

All Addison wanted was to go upstairs and crawl

into bed. She didn't even care if she undressed. Instead she said, "I'm not fit company tonight, so if you'll excuse me—"

"Sit down, Addison," Ava gently commanded. "Wade called and told me what happened. And that you disappeared without giving him a chance to explain. He's worried sick that you may have gotten into a vehicle with some maniac."

Addison's voice bit harder than she intended. "He should have told me he was married."

Nell said, "We all share the blame in this. Brenda told me yesterday that she thought she'd seen Gracie. I didn't believe her. That's neither here nor there. We wanted you to hear about it from Wade." She patted the cushion. "Sit and listen, please. Once you've heard the entire story, then the rest is up to Wade and you."

Nell reached for the coffeepot and poured a cup for Addison, who sat next to her foster mother and kicked off the high heels. "I suppose I have nothing to lose."

Lucy reached over and held her daughter's hand, as if she needed courage to say what she had to say. "First, Wade and Gracie were divorced a long time ago. He had planned to tell you about her tonight."

The statement didn't appease Addison. She still felt like the life had been drained out of her. "Go ahead. I'm listening."

Lucy began.

"He had loved Gracie all through school. The two of them were inseparable. He was the captain of the football team and she was captain of the cheerleading squad. Wade wanted a military career. Gracie planned to attend nursing school. Before high school graduation he joined the Marines. After graduation he left for San

Diego to attend boot camp.

"The news wasn't good when he came home for a short stint. His unit was to deploy thirty days after boot camp. Gracie insisted she and Wade marry before he left. He promised that when he returned from Iraq they would have her dream wedding.

"They were young and in love and immature. We naturally didn't give it much thought when Wade called to tell us the happy news that he was about to become a father. We figured they had forgotten to use protection on their wedding night and every night thereafter until he left.

"By this time Ava was away at Harvard, studying medicine. Alice, that's Gracie's mother, and I were never close friends, but for the children's sake we formed a bond. Ward and I treasured those rare times we got phone calls from Wade, because Iraq was a hot spot.

"Gracie kept promising that she'd enroll in nursing school when the baby was born and old enough for her to leave for a few hours. We thought she meant the local college. Thankfully, Wade was able to get leave and was here for the baby's birth. A beautiful baby girl with blue eyes and a head full of blonde ringlets. They named her Meadow Lark. Unfortunately, Wade had to return to his unit to finish out his fifteen months. We thought he would get an assignment stateside. Instead he was sent to Africa.

"When Meadow was about nine months old, Alice found a note in Gracie's bedroom saying she didn't want to be a mother and that she had left for California to pursue an acting career. I think that's about the same time Wade got the divorce papers. To say the least, he was devastated. He said he'd tried numerous times to get in touch with Gracie, but she didn't answer her phone. He signed the papers and mailed them to me. He wanted to make sure they got filed. He also asked if I'd raise the baby.

"Well, I couldn't just take her away from Alice. She and I agreed to share the responsibility as grandmothers."

Lucy drew a deep breath and was quiet for a moment while she massaged her temples. It was almost as if she needed to collect her thoughts before proceeding. "In the meantime, Alice decided not to send Gracie any money, in the hopes the girl would come to her senses and return home. She did, all right. She came back with Tony Costa, Wade's best friend. We didn't even know they had left together."

She again sat quiet for a moment before she continued. "Whatever happened to them in California changed them. Drugs, maybe." She shrugged. "Anyhow, Tony and Hubert, that's Gracie's father, got into a physical altercation. It wasn't pretty. Hubert suffered the worst end of the fight, with a broken nose and a couple of busted ribs.

"The next thing we knew, Ward was getting a call that someone had broken into BB's Café. Brenda was found lying on the floor unconscious, with a gash over her forehead, and the cash register drawer was open and empty. Brenda knew her attackers—personally.

"You have to understand that Alice and Hubert Howard were good God-fearing citizens and mortified at what their daughter and her boyfriend had done. Wade was still in Africa when we notified him. He petitioned the court for his dad and me to get legal custody of Meadow. With his father being in law enforcement and my career as a nurse, the judge ruled in our favor. We naturally let Meadow visit her other grandparents as often as they wanted."

Addison listened in stunned silence. Finally she asked, "What happened to Gracie and the guy?"

"They both went to prison." Lucy shook her head and sighed. "It gets worse."

Addison gave a tentative smile to encourage Wade's mother to continue. She couldn't imagine how much worse the story could get. The woman's pale blue eyes briefly met Addison's and then looked away.

"Because of Wade's job in the Marines, he didn't get to the States often. He had it set up that support money was sent to our checking account monthly to take care of his baby girl. When Skype came available, his dad and I bought a computer and had Skype installed. It was a blessing because Wade got to see Meadow take her first step, and when he had time, he read stories to her. I can't begin to tell you how ecstatic he was when Meadow called him Dada, and when we taught her how to throw kisses to him with her little hand, to say 'bye-bye' and 'I wuv you.' "

For a moment, Lucy broke down and wept. "When Meadow was two years old, she got sick, and by the time she was three, she needed a bone marrow transplant. Wade's unit was in some remote mountainous area in the Middle East. Somehow he wangled an emergency leave. As Meadow's father, he was the perfect donor. Nell and Brenda came to the hospital to offer their support. We were all there."

Lucy's voice trembled, and it was clearly an effort for her to continue. Nell shifted to grip her friend's hands. Nell cleared her throat. "I still get angry enough to strangle that little bitch for what she did."

Lucy drew her eyebrows together. "Me, too, Nell. I'll never forget the look on Wade's face when he came to the waiting room to tell us that he wasn't a match for Meadow's DNA."

This wasn't the confession that Addison had expected. "You mean Wade isn't Meadow's father?"

"That's right. The doctor assured us that the test was ninety-nine point nine-nine-nine percent accurate that Wade was not Meadow's father. Ward immediately contacted the prison where Tony was housed. According to Alice, Gracie was O negative. As it turned out, Tony wasn't the father either. Meadow's blood type was rare. The doctor said less than six percent of the population carried her type." Lucy heaved a huge sigh. "Gracie admitted that she didn't know who the father was. She actually laughed when she admitted that she'd slept with most of the football team and some of the young male tourists, and she was pregnant when she and Wade married. That was the reason for the hurry-up wedding."

"I hesitate to ask." Addison's voice was faint. "Where is Meadow now?"

Lucy's voice trembled. "She's buried in the Meadow Creek Church cemetery. Had she lived, she would turn seventeen this coming May." She picked up her cup and, finding it empty, set it back down. "Wade was devastated…nearly broken. Afterward, he started volunteering for every dirty job the Marines offered. I think he had died emotionally and hoped a bullet would finalize his death.

"Shortly afterward, the Howards sold their home

and moved to South Carolina. They simply couldn't face the friends they had known forever, after what had happened to Brenda and then with the baby's death. We never heard from them again."

Nell had sat quiet during the entire explanation. She could do nothing but sigh. "I owe Brenda an apology for not believing she thought she saw Gracie yesterday."

Addison pressed the tips of her fingers to her eyes. "My emotions are going haywire. Why didn't Wade tell me?"

Nell said, "You of all people should understand, Addison. It was too hard for him to relive the hurt."

"Of course. I'm sorry. He must think I hate him."

The wariness in Lucy Grey's voice was unmistakable. "The question is why did Gracie return to Meadow Creek? She's been out of prison for at least ten years. So what does she want from Wade?"

Ava reached over and clasped her mother's hands. "Her returning may be a good thing, Mom. He's never been clear about his feelings for Gracie. One minute he still loves her, the next he hates her, the next he's befuddled." She directed her attention to Addison. "I'm going to ask you straight out, and please be honest—do you love my brother and are you willing to fight for him? If not, cut it off. *Don't* leave him dangling."

Addison drew a deep breath as Wade's image appeared in her mind—a far fresher image than his sister could imagine. She lifted her chin. "There are still a lot of unanswered questions, but unequivocally yes! I am in love with Wade, and Gracie has met her match."

Chapter Thirty-Two

Wade spoke between gritted teeth. Her black dress, short hair spiked with gold tips, and black makeup that reminded him of a zombie didn't resemble the girl he'd married. "What the hell are you doing here, Gracie?"

She reached for her glass of wine. "Oh, pookie, aren't you happy to see me?"

Mustering his self-control, he said, "You didn't answer my question. How did you know I'd be here, and with Addison?"

Letting her breath out in an exaggerated sigh, Gracie offered a smug smile. "I was the one who bid the five hundred on you. I was about to shit my britches hoping someone else would bid higher, 'cause, man, I didn't have the dough, you know." She sniggered at her joke. "Anyhow, I was standing practically on top of you when you opened the envelope and said it was for dinner at Le Chalet."

The puzzled look on his face prompted her to say, "When I was trying to be an actress I learned the art of disguise." She giggled. "Fooled you, didn't I?"

Rage trembled through him as he pushed back his chair. "Why are you dressed like a Halloween goth witch?"

She answered with a condescending shrug. In a slightly uncoordinated movement, Gracie lifted the goblet but missed her mouth. Wine spilled down her chin. She seemed to be drifting away when Wade rescued the wineglass before it toppled from her fingers.

She giggled a hiccup. "Oops! I seem to have made a mess."

Using his thumb to guide her face toward his, he looked past the dark owlish makeup and into her eyes. He leaned forward and kept his voice low. "You're stoned. What did you take?"

She rolled her eyes. "Pookie, don't be mad. It's just a little feel-good medicine."

"Stop calling me that name." Setting his jaw, he hooked his arm through hers and hissed, "Come on—and as you said—*don't* make a scene."

She wobbled as he helped her from the chair. "Chill out, Pookie. All I want is you."

At the courtesy desk, the hostess said, "Sheriff Grey, is something wrong? The other lady seemed upset. She left in a white van."

He forced a smile. "A little misunderstanding with an unexpected guest." He pulled the white envelope from his suitcoat pocket and laid it on the desk. "The festival committee and I appreciate Mr. and Mrs. Bettencort's kind gesture."

The hostess shifted a perceptive glance from the sheriff to the woman. She used the tip of her finger to shove the envelope forward. "I can clearly see the intrusive mistake, Sheriff. Since you hadn't yet ordered, we would be pleased if you keep the certificate and be our guest another time."

Wade thanked the hostess. He returned the envelope to his pocket. "What do I owe you for her glass of wine?"

The hostess shook her head. "She paid for it."

He grabbed the black wrap Gracie indicated from a hook by the door and escorted her into the cold.

The doorman said, "Will you be going for a sleigh ride, Sheriff?"

"Not this time, Billy."

He practically dragged Gracie down the snow-covered walk to his truck. He wrenched open the passenger door and lifted her inside.

It was much darker out than it had been twenty minutes ago, and it had begun to snow. Hunched against the cold, he hastened to his side of the truck and climbed in. He turned the key in the ignition. While waiting for the heater to work its magic, Wade dialed Millie's number. He tapped his finger against the steering wheel waiting for her to answer.

"What's up, Wade?"

"Millie, I know you're off duty. I'm bringing in a female and need you to process her."

"I thought you were on a date with Addison."

"Something came up. Tell Pop I'm bringing Gracie in, and if he'd rather not be there I'll understand."

"Gracie...*your* Gracie? No...forget that. I'll relay the message to your dad."

"Also, call my sister. Gracie's in a bad way. She'll need something to get her through the night."

He disconnected and shifted the truck into gear. Gracie scooted close. Her hand found its way to his thigh and then between his legs where she gripped him. She purred, "Feeling you inside me—that's all I want right now."

Shit. He fought to keep his deprived libido from

responding to her.

He reached down and removed her hand. "There was a time when I would've taken you up on it." He kept his eyes on the snowy road. "Not anymore."

She snuggled against him. "If you're worried I'll get pregnant—don't. I had my incubator removed years ago."

When he didn't answer, she shifted her gaze to look at him. "Look, I've screwed up my life plenty." She let out a breath and a shaky laugh. "Don't you want me?"

"You didn't answer my question, Gracie. Why did you come back to Meadow Creek?"

She scooted down in the seat, her chin resting on his thigh. Her fingers found the way to his zipper. "I'm horny as hell, Wade. I've always been horny. I can't seem to get enough sex to satisfy me."

Wade slammed on the brakes. He gripped the steering wheel to hold the skidding truck steady until it rolled to a stop. Grabbing the keys from the ignition, he opened the door and practically jumped from the truck. He sucked in gulps of air, allowing the cold to chill his heated body. Damn his body for responding. He jogged to the passenger side and yanked open the door. He opened the glove compartment and removed a pair of handcuffs.

"Sit up and lean forward," he barked out the command.

When she obeyed, he cuffed her hands behind her back. "Blow out a breath."

In the truck's overhead light Gracie's flush was obvious. Her reply was ballsy. "Okay, I confess. I took a speedball. So arrest me."

He growled. "That's exactly what I intend to do."

He slammed the door and returned to the driver's side. The wheels spun on the icy road as he eased the truck forward. "In high school you were smart, and beautiful, and with a great future. Help me understand what happened to you."

Gracie slid her petite frame down in the seat and curled into a ball. She sounded more like a child than a grown woman. "I didn't want to be a nurse, or a wife, or a mother. My parents were always yammering at me about going to college, about being responsible. I wanted to live life—to be a party girl." Her voice grew contemptuous. "I wanted money, lots and lots of money, and jewelry, a mansion with a swimming pool, and sexy pool boys at my beck and call."

She swung her body into a sitting position. "You were boring, Wade Grey, captain of the football team, big man at school. Even your one position sex was b-o-r-i-n-g! I couldn't wait to put *you* and this one-horse town behind me."

And then she broke into hiccupping sobs. Tremors shook her body. She moaned and gagged and lifted beseeching brown eyes to him. "I don't have any money." She clutched her abdomen. "The cramps are setting in. Please, Wade, we can go to a motel, or we can do it right here in the truck." She struggled to sit upright. Her voice quavered as she added, "I'll make it worth your while if you'll please get me a hit of dust."

When he didn't answer, she mewled, "I want my mommy." Then in an agitated breath, she moaned, "Where the hell are my friggin' parents? I went to their house, and the woman said to get the hell off her porch or she'd call you."

Wade knew Gracie was in agony. He'd seen what withdrawals did to addicts. Still he kept his eyes on the road and remained silent, suffering his own anguish.

She screamed and started kicking the dashboard. "You sanctimonious bastard, you gotta get me a hit."

"Not on your life." Relief washed over him when the lights of town came into view.

In front of his office, he slammed the truck into park and cut the ignition. He pulled Gracie into his arms and carried her up the steps. Millie held the door wide for him. His father stood next to an open cell door and waited for Wade to lay Gracie on the cot and cover her with a blanket.

Ward asked, "What happened? Drunk?"

Wade hated seeing his father's eyes filled with outrage. Yet he fully understood the emotion. He fought against the tie that felt like a noose around his neck. "No, speedball."

Ward expelled a disgusted snort. "In any form, cocaine's bad stuff."

Millie asked Wade if he wanted a cup of coffee. He acknowledged with a nod as he locked the cell door.

"I'm sorry as I can be, son. For you, your mother, me," he nodded toward the sleeping woman, "and even her."

Ward hobbled over to a chair and sat down. It was plain his gout was still bothering him. He accepted the cup from Millie, and said, "You might as well show him. Bad as it is, it's a blessing in disguise."

Millie motioned Wade to her desk. She moved the computer's mouse to awaken the screen. A disheveled image of Gracie stared back at him. He released a whistling sigh. "Active warrant: Wanted for passing bad checks and credit card fraud." He scrolled to another page and read: "Prostitution, extortion, dealing."

"I'm sad for her, Pop. What a waste."

"She's put you through hell. You gonna be okay, son?"

Tamping down emotions he'd been wrestling with, Wade forced a smile. "Whatever feelings for Gracie I've been holding onto all these years have completely vanished." Lying like a lump under an olive green blanket, she suddenly reminded him of roadkill, and he found the sight of her disgusting.

He kept a steady voice. "Millie, notify Los Angeles PD that we're holding their perp. They can pick her up any time."

He sent his father home and ordered Millie to retire to the cell reserved for deputies. He dimmed the office lights. For a bit he watched the fish, which seemed to be asleep. And then he opened his phone. It was late, too late to make a phone call. His thumbs moved across the keys.

He sent the first text to his sister explaining about Gracie's drug use, and the possibility of needing to send her to the hospital. Ava responded that she'd come right over to check on Gracie.

To Addison he texted: *—We belong together. Don't give up on us—*

Addison:—*I won't if you are always honest with me—*

Wade propped his feet on the desk. *—Tomorrow. I'd like to explain about G—*

Addison: *—No need. Your mother filled me in. I'm so sorry about Meadow—*

Wade: —*Thanks. I'd still like to see you*—
Addison signed off with a heart emoji and: —*Tomorrow. G'night*—

Chapter Thirty-Three

J.J. tossed her duffel bag into the police car's back seat. "Not many people out on New Year's Day. I guess most of them partied too much last night."

Wade smiled over at J.J. "Most of the tourists have gone back to wherever they came from. Which is nice because we can kick back and relax a little until the season gears up again."

"Thanks for picking me up."

"You bet. By the way, I've got you enrolled at the academy. You'll actually begin classes next Tuesday. We'll work your duty schedule around your class schedule. Tomorrow, I'll officially swear you in as my deputy."

"Honestly, Sheriff, I'd like to squeal like a silly girl. That's how happy I am."

Wade laughed. "There's nothing wrong with a little happy squealing, J.J."

As Wade approached Millie's duplex, he said, "Hmm, there's a strange car parked out front. Millie doesn't own a car." He pulled the cruiser in behind the vehicle. "Just as a precaution, let's check it out. Stay behind me."

On the porch, he bent and pulled the key from under the doormat and held it up. "Let this be a lesson to you. The first place an intruder always looks." He inserted the key and, using caution, eased the door open. He stepped inside the room with J.J. on his heels.

Voices rang out, "Happy New Year and Welcome Home!"

Joey and Julie raced to their startled mother's open arms. After hugs and kisses, she said, "This is too much! I don't know what to say."

The crowd of friends parted to open up a view of the room. Nell stepped forward. "The sofa and chair are from Emmett. Millie made curtains for all the rooms. Brenda stocked the refrigerator with enough food to feed an army."

Nell's unintentional pun brought a round of guffaws.

She went on to say, "Addison wanted the twins to have their own beds and quilts, and the rest of us made sure your electric is paid for an entire year. It's our way of thanking you for putting your life on the line for all Americans, and to let you know that you and the twins are part of our family."

J.J. wiped the tears from her eyes. "Soldiers aren't supposed to cry. I'm breaking that rule."

Wade dangled the key chain in front of J.J. "Welcome home."

****

Later in the afternoon, Addison left Nell and Emmett chatting with Brenda at the café and strolled to the sheriff's office. She wasn't surprised to see Millie alone at her desk, reading a romance novel. They chatted for a few minutes about the welcome home party for J.J. and how much Millie looked forward to spoiling the twins.

Addison's voice filled with disappointment. "I

suppose Wade is on a call?"

Millie closed the book. She gave a woeful sigh. "No, I guess having Gracie showing up out of the blue, and first thing this morning watching LAPD haul her off in cuffs, followed by the twins' excitement over seeing their mother—it all kinda wore him down a little."

"Did he go home?"

Millie answered in a melancholy voice. "No, he went to visit Meadow. He does that sometimes when life gets him down."

Addison walked to the double doors and gazed toward the quaint church. "I thought being abandoned in a bus station was horrible." She shook her head. "What Gracie did was execrable."

She zipped her jacket, pulled on her gloves, and adjusted her knit sweater cap. "Enjoy your book, Millie."

"Shall I tell Wade you were here?"

Addison shook her head. "It isn't necessary. He'll know."

Tears balanced on her lashes and dropped to her cheeks. She blinked to clear her vision as she crossed the street and turned toward the church. It took but a few minutes to walk to the rear of the building and through the wrought iron cemetery gate. He stood, hat in hand, his spine stiff, head bowed. Even from this distance Addison was certain the pain he suffered had pierced her own heart.

He felt her arms come around him, and he completed the circle of her embrace. They stood silent. No words necessary.

"Even though she wasn't mine, I loved her." He

heaved a deep sigh. "I think a part of me knew I wasn't the father. There's no one in our family with blue eyes and blonde curly hair. Not even in Gracie's. I just didn't want to believe what was right in front of me."

Addison laced her fingers in his. "In time there will be other children."

He looked down at her, his eyes filled with hope. He leaned in closer. Their lips fit perfectly together, and neither hesitated to open to the other. He tightened his hold on her.

Her heart murmured, *You love him—what are you waiting for?*

Addison pulled away and looked up at him. Her breath created wispy vapors as she spoke. "The children will be ours—yours and mine."

****

Wade dropped to one knee. He held Addison's gloved hands. Suddenly he had no sense of time. All he knew was the sky was blue and cloudless, and that he loved this woman with all his being. He saw a life for them here in Meadow Creek.

"I'm certain a cemetery isn't the proper place to propose marriage, but before God and baby Meadow Lark, I want the simple joys of sharing life with you, raising our children together, spending a lifetime of making memories to tell our grandchildren, and doing everything within my power to make you happy always. Addison James, heart and soul—I love you. Will you be my wife?"

She knelt in the snow and cupped his face with her hands. "I don't want courtship, Wade. I think we're old enough and with enough life experiences that we've moved well beyond those days. I'm ready to move forward with no looking back. I'll treasure growing old with you, and helping you make those memories. I don't want to waste another day. I love you, Wade Grey. Yes—a thousand times—yes."

He pulled her close so that she molded against him. A sudden gust of snowy wind swept through the cemetery and swirled around them like a spinning top, then continued wending its way through the headstones until it disappeared.

Addison smiled. "I believe Meadow Lark just gave us her blessing."

Wade covered her mouth with his. A strange sensation of peace engulfed him. "I'm ready to get this marriage under way. Is tomorrow soon enough to visit the justice of the peace, or do you want a big wedding?"

Her lips hovered closed to his. "I've had enough glitz and glamour to last almost the rest of my life. The justice of the peace is perfect. All I want is a simple wedding."

Wade smiled against her lips. "Your wish is my command."

Her long agile fingers caressed the back of his neck. After a moment of silence, her voice was deep and husky with passion. "Would you think badly of me if I suggested we go to your house and engage in a little pre-honeymoon celebration?"

He could hear his own breathing against hers. "It's like you just read my mind." He clasped her hand in his and led her from the cemetery to where he'd parked his pickup truck.

****

Waking came with a brightness that seemed almost painful. Addison's mind became slowly aware of the disturbing glare. Light filled the entire room, and although she lay with her back toward the windows, it still intruded, shining through her closed eyelids, penetrating into her brain. She stirred sleepily as a hand began to caress the small of her back, kneading away the stiffness that she sensed more than felt. Lazily she stretched like a contented feline and rolled to her stomach to let the strong fingers do their work. She released a throaty moan and arched her back against the gentle massaging as it soothed her achy muscles. The hand plied her back and shoulders, sending waves of weakening pleasure up and down her spine.

Languidly she rolled toward the source of her enjoyment until her bare breasts pressed against a firm, hairy chest. She lifted to allow her head to loll against his shoulder. Her eyes came open, and all memory of last night flooded back as she stared into Wade's smiling gray eyes. She heard the gentle voice with a hint of laughter behind it. "Good morning. I trust you slept well."

She crooned. "I had the most luscious dream. It was about a naked man and woman making wild passionate love. If only dreams came true."

Wade inclined on his side, head propped casually in his hand. His eyes played with hers, glowing devilishly, his arm curled warmly around her, until he leaned down, a soft breast crushed against his lean, hard chest, their thighs caught together, and Addison became aware that he was more than willing and certainly ready to make her dream come true.

She smiled softly into his eyes. Her silken thighs opened to his seeking hand, and his wandering caresses brought soft, breathless cries of trembling joy. She closed her eyes as his kisses devoured her, fierce with love and passion, then traced lower to spread their heat over her throbbing nipples, which thrust forward in eager anticipation. Addison savored the bliss as his greedy mouth swept her every nerve with intense excitement. She felt the bold urgency of him as he entered her, consuming, searing, setting fire to her until the rippling, molten waves of ecstasy flooded her with almost unbearable pleasure. She heard his rasping breath and the sweetly whispered words of love. His heart beat wildly against her naked breast, and beneath her hands the hard muscles of his buttocks flexed with manly vigor. They were caught together in a shimmering, surging, swelling tide of bliss.

In the aftermath of their storm, Addison lay wrapped in Wade's arms. Their voices were hushed and lazy, yet seemed to echo in the silence of his bedroom. The room had chilled, and he reached to cover them with a blanket before they gently entwined fingers in a knot of love. Wade's lips nibbled at the soft flesh of her shoulder and sank warmly against her creamy throat, then paused to taste an ear lobe. She moaned as his lips moved to leave a trail of burning kisses down her throat between her breasts and further to the blonde apex between her thighs.

He placed his hand to the small of her back and lifted her, allowing his tongue to work its magic. She arched her back, grasping a handful of sheet in one hand. "Wade," she whispered, wrapping her arms around his shoulders, trying to draw him closer. "Please..." She let her eyes drift shut and moaned with pleasure. She felt as if she were drifting on a cloud and barely realized when he entered her, his manhood full and throbbing as he thrust his hips forward and she rose to meet him. She found herself laughing and crying at the same time she found fulfillment.

A heartbeat later, Wade moaned and fell forward, burying his face in the crook of her neck. Both lay there panting for a moment, and then he withdrew from her. She curled in the crook of his arm and allowed him to cover them with a blanket.

"Addison?"

"Hmm."

"I just realized I didn't use protection. Are you angry?"

She pushed him to his back and then straddled him. She could have sworn she saw moisture in his dark stormy eyes when she said, "I guess you'd better make me Mrs. Wade Grey as soon as possible."

He gave her a wry grin, and her stomach tumbled when he wrapped his arms around her waist and pulled her to his chest, kissing the top of her head and then each breast. He rolled her onto her back, lowering over her and gazing into her eyes. He whispered, "Mrs. Wade Grey. I like the sound of that."

She smiled, so happy, and wondered if she was dreaming. If so, it was the longest and best dream she had ever experienced.

Epilogue

The first day of June arrived. Horses grazed in the pasture, and in the freshly cultivated tree farm the blue spruce trees grew in neatly manicured rows. It seemed the entire township of Meadow Creek had gathered around the newly constructed gazebo overlooking the Kootenay River at Hope Ranch. Wade and Addison stood in the middle of the beautifully decorated summerhouse. They held hands as they stood behind a long table laden with food and an extra-long sheet cake decorated in pink, blue, yellow, and green flowers, set in the table's center.

Wade welcomed everyone. "Today is a special day in more ways than one. Hope Ranch is officially an event and vacation destination resort." He extended his hands toward the crowd. "My lovely wife and I extend our appreciation to all of our friends and welcome you, the first of our guests."

A large easel covered with a baby blanket stood behind Wade.

Nell yelled, "The suspense is killing us. How long are you going to keep us waiting?"

A round of cheerful disgruntlements hooted.

Ruby Raye stood with her arm looped through Nell's. She beamed up at Addison. "Come on—is it a girl or a boy? We wanna know."

Wade held up his hand to quiet the crowd. He

turned to Addison and smiled as he nodded. He said to their family, friends and guests, "Give us the count down."

Voices rang out, "Five…four…three—"

When the count ended with one, Wade and Addison each grabbed a corner of the blanket and folded it over the easel to reveal a poster-sized hand-crafted baby announcement that read:

Roses are Red
Violets are Blue
We are due with
Not one, but
TWO!
Sadie and Sawyer
Expected to arrive
Christmas Day!

A proud gleam flashed in Wade's gray eyes. Addison gave him her own proud gaze in return. His laughter was warm and rich as he wrapped her in his arms.

Loretta C. Rogers

Aunt Nell's Gingerbread with Rum Whipped Cream

Ingredients:
- ½ cup butter (1 stick of butter)
- ½ cup white sugar
- 1 egg
- 1 cup molasses
- 2 ½ cups all-purpose flour
- 1 ½ tsp baking soda
- 1 cup hot water
- 1 tsp ground cinnamon
- 2 tsp ground ginger
- 1 tsp ground cloves
- 1 tsp lemon extract
- ½ tsp salt

Directions:

Preheat oven to 350 degrees F (175 degrees C). Grease and flour a 9-inch square pan.

In a large bowl, cream together the sugar and butter. Beat in the egg, and mix in the molasses.

In a bowl, sift together the flour, baking soda, salt, cinnamon, ginger, and cloves. Blend into the creamed mixture. Stir in the hot water. **(See Aunt Nell's secret ingredient.) Pour into the prepared pan.

Bake 1 hour in the preheated oven, until a knife inserted in the center comes out clean. Allow to cool in pan before serving.

**Shh! Don't tell anyone, but here is Aunt Nell's secret ingredient: add ½ cup chopped crystallized ginger.

Rum Whipped Cream

Ingredients:
- 1 cup (1/2 pint) cold heavy cream
- 3 tablespoons sugar
- ½ teaspoon pure vanilla extract
- 1 tablespoon dark rum (substitute: rum extract)

Directions:

Whip the cream in the bowl of an electric mixer fitted with the whisk attachment. When it starts to thicken, add the sugar, vanilla, and rum. Continue to whip until it forms stiff peaks. Serve cold large dollops on warm gingerbread.

German Glühwein

Part of my ancestry is German. Each year at Christmas my grandmother made her Glühwein, just as Aunt Nell does in this story. Because the alcohol cooks off and leaves the flavor, the children were permitted to have a small cup (minus the rum or amaretto) to celebrate after the gifts were open.

Serves: 4 to 6

Ingredients:
- Juice of 1 medium orange (strain to avoid seeds and pulp)
- 3/4 cup water
- 1/4 cup granulated sugar
- 10 whole cloves
- 2 cinnamon sticks
- 2 whole star anise
- 1 (750-milliliter) bottle dry red wine
- 1 shot of rum or amaretto, for serving (optional)

Instructions:
- Use a vegetable peeler to remove the zest from the orange in wide strips. Avoid cutting in to the white pith; set aside. Juice the orange and set the juice aside.
- In a large sauce pot, combine the sugar and water. Bring to a boil and stir until the sugar has completely dissolved.
- Reduce the heat and add the cloves, cinnamon, star anise, orange zest, and orange juice. Simmer until a fragrant syrup forms—about 1 minute.
- To avoid a flare-up, remove the pot from the stove. Add the wine. Reduce the heat to low, gentle simmer. Return pot to burner. Let liquid barely

simmer for at least 20 minutes or up to 1 hour. Stir occasionally.

Keep an eye out that liquid doesn't come to a full simmer.

Strain and serve in small mugs.

Optional: add a shot of rum or amaretto; garnish with orange peel curls if desired.

If you enjoyed this book you may want to read Loretta C. Rogers' book *WHEN COMES FOREVER*...

Jesse Starr, son of a Kiowa princess and an English lord, was raised in England but constantly persecuted by his jealous half-brother, who eventually had him shanghaied. Now on his way home, Jesse determines to find the mother he never knew, then return to England to avenge his father's death at the hands of the half-brother. When he finds beautiful and very pregnant seventeen-year-old Rebecca Throckmorton abandoned in a remote cabin deep in Oklahoma territory, his plans go awry. Rebecca rues the day she eloped with a con man. All she wants is to return to Chicago, hoping her family will welcome her and the baby. Yet despite her vow never to trust her heart to another man, she can't help being attracted to Jesse, the rugged adventurer who rescues her. If her society-conscious family won't forgive her, what will she do? Jesse, drawn to Rebecca but intent on his revenge in England; has no thought of her accompanying him…until he must rescue her and change his plans again.

~

Available online now wherever books are sold.

A word about the author…

A native Floridian and proud of her Scots-Irish heritage, Loretta C. Rogers is a bestselling author. She writes in all sub-genres of romance. There is always a little bit of mystery and suspense in her novels. Her books are in libraries throughout the USA and Europe. When not writing, she is an avid traveler, and enjoys researching her family genealogy.

~*~

HAPPY!
If you enjoyed reading *Christmas at Hope Ranch*,
your review is highly appreciated.
Visit Loretta at:
www.lorettacrogersnovels.com

Thank you for purchasing
this publication of The Wild Rose Press, Inc.

For questions or more information
contact us at
info@thewildrosepress.com.

The Wild Rose Press, Inc.
www.thewildrosepress.com

Lightning Source UK Ltd.
Milton Keynes UK
UKHW021827141120
373340UK00010B/230